ALSO BY YIYUN LI

Tolstoy Together: 85 Days of War and Peace with Yiyun Li

Must I Go

Where Reasons End

Dear Friend, from My Life I Write to You in Your Life

The Story of Gilgamesh

Kinder Than Solitude

Gold Boy, Emerald Girl

The Vagrants

A Thousand Years of Good Prayers

THE BOOK OF GOOSE

The Book of Goose

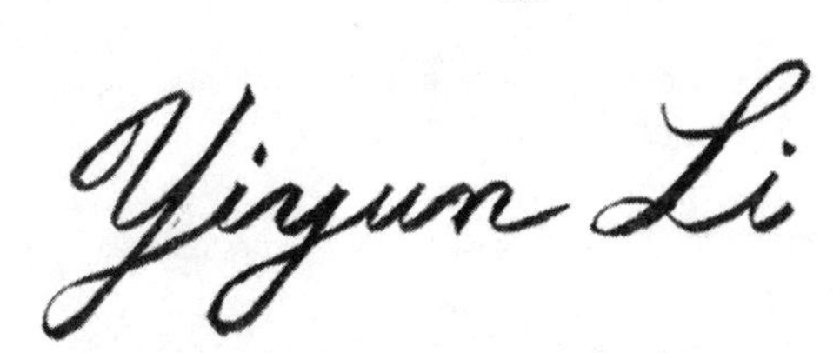

FARRAR, STRAUS AND GIROUX • NEW YORK

Farrar, Straus and Giroux
120 Broadway, New York 10271

Printed in the United States of America
First edition, 2022

Title-page hand-lettering and chapter-opener ornament by Na Kim.

Library of Congress Cataloging-in-Publication Data
Names: Li, Yiyun, 1972– author.
Title: The book of goose / Yiyun Li.
Description: First edition. | New York : Farrar, Straus and Giroux, 2022.
Identifiers: LCCN 2022022703 | ISBN 9780374606343 (hardcover)
Subjects: LCGFT: Novels.
Classification: LCC PS3612.I16 B66 2022 | DDC 813/.6—dc23 /eng/20220516
LC record available at https://lccn.loc.gov/2022022703

Designed by Abby Kagan

www.fsgbooks.com
www.twitter.com/fsgbooks • www.facebook.com/fsgbooks

1 3 5 7 9 10 8 6 4 2

For Dapeng and James

and for Vincent, a monumental child

THE BOOK OF GOOSE

~

YOU CANNOT CUT AN APPLE with an apple. You cannot cut an orange with an orange. You can, if you have a knife, cut an apple or an orange. Or slice open the underbelly of a fish. Or, if your hands are steady enough and the blade is sharp enough, sever an umbilical cord.

You can slash a book. There are different ways to measure depth, but not many readers measure a book's depth with a knife, making a cut from the first page all the way down to the last. Why not, I wonder.

You can hand the knife to another person, betting with yourself how deep a wound he or she is willing to inflict. You can be the inflicter of the wound.

One half orange plus another half orange do not make a full orange again. And that is where my story begins. An orange that did not think itself good enough for a knife, and an orange that never dreamed of turning itself into a knife. Cut and be cut, neither interested me back then.

My names is Agnès, but that is not important. You can go into an orchard with a list of names and write them on the oranges, Françoise and Pierre and Diane and Louis, but what difference does it make? What matters to an orange is its orange-ness. The same with me. My name could have been Clémentine, or Odette, or Henrietta, but so? An orange is just an orange, as a doll is a doll. Don't think that once you name a doll, it is different from other dolls. You can bathe it and clothe it and feed it empty air and put it to bed with the lullabies you imagine a mother should be singing to a baby. All the same, the doll, like all dolls, cannot even be called dead, as it was never alive.

The name you should pay attention to in this story is Fabienne. Fabienne is not an orange or a knife or a singer of lullabies, but she can make herself into any one of those things. Well, she once could. She is dead now. The news of her death arrived in a letter from my mother, the last of my family still living in Saint Rémy, though my mother was not writing particularly to report the death, but the birth of her own first great-grandchild. Had I remained near her, she would have questioned why I have not given birth to a baby to be added to her collection of grandchildren. This is one good thing about living in America. I am too far away to be her concern. But long before my marriage I stopped being her concern—my fame took care of that.

America and fame: they are equally useful if you want freedom from your mother.

In the postscript of the letter, my mother wrote that Fabienne died the previous month—"*de la même manière que sa sœur Joline*"—in the same manner as her sister. Joline had died in 1946 in childbirth, when she was seventeen. Fabienne died in 1966, at twenty-seven. You would think twenty years would make childbirth less a killer of women, you would think the same calamity should never strike a family twice, but if you think that way you are likely to be called an idiot by someone, as Fabienne used to call me.

My first reaction, after I read the postscript: I wanted to get pregnant right away. I would carry a baby to term and I would give birth to a child without dying myself—I knew this with the certainty that I knew my name. This would be proof that I could do something Fabienne could not—be a bland person, who is neither favored nor disfavored by life. A person without a fate.

(This desire, I imagine, can be truly understood only by people *with* a fate, so it is a desire akin to wishful thinking.)

But you need two people to get pregnant; and then two people do not necessarily guarantee success. Getting pregnant, in my case, would involve looking for a man with whom

I could cheat on Earl (then what—explaining to him a bastard would still be better than a barren marriage?), or divorcing him for a man who can sow and reap better. Neither appeals to me. Earl loves me, and I love being married to him. The fact that he cannot give me a child may be disheartening to him, but I have told him that I did not marry him to become a mother. In any case we are both realists.

Earl left the Army Corps of Engineers after we moved back from France and now works for his father, a well-respected contractor. I have a vegetable garden, which I started in our backyard, and I raise chickens, two dozen at any time. I was hoping to add to my charges some goats, but the two kids I acquired had a habit of chewing the wooden fence and running away. Lancaster, Pennsylvania, is not Saint Rémy, and I cannot turn myself back into a goatherd. "A French bride" is how I was first known to the local people, and some, long after I stopped being a new wife (we have been married for six years now), still refer to me by that name. Earl likes it. A French bride adds luster to his life, but a French bride chasing goats down a street would be an embarrassment.

I gave up the goats and decided to raise geese instead. Last spring, I acquired my first two, a pair of Toulouse geese, and this year I purchased a pair of Chinese geese. Earl read the catalogue and joked that we should go on adding American geese and African geese and Pomeranian geese and Shetland geese each year. Let's have a troupe of international brigands, he said. But he forgot that the two couples will soon be parents. In a year I will be expecting goslings.

The geese, more than the chickens, are my children. Earl likes the geese, too, and he was the one to suggest that we give them French names. His French is not as good as he thinks, but that has not stopped him from speaking the language to me in our most intimate moments. I always speak English to the people in my American life. I speak English to my chickens and geese.

The garden produces more vegetables than we can consume. I share them with my in-laws—Earl's parents and his two brothers and their families. They are all nice to me, even though they find me foreign, and perhaps laughable. They call me Mother Goose behind my back. This I learned from Lois, my sister-in-law, who is unhappily married and who hopes to turn me against the Barrs family. I don't mind the nickname, though. It may be insensitive of them to call a childless woman Mother Goose, but I am far from being a sensitive or sentimental woman.

When Earl asked about my mother's letter, I told him about the birth of my grandniece, but not the death of Fabienne. If he detected anything unusual, he would assume that another baby's birth reminded me of the void in my life. He is a loving husband, but love does not often lead to perception. When I met him, he thought I was a young woman with no secrets and few stories from my childhood and girlhood. Perhaps it is not his fault that I cannot get pregnant. The secrets inside me have not left much space for a fetus to grow.

I was in such a trance that I forgot to separate the geese from the chickens at their mealtime. The geese had a busy time terrorizing and robbing the chickens. I chastised them without raising my voice. Fabienne would have laughed at my incompetency. She would have told me that I should simply give the geese a good kick. But Fabienne is dead. Whatever she does now, she has to do as a ghost.

I would not mind seeing Fabienne's ghost.

All ghosts claim their phantom skills: to shape-shift, to

haunt, to see things we don't see, to determine how the lives of the living people turn out. If dead people had no choice but to become ghosts, Fabienne's ghost would only scoff at the usual tricks that other ghosts take pride in. Her ghost would do something entirely different.

(Like what, Agnès?

Like making me write again.)

No, it is not Fabienne's ghost that has licked the nib of my pen clean, or opened the notebook to this fresh page, but sometimes one person's death is another person's parole paper. I may not have gained full freedom, but I am free enough.

HOW DO YOU GROW HAPPINESS?" Fabienne asked. We were thirteen then, but we felt older. Our bodies, I now know, were underdeveloped, the way children born in wartime and growing up in poverty are, with more years crammed into their brains. Well-proportioned we were not. Well-proportioned children are a rare happenstance. War guarantees disproportion, but during peacetime other things go wrong. I have not met a child who is not lopsided in some way. And when children grow up, they become lopsided adults.

"Can you grow happiness?" I asked.

"You can grow anything. Just like potatoes," Fabienne said.

I thought she would have given a better answer. Growing happiness on the top of a maypole, or in a wren's nest, or between two rocks in a creek. Happiness should not be dirt-colored and hidden underground. Even apples on a branch would be better suited to be called happiness than apples in the earth. Though if happiness were like apples, I thought, it would be quite ordinary and uninteresting.

"You don't believe me?" Fabienne said. "I have an idea. We grow your happiness as beet and mine as potato. If one crop fails, we still have the other. We won't be starved."

"What if both fail?" I asked.

"We'll become butchers."

Such were the conversations we often had then, nonsense to the world, but the world, we already knew, was full of nonsense. We might as well amuse ourselves with our own nonsense. If the thumb on the left hand got crushed under a hammer, would the thumb on the right feel anything? Why did god never think of giving people ear-lids, so we could close our ears as we shut our eyes at bedtime, or anytime when we were not in the mood for the chattering of the world? If the two of us prayed with equal seriousness but with the opposite requests—dear god, please let tomorrow be a sunny day; dear god, please let tomorrow be an overcast day—how did he decide which prayer he should honor?

Fabienne loved making nonsense about god. She claimed she believed in god, though what she meant, I thought, was that she believed in a god that was always available for her to mock. I did not know if I believed in god—my father was an atheist and my mother was the opposite of an atheist. If I had been closer to one or the other, it would be easier for me to choose. But I was close only to Fabienne. *Perturbatrice* of god, she called herself, and said I was one, too, because I was always on her side. In that sense we were not atheists. You had to believe that god existed so you could make mischief and upend his plans.

"If we can grow happiness, can we also grow misery?" I asked her.

"Do you grow thistles or ragworts?" Fabienne said.

"Do you mean misery grows by itself, like thistles and ragworts?"

"Or by god," Fabienne said. "Who knows?"

"But happiness, can it grow by itself?"

"What do you think?"

"I think happiness should be like thistles and ragworts. Misery should be like exotic orchids."

"Only an idiot would believe that, Agnès," Fabienne said. "But we already know you're an idiot."

~

I DID NOT TELL FABIENNE then that I thought our happiness should be like the pigeons M. Devaux kept. They went away, they came back, and what happened in between was no one's business. Our happiness should not be rooted and immobile.

M. Devaux: I should say a few words about him. He, like Fabienne, begins this story, but he was already in his sixties when we were thirteen. I suspect that he is dead now. He should be. Fabienne is dead, and he should not have more rights to life than she.

M. Devaux was the village postmaster, an ugly and sickly-looking man. Fabienne and I had paid as much attention to him as we had paid every adult, which was very little. We liked his pigeons, though. For a while we talked about keeping a pair of pigeons ourselves. One would go with Fabienne to the pasture during the day, one would accompany me to school, and they would fly over the fields and alleys, delivering our messages to each other. But the scheme, like that to grow happiness, entertained us for some days and was then replaced by a new one. We never seriously carried out any of our plans. It was enough to feel that we could, if we wanted, make things happen.

One day Mme Devaux died. She had been a robust woman, younger than her husband, coarser and louder. It was said that she had never been ill for a day in her life, until she came down with the fever. Three days and she was gone.

I do not remember if they had children. Perhaps M. Devaux could not give her a child. Earl cannot be the only man who has to endure that fate. Or their children had grown up and left the village before our time. The questions that did not occur to me to ask at thirteen feel important now. I wonder if Fabienne knew the answers. I wish I could ask her. This is the inconvenience of her being dead. Half of this story is hers, but she is not here to tell me what I have missed.

Mme Devaux was buried on a Thursday, that I remember. A funeral was not an excuse for Fabienne not to take her two cows and five goats to the meadow, or for me not to go to school. But in the evening, we went to the cemetery, looking for the freshest grave. There was more than one new grave that fall.

On the way there, Fabienne gathered some marguerites and gillyflowers and handed the bouquet to me. We were not the kind of girls who put flowers in our hair or made wreaths out of boredom, but if someone caught us wandering in the cemetery, we would say we were leaving flowers for Mme Devaux.

I do not think Fabienne explained the necessity of the

flowers to me. I simply understood it. Back then we often knew what we were doing without having to talk things over between ourselves. But was it such a surprise? We were almost one person. I do not imagine that the half of an orange facing south would have to tell the other half how warm the sunlight is.

When we found the patch of fresh dirt, Fabienne took some of the flowers from me. There was a bouquet left near the wooden cross, and she scattered our flowers at the foot of the grave, one at a time. "Some flowers to hem into your robe," she whispered. "And these are for your slippers." I imitated Fabienne, though I did not say anything to the dead woman. We did not know Mme Devaux well. Most adults struck us as peripheral, some more annoying than others. But we liked the ceremony, the grave of a recently dead woman strewn with the more recently dead flowers.

Afterward, Fabienne lay down on a stone nearby. I arranged myself next to her, looking at the inky blue sky and the stars, as I believed she was doing. The stars, those we could see with our eyes and those we could not see, had been named, but my learning that fact at school did not help us at all. Fabienne had not made the stars into a story or a game for us, and I knew exactly why: the stars were too far away, and they looked too much alike.

Neither of us spoke. Underneath us were a couple who had lived and died long before our time. We preferred the cemetery at nighttime. During the day there were often people around, old women in black with brooms, a caretaker cleaning away the stale flowers. It was not that we minded being seen, but we believed that ghosts, if there were any, would not show themselves to us if someone else was around.

It was October 1952. Fourteen years have passed since then. Soon I will be many decades removed from Fabienne. But years and decades are mere words, made-up names for units of measurement. One pound of potato, two cups of flour, three oranges, but what is the measuring unit for hunger? I am twenty-seven this year, and I will be twenty-eight next year. Fabienne was, is, and will always be twenty-seven. How do I measure Fabienne's presence in my life—by the years we were together, or by the years we have been apart, her shadow elongating as time goes by, always touching me?

The evening air was chilly, and the stone underneath us retained no warmth from the day. I felt the cold in my body. It was a different kind of cold than when we jumped into the creek too early in the spring. The shocking iciness of the water would take our breath away, but only for a moment, and then we would scream with giddiness, the air in our lungs making us feel strong and alive. On the gravestones, the cold was heavy, as though it were not us who were lying on the stones, but the stones lying on us. I listened to Fabienne's breathing, which was becoming slower and shallower, and I tried to match mine to hers.

She must have been as cold as I was. I waited for her to sit up first so I could follow. Sometimes we lay on the gravestones for a long time, until our bodies turned stiff, and afterward, we had to jump up and down to warm ourselves, our bones and teeth rattling. Fabienne believed that we must always test the limits of our bodies. Not drinking until thirst scratched our throats like sand. Not eating until our heads were lightened by hunger. There was not much to eat, in any case. Some bread, and, if we were lucky, a piece of cheese. Sometimes we would face each other and hold our breath, counting with our fingers, seeing how long we could go and how red we would turn before we had to take our next breath. When we lay on the gravestones we did not stir until we felt as cold and immobile as death. If we wait to do something until it becomes absolutely necessary, Fabienne had explained to me, we will leave little opportunity for the world to catch us. Catch us how? I had asked, and she had said that she saw no point explaining it if I could not understand. Just follow me, she had said, you do nothing but what I tell you to.

"What do you think M. Devaux is doing at this moment?" Fabienne sat up and asked.

I felt a rush of gratitude. I would not have been surprised if she had decided not to move until sunrise. I would have had no choice but to lie next to her. My parents, unlike Fabienne's father, would have noticed that I had missed my bedtime.

"I don't know," I said.

"Let's pay him a visit," Fabienne said.

"Why? We don't know him."

"He needs something to occupy himself. All widowers do."

Fabienne's father was a widower, so she must have known something about widowers. "What can we do for M. Devaux?" I asked.

"We can tell him we come to offer our friendship."

"Does he need friends?"

"Maybe, maybe not," Fabienne said. "But we'll say we need him to be our friend."

"Why?" I asked. Back when Fabienne still went to school, some girls used to ask to be our friends, but they had quickly learned the humiliation of wanting something from Fabienne, who would study the girls with a malicious curiosity and then speak slowly: *I don't understand how you came up with the notion that we want you as a friend.*

"A man like M. Devaux can be useful," Fabienne said. "We can say we want his help to write a book."

"A book?" Fabienne had not been to school for the past two years. Sometimes she studied my readers to keep up with me, but neither of us had seen a real book in our lives.

"Yes, we can write a book together."

"About what?"

"Anything. I can make up stories and you can write them down. How complicated can it be?"

It was true that I could write my letters better than Fabienne. In fact, my handwriting was good, and every year I won the school prize for penmanship. And it was true that Fabienne could make up stories about pigs and chickens and cows and goats, and birds and trees and Mère Bourdon's window curtains and Père Gimlett's horse cart. And Joline, Fabienne's older sister, who had died a long time ago. I no longer remembered what Joline looked like, but Fabienne had several stories made up for Joline's ghost, and the ghost of her baby. Fabienne called him Baby Oscar even though he had died before there was time for anyone to come up with a name for him. And then there was the ghost of Joline's American sweetheart, Bobby. Bobby, who was a Negro, had been court-martialed and hanged after Joline got pregnant.

All those deaths had happened when Fabienne and I were six going on seven. I remembered Joline whipping Fabienne and me with a bundle of nettles when she caught us sneaking behind her and Bobby, and I remembered the chocolates he had thrown to us, to make us stop following them. Fabienne and I talked about what Bobby was doing to Joline in the Jeep or when he drove with her to someplace we could not reach by foot. We tried to act those things out according to our imagination. We felt old enough for everything in the world, including the stillborn baby, his color darker than our nanny goat Fleur. Fabienne and I both touched his head, sticky and gray and lukewarm, when all those women's attention was on Joline, who was bleeding and dying quickly, making terrible noises.

In Fabienne's stories, all three of them were all right now, not really a happy family, but three happy ghosts, busy with their own games.

The ghosts gave me a chill sometimes, but more often they made me laugh. Look there—Fabienne would point to the creek—did you see? What? I would ask. I knew I would never see anything she saw, and it was for that reason I could have no other friend but Fabienne. She was eyes and ears for both of us. It's Baby Oscar, she would whisper; he's lancing eels with a bayonet. Oh, he's learned swimming, I would say, and Fabienne would reply that she wasn't sure how good a swimmer he was, as he was sitting on that lily pad like a frog. In other stories, Joline's ghost wove willow branches into a snare and caught any man leaving the bar too late at night. What did she do with them? I asked. She tickled them so they couldn't stay drunk easily, Fabienne would say; do you know how funny and terrible it is for those men when they cannot focus on being drunk?

And then there was Bobby's ghost, my favorite. He blew air into a cow's ears. He tied the tails of a litter of piglets together and threw a firecracker at them. He put cigarettes under children's pillows and stuffed fragrant soaps in men's pants. He hid oranges behind the rocks or in the woods. The oranges, in Fabienne's stories, were always for us only. In truth we had seen oranges no more than a handful of times in our lives, back when Bobby was still alive. The first time he brought an orange for Joline, Fabienne sent me to beg her to let us hold the fruit in our hands for a moment. We had never seen anything in that color till then.

I never made up stories, but I was good at listening to Fabienne.

~

EVERY STORY HAS AN EXPIRATION DATE. Like a jar of marmalade or a candle.

Does marmalade have an expiration date? Yes, marmalade only makes fruit live longer, not forever.

Does a candle have an expiration date? It may not come with one, but once past a certain point in its life, it is corrupted, even if it still burns.

Time corrupts. And we pay a price for everything corruptible: food, roof beams, souls.

This story of mine expired when I heard of Fabienne's death. Telling a story past its expiration date is like exhuming a body long buried. The reason for doing so is not always clear to everyone.

I have been thinking about Fabienne's baby. My mother did not say in her letter if that baby survived his or her birth. Nor who fathered the baby. Certainly my mother saw no point in sharing the information. Perhaps she has even forgotten my friendship with Fabienne. More often now my mother, in her letters, includes the news of this or that death from the village. She has long accepted that I will not return to Saint Rémy during her lifetime. Her hope, she said in one letter, is that I will at least return for her funeral.

Perhaps I should plan a visit to Saint Rémy. Earl would not grudge me the fare. If I lie on Fabienne's stone, I wonder if I will feel the same heaviness as we once did. There will be no waiting for her to decide when to stand up and walk away. Any choice will have to be mine: to up and leave, or to remain immobile above her grave forever.

~

I HAD SOME ADVANTAGE OVER FABIENNE when we were thirteen. I could read and write better. I was taller and my body had begun to fill out a little, not as bony as hers. My forehead was wider, my cheeks had a nicer contour. In general I had a more pleasant look. And I did not mind smiling at people, or carrying a basket for an old woman without her pestering me too much, or behaving obediently toward anyone who had some power over me. Fabienne minded all those things.

I did not know these were advantages back then. Fabienne could climb a tree in a few seconds while I was barely hanging on to the lowest branch. She could hold her breath underwater until it seemed that she would never surface again. I went upward, always, like a freak fish with extra-large swim bladders. Her cows were afraid of her—even before she raised her stick they cowered. No dogs nipped at her. The bees in the woods stung only me.

Some people are born with a special kind of crystal instead of a heart. No, I am not talking about witchcraft, but it is a mystery that these people, who look no different than others, can sail through life without illness, injuries, or broken hearts. There are not many of them around, but Fabienne is one. Was. Was one, until she was trapped by childbirth.

That crystal in place of a heart—it makes things happen. To others.

But I did not know this back then. On that day, when we knocked on M. Devaux's door, in the dark, all I was trying to do was stifle my giggles. It would have been rude to laugh in a man's face the day his wife had been buried.

M. Devaux did not immediately answer the door. Fabienne told me to take off one of my clogs. Why? I said, but I often asked questions automatically, not expecting an answer. I handed it to her, and she pounded on the door with its hard rubber sole.

M. Devaux said from behind the door, "Who's there?"

"It's us," Fabienne said.

I was not sure if M. Devaux could tell who we were, but perhaps anyone alive would have seemed the same to him when he was waiting for his dead wife's ghost, and a ghost did not have to knock on the door. It was said that he had loved his wife. If a man loves a woman and if the woman dies, will he love her ghost equally? I wished I could ask Fabienne the question as we stood there. It was the kind of question we liked to ponder.

"What do you want?" M. Devaux asked.

"We want to talk to you," Fabienne replied.

"About what?"

"Let us in first," Fabienne said. "It's a secret. We can't let others hear us."

This was how it had unfolded in my memory. It was possible that it did not happen exactly so, but between facts and memories I always trust the latter. Why? Because facts do not make myths. And I was made into a minor myth by that visit. If I told people that I was once a myth, nobody would believe me. But is it a myth's job to make you believe in it? A myth says, Take me or leave me. You can shrug, you can laugh at its face, but you cannot do anything about it. You are the one to change your mind, or not to change—either way, a myth is a complete thing, and you, a nonmyth, are a nonentity.

No one is born a myth. All babies, whether delivered in a barn or in a palace, need the same things to stay alive. Later, some people are smart enough to turn themselves into myths. Some people turn others into myths. Yet what is myth but a veil arranged to cover what is hideous or tedious?

People are oftentimes hideous or tedious. Sometimes they are both. So is the world. We would have no use for myths if the world were neither hideous nor tedious.

WHAT'S THE SECRET you can't let others hear?" M. Devaux asked. He did not invite us into his house. His thin frame fit nicely in the crack of the door he left open.

"We're writing a book," Fabienne said. "We need your help."

"What do you know about books?" M. Devaux said.

"They're written by people. Are they not?"

"Not by people like you."

"That's what you think."

"You need to know how to spell your name and write your sentences," M. Devaux said.

"She knows how to do those things," Fabienne said, draping an arm over my shoulders. I bent my knees slightly, making myself not much taller than her. She might have said, This cow milks well, and it would have been all the same to M. Devaux.

"Who's writing the book?" he asked.

"We both are," Fabienne said. "It's like we're one person."

"You need a nom de plume, then."

"A what?" Fabienne asked.

"You can't be wanting to write a book without knowing what a nom de plume is," M. Devaux said.

"Agnès Moreau," Fabienne said. "We'll use Agnès's name for our book."

"Why not yours?" I asked her.

"Because writing a book is my idea," Fabienne said. "You have to give something, too."

M. Devaux looked at us this whole time, not hiding his contempt. He was truly an ugly man. With tufts of hair sticking out from the sides of his head, and round eyes hooded by heavy lids, he looked like an old and starved owl. "I'm about to go to bed," he said, and then he bade us good night.

Fabienne placed a foot inside the door so he could not close it. "We haven't finished," she said. "Will you help us or not?"

"I don't know how to help you."

"I have it all planned out," Fabienne said. "I'll make up the stories, Agnès will write them down, and you'll make them into a book."

M. Devaux mumbled something, an exchange with god or with his dead wife. But Fabienne would not withdraw her foot until he agreed to read what we would be writing.

"See, he just needs some distraction," Fabienne said later, before we parted near my house.

"Distraction from his wife's death?" I asked.

"Boredom," Fabienne said. "Sad people don't often know that they are sad *and* bored."

"WHY DO YOU WANT TO WRITE A BOOK?" I asked Fabienne. We were lying on the grassy slope adjacent to Père Gimlett's potato field. He was decent enough to let Fabienne graze her cows and goats there as long as they didn't trample his field. A good Christian, Fabienne said of him a few times, always with a sneer.

It was a public holiday, but cows and goats and pigs and chickens did not celebrate the holidays. Sometimes they were killed for a celebration. Not on this day. It was one of those minor holidays that did not require bloodshed.

"It'll be amusing to us," Fabienne said.

A lot of things were amusing to us one day but not the next day. "How?" I asked. "I don't see why we need to amuse ourselves by writing a book."

"You don't see many things," Fabienne said. "We write a

book so other people will know how we live. And they'll know how it feels to be us."

The two cows stood nearby, chewing so slowly, as though they had all the time in a world where grass would never run out for them. Their names were Bianca and Millie, and they were the reason Fabienne no longer went to school. Everyone with a mouth to be fed had to earn his or her keep—children without a mother met that reality earlier. Nobody found it extraordinary, the least Fabienne and me. Her two older brothers worked on their farm. Once upon a time Joline used to get cartons of American cigarettes from her boyfriend. You could barter for anything you wanted if you had American cigarettes, so Joline, even though she had not liked to do farmwork, had earned her keep, too.

A goat wandered off, approaching the creek. I thought of warning Fabienne but decided not to. She would only laugh and pucker her lips to give an earsplitting whistle. She had many ways to make the animals follow her orders.

A bee landed on a chicory, making the head of the flower bow. Soon the bee would go to another flower. I could not see which part of our lives was worth other people knowing about. My days at school were all the same, and Fabienne's life, with her cows and goats, could not be so different from one day to the next. Growing up required patience, but even if we had all the patience in the world, where would that lead us? Someday we would get married. Then we would have to raise children, if we were lucky enough not to end up dying in childbirth, as Joline had. We would have more work to do then, more mouths to feed. Would Fabienne and I still be able to spend all this time together? I used to think that she and I could find a pair of brothers to marry so we would never part, but perhaps it would be better, I thought, if we could stay unmarried. "Why do we want people to know what it feels like to be us?" I asked.

"Why not?"

"Who are those people?" I asked. Nobody, I thought, but my role was to ask questions, not to answer them.

"I don't know yet," Fabienne said. "But you can always make people think they want something."

"How?"

"We'll sort that out later," Fabienne said. "For now, we must write. You have your pencil and workbook with you?"

I had brought my school satchel as she had told me to. I had told my parents that I would do my homework while spending the day with Fabienne. Maybe they believed me, maybe not. But at this moment, it suited them that I was not around too much. My brother, Jean, was dying. He had not been well enough to do heavy farmwork since he returned from a German labor camp six years earlier, but in the past few months he had gotten worse. He lay in bed all day long, staring at the ceiling when he wasn't coughing up blood. I looked too healthy, too fat, too happy in comparison. Sometimes my sisters, all three of them married, visited and spent time with him. My parents never felt uneasy with my sisters around Jean, so they must have seen something wrong in me, which did not bother me. I did not speak with my parents unless I had to. I did all my chores without their bidding because I hated to give them an opportunity to disturb the blanket of quiet mystery I carried around myself at home. I was not a child who could bring comfort to anyone, and I had no such desire.

"All right, write down what I say," Fabienne said. In a deeper voice, she said, *"Le jour où bébé François est mort* . . . On the day when baby François died . . ."

"Who's François?" I asked. Joline's little dead baby did not have a name, but we always called him Oscar.

Fabienne ignored me, and continued in the same eerie tone. I looked up several times to make sure she was still the Fabienne I knew. She was speaking as someone else, and whoever that woman was, she was already dead, and she was speaking with a dramatic despair that would usually strike Fabienne and me as comical. But she did not have her usual mocking smile. When she—no, the woman she was speaking for—asked god why he had sent her baby to the earth only for him to die, I stopped writing. "That's a funny question the woman is asking," I said.

"What's so funny?"

"All people are sent to the earth to die," I said. "God even sent his own son to the earth to die."

Fabienne shushed me.

I will not pretend that I remember every word she dictated to me, but I know the first few sentences by heart. I can see Fabienne's words in my neat handwriting. I was not bad at penmanship. She was not bad at speaking like a dead woman.

The dead woman in that story was not Fabienne, but how strange—I have been thinking in the past few days—that one day she would become that woman.

We did not finish the story by the end of the day. I asked Fabienne if she needed more time to make up the rest, and she said of course not. She knew the story by heart, but knowing a story by heart was different than taking the time to write it out.

"What's the difference?" I asked.

Fabienne thought for a moment and said she didn't understand why I was behaving like an idiot and asking stupid questions. I lay down and covered my face with my satchel.

To a stranger it might have looked like I was sulking. But the truth was, I was smiling under the canvas bag. Fabienne was right that I asked too many questions, but she got mad at me only when she was unable to offer a good answer.

What's the difference between knowing a story and writing it out? But the questions I should have asked, which I did not know how when we were younger, were: Isn't it enough just to know a story? Why take the time to write it out?

I now have the answer, for her and for myself. The world has no use for who we are and what we know. A story has to be written out. How else do we get our revenge?

(Revenge against what, or whom, precisely?

Don't, Agnès, fall into the trap and answer that question.)

~

When we finished the story of Baby François, we showed it to M. Devaux. He asked us how many more stories like this we had. Seven, Fabienne replied. All about dead babies? he asked. She said not all of them were about dead babies, but all were about dead children. He nodded and said he imagined that would be the case. How did he know while I did not? I decided that to dislike him was not enough. I must hate him.

M. Devaux was a reader of poetry and philosophy. He told us he had written some unsuccessful plays that had never seen the stage, and he still composed a poem a day, after he came back from the post office. Fabienne asked if we could read his poems, but he said we should be spared, as he read his poems aloud only to his pigeons.

"You should keep some parrots instead," Fabienne said. "They could read your verses back to you."

M. Devaux gave her a strange look.

"You know I'm joking," Fabienne said.

"I don't like jokes," M. Devaux said. "Jokes have barbs."

"Fishhooks have barbs, too," Fabienne said. "Still, fish like to swallow them."

"I don't like fish. They're not intelligent," M. Devaux said.

Had I been a tempestuous person, I would have cut in and told M. Devaux that he was as stupid as a fish. I did not like the way Fabienne talked with him, too much like the way she talked with me. But I did not interrupt them. There were many corners in M. Devaux's house where the light of the hanging bulb did not reach, and I preferred sitting in one of those corners and keeping my face in the dimness when I studied M. Devaux and Fabienne. Neither of them was good-looking. Watching his face and knowing he was ugly gave me some pleasure. Watching her face and knowing that it made no difference whether she was pretty or not—that, too, gave me pleasure.

"You call the fish unintelligent, but that's because they're animals," Fabienne said. "Animals are stupid."

"Some animals are intelligent," M. Devaux said. "My pigeons, for example. I respect them as I respect talented people."

"They have enough intelligence to coo over you."

"No, they have highly developed brains. If they wanted to live in the wildness I would let them."

"It's foolish to let animals decide what they want," Fabienne said.

"Watch out, mademoiselle," M. Devaux said. "You follow that logic, next thing you say is that it's foolish to let people decide what they want."

Fabienne shrugged. "But tell me, what if your pigeons decide not to return to you one day?"

"They won't. I know them," M. Devaux said. "They know me, too."

Fabienne laughed, and I shivered with excitement. For others, that laugh might sound as silly as any girl's, but no one knew her as well as I did. Fabienne laughed like that only when she planned to amuse herself—hurling a cat on top of a roof, crushing a bird nest in her palm, or telling a nasty joke about her dead sister, Joline. Once, when I was meeting her after school, she ambushed me and pushed me into the creek when the ice was not yet gone, her shrill laugh the last thing I heard before the rushing blood and the thawing creek filled my ears with rumbling. I scrambled onto the bank and nearly wept with fury, but she shushed me and pointed to a pile of old clothes next to a tree trunk. I was appeased right away. When she hurled a cat onto the roof, she meant to watch it tremble with fear. When she set her heart on destroying a bird's nest, it was because she wanted to watch an egg dropping from the height of the branch she was sitting on. But she did, after all, care about me enough to prepare a change of clothes. They were Joline's, I could tell from the way the blouse hung over my hips and the pant legs dragged on the ground.

"I'm glad that your pigeons are loyal to you," Fabienne said.

M. Devaux nodded. He did not yet know that she could hurt him. She could catch one of the pigeons, wring its neck, and bring the body back to him, just to see the look on his face. The more I thought about it, the more certain I felt of Fabienne's plan. In my imagination I even suggested that we roast the bird so it wouldn't be a wasteful death. Bringing the bones and the feathers back to M. Devaux would be enough to punish his stupid pride in his pigeons.

But for weeks, they came and went as they always had.

AFTER THE START OF THE NEW YEAR, Fabienne and I had eight stories. Eight dead children and a number of dead animals. All but one of the dead children were buried, yet when the book was eventually published, the one unburied child drew much more attention than all the others. It was a one-day-old baby, alive at his birth, dead because his mother, a girl no older than Joline and also unmarried, had to hide the fact that he was born. It was sensible that such a poor thing could not get a proper burial. Still, I must confess that even as I was writing out what Fabienne dictated, I felt a nausea and a tingling at the back of my throat. I did not protest the way she made the baby disappear, though for some time after, I fed our pigs hastily, never lingering at the trough a second longer than necessary.

There were also some dead men and women in those

stories, but who they were and how they came to meet their deaths were of little importance. They were, like the adults in our lives, no more than wooden posts by the roadside. But their ghosts, like the cemetery, held our interest.

The number of people you kill in your stories, M. Devaux grumbled—but how could he not see what we knew already? Mathematics matters little when it comes to death.

(Mathematics may not be that important even in life. You need only to be able to count and to add. And those skills may still be superfluous. If god said he was to take something, your sight or your hearing or your arithmetic aptitude, would you find being blind or being deaf preferable to being unable to do arithmetic? Someone is bound to disagree with me, old Pascal in his grave, whom M. Devaux often quoted as though they had been friends who met for a daily walk. If not for M. Devaux, I might have gone through all these years without knowing Pascal. What a shame it would have been. Pascal, in fact, is the perfect name for one of my geese, who is less frivolous than his other three companions. Even as a gosling, Pascal walked with a gravitas. He follows the other geese when they get into mischief, but you can see that his heart is not quite in it. He charges at the postman and terrifies the chickens only because he has to fulfill a goose's fate. He is, I believe, a philosopher.)

Macabre, M. Devaux called the stories, but he opened his door to us without fail whenever we visited. He had not minced words when he talked about our work: puerile, incoherent, morbid, repetitive, unbalanced, carelessly written. Sometimes he hissed at a page. Or groaned. But we could see that he waited for our stories with interest. With greed, even. If we did not show up for a few days, he would complain when we next visited. "What do you expect?" Fabienne said. "We aren't hens, and we don't lay eggs every morning and run around clucking."

M. Devaux said that he would rather we were as reliable as hens. "Only," he said, "don't be too loquacious."

One day he told us that some people had noticed our frequent visits to his house. Fabienne said it would be strange if no one noticed. "The only job everyone loves is to be in other people's way," she said.

M. Devaux said he had explained that he was giving us some education because he hated to see us squander our lives away. I'm going to school, I argued, and he said, Yes, but Fabienne needs to learn, too. I thought she would refute that notion and say something nasty to his face, but she only shrugged and said we were his pupils because we decided to be. "Or . . ." She looked around the house and then said, "You can tell people we come to you because we're hungry. You can say food is the best bait for young girls."

M. Devaux's face flushed, looking insulted. "Mademoiselle, I treat you honorably because I respect your intelligence."

"Like you respect your pigeons' intelligence?"

I laughed, though neither M. Devaux nor Fabienne heard me. They studied each other like two goats getting ready for a fight. But such moments came and went. Oftentimes it was Fabienne who found something else to talk about, and then they behaved as though nothing awkward had happened. Only once did M. Devaux, retreating from Fabienne's stare, change the subject, saying that he did not know if we had heard, but Stalin had died. When Fabienne did not respond right away, I said, in a tone half as sharp as hers, that I did not see how that news had anything to do with us. Then I got both their attention, M. Devaux calling me ignorant and Fabienne shushing me, telling me to stop behaving like an idiot. I was not disheartened by their contempt as much as amazed by a new stupidity that I had discovered in myself: I used to be able to stay quiet when I sat in a corner, observing them; I should have known better than to give them an opportunity to find something in common between themselves.

Had M. Devaux been a more perceptive person, he would have taught us a few things about geometry. The three of us made a volatile triangle. I, Agnès, would be just fine with only Fabienne in my life, but she needed more than I could give her. M. Devaux was not much, but there were things he offered Fabienne that I could not.

The last thing on our minds was to wonder what he wanted from us. He must have figured it out, and decided that however little we gave him was better than nothing.

When Fabienne told M. Devaux that we were finished with the book, he scowled. "Finished? It's only beginning," he said. He told us that we did not really know how to write. "You can't even write a single proper sentence," he said to me.

"But they're not my sentences," I said. "They're Fabienne's. I only wrote down what she told me to."

"Well, then, you'd better start all over again. And this time, you write down what I say. And you—" He turned to Fabienne. "You go on dreaming up your tales."

"Like it's your job to tell a hen to keep laying eggs," Fabienne said.

~

WHEN WE—M. DEVAUX AND I—FINISHED the second version, the stories felt different from the ones Fabienne had dictated to me. What exactly had happened I could not tell, but the new stories felt less like hers, more like mine. Not that it was me who had written them, I was only taking down what M. Devaux dictated. But if you put the new version next to Fabienne's, it was like putting me next to her. Fabienne was savage. I was only crude.

There was a reason M. Devaux made the stories more like me. Had I been a good pupil, I would have placed the two sets of exercise books side by side to see how M. Devaux had changed a few words in every sentence. But I was not interested in that. The truth was, this book-writing game wearied me. All spring my body felt heavy with torpor. I thought about the inside of my body, the strange shapes with their strange softness, and I could not tell if it was dread or disgust that made me wake up in the middle of night, drenched in sweat. When I could not fall back to sleep, the frogs and the owls took turns to speak some sort of message to me. Sometimes older boys who were already out of school would whistle at me or say something obscene to my face, and then break out laughing. A few years earlier they threw rocks at Fabienne and me, but now they seemed to have lost interest in her.

I did not tell Fabienne all those things that troubled me. As long as I was next to her, I could be the same Agnès. My body was getting heavier, slowing down my mind, which was not fast to begin with, but Fabienne's lightness and quickness still carried me. Sometimes I lay at the foot of a tree and looked up at her dangling legs above me. "Climb up here," she said, even though she knew I could never reach that high. I smiled stupidly back. It did not matter at all that I could not catch up with her. I lived through her. What was left behind was only my shell.

But there was one thing I could not leave behind. From spring to summer I helped care for my brother, Jean, more than before, but he rarely touched the food and drink I brought into his room. My mother told me to walk without making a sound and not to bother him with any conversation unless he wanted to talk first. He never did. I knew my mother did not trust herself to be able to stay quiet and calm around him. She could easily throw herself onto her knees and beg him to eat, to speak, to live. He could not, and would not, for her or for anyone. I could see my mother's fear, and my father's resignation. They were to lose him a second time, and they could do nothing about it, as they had not been able to do anything when he was taken away by the Germans. I could see also that Jean felt neither pity nor warmth toward us. We, like the pigs in the sty and the sparrows on the windowsill and the crickets in the grass, were on the other side of where he was. Why would he care about how we felt—if I were him I would have held the same indifference toward everyone and everything in the world. In fact, I did not have to be so near death as Jean was to feel that way. That summer, my family, my neighbors, my schoolmates, M. Devaux, and all the people busy in the world were on the opposite side of where I was. Only Fabienne was on my side.

One day, when Fabienne asked about Jean, I said that a sudden clean death would be ten times better than a slow one.

"No," she said. "Being alive is a hundred times better than being dead."

"We're talking about different things, no?"

"But why do you even concern yourself with being dead? We won't die for a long time."

"Then why are our stories all about dead children?" I asked. I thought about Jean's eyes, hollow with a blind look, and his collarbones protruding in such a horrible way that sometimes I felt the urge to wrap a scarf around his neck, to cover any exposed part of his body, which must have been nearly a skeleton underneath the blanket.

"Precisely for the reason that they're dead and we're not," Fabienne replied. "Stop being morbid."

What a strange accusation that was. Fabienne was ten times more morbid than I was. The difference between us was that I respected and feared death, and would rather not think about it unless I was forced to. To her, death was a prank. Only the weak, the foolish, and the unlucky would fall for it.

She then told me that she had something else in mind, a second book, but she wasn't ready to make me write it down yet. She had a few things to sort out in her head.

"Are there more dead children?" I asked.

"No one will die this time," she said. "I promise."

That did not convince me. Fabienne made promises to me all the time. She knew I would never expect her to keep them.

We still went to M. Devaux's house regularly, and sometimes we stopped at the post office to drop a bouquet of wildflowers on his counter. It was Fabienne's idea, which surprised me. We looked down upon the girls who softened their edges with pretty things—bracelets made of red berries around their wrists or satin ribbons in their hair. When this went on, I asked her whether we would be giving M. Devaux the wrong idea that we liked him more than we did. He had placed a glass jar on his counter to receive our flowers.

"That's the point," Fabienne said. "Why would we want to give anyone the right idea about anything? We want him to think he's important to us."

"Why?"

"We like to see people proved wrong," Fabienne said. "Don't you think?"

"Oh yes," I agreed quickly.

"Then stop pestering me with all these whys."

M. Devaux was still sickly looking, but now that we knew him better, he looked less ugly. He tried a few times to make us read the books on his shelves. I wanted to open one of them, just to see what was inside, but Fabienne always shook her head, saying we had better things to do, and that we had no time for his books. When he continued to press us, she said those books were of no use to us.

"Of no use?" M. Devaux raged, and called us idiots.

"We'd be idiots if we thought those books would do us any good," Fabienne said. "Which one of these books can herd my cows for me? Which one can feed Agnès's pigs?"

"These books will make you think about more than your cows and pigs," M. Devaux said. He went on a long rant about philosophy and poetry.

"We have our own philosophy and poetry," Fabienne said. "And you don't get to know anything about them."

M. Devaux turned away from her stare and put the books back on the shelf, each to its original place. He often fumed, but his anger rarely lasted. He mumbled that no one should dismiss others' philosophy and poetry without even knowing them.

"Why not?" Fabienne said. "Do you think anyone cares about our philosophy and poetry?"

M. Devaux did not seem to have an answer to that. He was a little intimidated by Fabienne, I could tell. That was not surprising. I was always intimidated by her, but I did not make the mistake he was making, speaking of poetry and philosophy and using words we had never heard of, as though that would make him superior.

~

The way we lived back then—the stench and the filth, the animals running amok, and the people crazier than animals—these things I had not found extraordinary until I was told, later in Paris and in England, that they were. In fact, those words—stench, filth, amok, crazy—were not mine, but other people's. My books described how we lived then, though I wonder if they are still around in the world. Where do dead books go? A graveyard somewhere? A crematory?

When I arrived in America, Earl liked to bring me to dinner parties at his friends' houses, to show off his young French bride. The husbands at those parties had healthy appetites, and the wives, moving around in their mint-green or coral-pink kitchens, were as pretty and mysterious to me as the pair of goldfish I had seen in a Parisian publisher's office, whirling in a crystal bowl. It was the first time I had seen goldfish, and they had struck me as the most luxurious beings in the world, their lives calm and carefree.

The women asked me about France, about French cuisine and French fashion, their faces taking up a girlish expression. I responded to them with an equal dose of girlishness, giving them what they thought they wanted to hear. Though sometimes, behind my voice, which softened in English, I could feel myself sneer: Are you sure you want to know about *my* France? I could tell you a few things, as many as you could stand, and gladly rob you of your appetite for dinner. And then tomorrow morning, when you looked at your mud-colored coffee, glistening bacon, and runny yolk, you'd remember the maggots unearthed by the torrential rain, or the screeching of the butchered pigs, their panting replaced by a liquid hiss, or the chickens that were half hatched and then died in their shells. And you'd also remember that we wasted nothing that had once lived, after it died. There were always hungry creatures waiting to eat so that they could postpone being eaten themselves.

Les Enfants Heureux—The Happy Children—was the title of the first book. M. Devaux was the one to come up with the title, adding an epigraph about how dead children remain the happiest children. Later, when the book was published, the press talked about the ferocious honesty on every page, and they called me a savage young chronicler of the postwar life with a mind drawn to morbidity. Me, savage? My mind, morbid? That would be like calling my chickens a band of robbers.

My mind was not morbid. It has never been. You have to be obsessed with death to be morbid, just as you have to be obsessed with love to be romantic. I am neither morbid nor romantic.

In those stories, the children, other than the fact that they all died in the end, lived the way Fabienne and I lived. The journalists and critics, mindless people, refused to see that the distance between life and death was always shorter than people are willing to understand. One step further, one breath skipped—it does not take much to slip from life into death.

From life to life? That is a long way. The cousins of my geese, the wild ones, fly over a continent. People leave their homes for new homes, new cities, new countries. But who can shorten the distance between two people so they can say with confidence that they have reached each other? In that sense perhaps Fabienne was one of the few who worked miracles. She made me her. She made us into one person.

When *Les Enfants Heureux* was published, the press debated what had driven a peasant girl like me to write a book. Ambition, some said. Necessity, said others. I did not understand what they were talking about then, but I have since seen ambition and necessity drive many people to prosperity, and as many to despair. Ambition and necessity: I've never felt either of them keenly. Fabienne was driven by both, though to the world she would appear the opposite. Ambition would have made her put her name on the book. Necessity would have made her see the material gain in such a fame. But that is only a worldly way to look at things. What Fabienne wanted to do, what she absolutely needed to do, was to make things happen. To peel a young tree's bark to see how fast it would die. To pet a dog and then give it a kick, just to cherish the confused terror in the poor beast's eyes. To push me into the water when my back was turned. To make me into a star, or a freak show, though she alone did not make me into a freak show. Many other people joined her, starting with M. Devaux.

M. DEVAUX ARRANGED A TRIP to Paris in May. He and I. What about you? I asked Fabienne, and she told me not to be an idiot. "When the book is published, it will only have your name printed on it. We don't want to confuse people."

"Why are you so sure someone will publish the book?" I asked.

"That's M. Devaux's promise," she said.

I did not want to remind Fabienne that she often made promises, most of which she had no intention of keeping. In the village she had a reputation of being a liar, but that was because people did not know her as I did. Say someone was looking for a runaway goat. If you told him that you'd seen the goat go into someone else's barn, you would be lying. Fabienne would never do that, not because a lie like that could lead to accusations or quarrels or even fistfights, but because people who could be so easily made into fools would give her less pleasure. Rather, she would offer the owner her assistance. She would say that she would watch out for the goat, and she would promise that she would get it back by the end of the day. People might not believe her, but what was their option but to thank her in advance, hoping that she would be in the right mood to fulfill her promise? Fabienne might not bring back their goats, but they knew she could make their goats disappear forever.

"But don't you want to go to Paris?" I asked.

Fabienne said that there would be time for that. She was in no rush to go anywhere at the moment. She had things to think about.

"Like what?" I asked.

"Like what," she mimicked me. "About our next book, of course. Once M. Devaux helps us publish this book, we'll follow up with another, and then more."

"We'll end up with a lot of dead children on our hands," I said. Like a pair of murderesses, I thought.

"I told you already that we're finished with dead children," she said.

"What are we writing next, then?"

"Anything that comes our way," she said. "Postmasters. Or Paris."

"What about Paris? How should I carry myself there?" I asked. She said M. Devaux would take care of that. When I asked him, he told me to just be myself. That was of no use to me. I could be myself only when I was with Fabienne. Can a wall describe its own dimensions and texture, can a wall even sense its own existence, if not for the ball that constantly bounces off of it?

M. Devaux paid a visit to my parents. He told them I had written a book and he had sent it to a few publishers in Paris.

He proposed to bring me to meet them. It could open a door to my future, he explained to my parents. I did not think they listened closely to what he said. Afterward they did not ask me about the book I had written.

I was the youngest of five siblings. Perhaps my parents did love me, but between the war and the liberation, between their relief that my three sisters were safely married and their waiting for my brother, Jean, to die, they had little time and aspiration left for me. I was glad that there was no need to lie to them. It was not that I had any moral issue with lying, but lying to someone would only make that person important to me. The single lie—or the variations of the same lie—I had told in those years was to Fabienne: I made her believe that I was like a vacant house, my mind empty of any thoughts of my own, my heart void of feelings.

I was not aware of my falsity then.

I had never been to Paris. The day before the trip, when I brought Jean his dinner, I told him that I was visiting Paris the next day. *Un voyage d'affaires*, I said, the words I learned from M. Devaux's notice on the door of the post office, saying it would be closed on Thursday.

I never spoke to Jean other than telling him that his meal was ready. Perhaps it was for that reason he turned to me with a strange look. "Are you coming back?" he asked.

"Yes," I said. I explained that I was only going for a day. M. Devaux and I were going to catch the early train, and we would take the night train back.

Jean did not seem to understand, or else he had simply lost interest. He closed his eyes, and I looked at his pale blue eyelids. Later, when I returned for the dishes, he had drunk half of a glass of milk, and left the bread and soup untouched.

"Make sure you come back," he said before I left his room.

"Of course I will," I said. I found his words strange, but it was a long train ride that had taken him to Germany, away from us for three years. Perhaps he had thought that his exile was permanent, but the train that had taken him away had also brought him back to us. At least he would die at home.

The next day we set out early. I had been on a train only twice, both for school trips. The train to Paris was longer, faster, though the wooden benches were dirtier and more worn than on the slow local trains. "What you need to do is watch people closely without speaking much," M. Devaux said to me when we settled down, facing each other by the window. "We want people to see a young girl from the countryside, who doesn't know a lot about the world but who was guided by her intuition to write a book."

I watched the fields and the roads out the window, the church spires, the houses with their vegetable plots, and the bridges over canals and rivers, all waiting for the day to start. I could have been born in any one of those villages. I would have still been me, but I would not have known Fabienne. That thought made me feel a tingling on my back, as I had felt the night before, when I studied Jean's thin eyelids, the bulges beneath unmoving. If he opened his eyes he would see my stupid stare, but he kept them shut, seeing nothing more than a blind man would see, formless gray. What a great terror it would be to be Jean, or to be born in a world without Fabienne.

"Agnès, did you understand what I said?" M. Devaux asked.

"What's intuition?" I said. "What's my intuition?"

He shrugged. "I don't suppose that's a question you should be asking," he said. "A girl with good intuition knows when to speak and when to keep quiet."

"I was keeping quiet," I said. "You wouldn't leave me alone."

"You weren't keeping quiet. You were playing dead."

I wished I could laugh at his face, the way Fabienne did. Did he only realize now that I had been playing dead all along when Fabienne and I spent time with him? M. Devaux did not think much of me. That I could tell. Between Fabienne and myself, he talked only with Fabienne. I wondered if he would rather have her name on the book, as he might prefer to travel with her. All the same, he had to carry out her plan. That made me pity him. I did everything Fabienne wanted me to, but that was how we were: I would never question her, and she would never think any other girl worthy of her friendship. M. Devaux, armed with his philosophy and poetry, still had to do what she wanted him to. All because he was a weak and unimaginative man.

M. Devaux took a cigarette out and tapped it on my arm. "You don't need me to tell you that you should leave most of the talking to me," he said.

"Can I have a cigarette?"

"Certainly not."

I smiled to show him that I had known that would be his answer, and that I did not mind at all. Long ago, when Joline was still alive, Fabienne and I had stolen a cigarette from her. We hated the taste.

"Hold it," he said. "Smile like that once more."

My face froze, and then I grinned.

"Now you truly look like an idiot," he said. "Smile like you did earlier. Give yourself an air."

"What air?"

"Mystery, humility, coquettishness."

I had no idea what he was talking about, so I only shrugged and turned to look at the field outside the window. M. Devaux was rude and ridiculous, but all grown-ups were, and I had no trouble putting up with them. Fabienne and I—we were friends for a reason. Only later, when I met more girls, when I got to know my nieces and nephews, did I understand that Fabienne and I shared something not often available to children (or adults, for that matter). Neither of us felt intense love toward our parents, or intense resentment. And the world was made of people who were not that different from our parents, so it was only natural that neither of us felt intense love or intense resentment toward anyone. We had each other, and for a long time that was enough.

IN PARIS I FIRST SMILED AT M. PERRET, a friend of M. Devaux's, and then at the men they brought me to meet in different publishing houses. My mother had given me permission to put on my best frock, cut from rose-colored plaid, with a round collar and tightly buttoned sleeves. It had been my mother's before her marriage, and it hung loose on me.

One of the men we met at a publishing house looked at me for a long moment and asked M. Devaux if truly I had written the book by myself. But of course, I said before M. Devaux replied. It was the first time I spoke, other than issuing greetings.

The man asked M. Devaux and M. Perret to stay in his office, and brought me to another room. "Here," he said, pushing a piece of paper and a pencil toward me. "I'm going to smoke a cigarette. While I'm doing that, you'll write a paragraph for me."

"About what?" I asked.

"Anything you like," he said. "No, let's make it specific: a man smoking a cigarette."

It was a test I could not fail. I watched him strike a match, his clean-shaven face taking up a warmer hue in the little bobbing flame. I took the pencil and did not think much before I started to write. My penmanship was one thing that gave me confidence. Even M. Devaux, who thought little of me, once said that no one would expect a girl like me to write like that.

Later, on the train back home, when M. Devaux asked me what I had done in the room with the man, I said we talked about how I came up with the stories, and the man also wanted to make sure I could write proper French. I wrote down what he dictated from a book on the shelf, I said. No, I don't remember what book, but he said he liked my penmanship. I was not sure if M. Devaux believed me, but it was not my responsibility to make him believe me or like me.

This is what I wrote on that day for the smoking man, which was later printed in the introduction to *Les Enfants Heureux*:

> Jonny the American was crying. His head was clutched in his hands, and his giant elbows rested on his giant knees. It couldn't be comfortable for him, sitting there in a position that would be much easier for a child. I asked him what was wrong with him, but today he seemed to decide he did not understand my French. He could not stop crying, so I picked up the jacket he had thrown on the ground. There was a pack of cigarettes in the right pocket. I had seen him take it out before. In the other pocket I found a matchbook, and I struck a match and lit a cigarette. It took me a few tries, and I put the cigarette in my mouth and inhaled as I'd

seen men do. It lit up, but I had to spit a couple times because I did not like the charred taste in my mouth. Jonny did not raise his head. I shoved my arm underneath his and tried to aim the cigarette at his mouth. He took the cigarette and threw it as far as he could. What a waste. I thought of going over and putting it out and bringing it back to my father, but before I could move, Jonny grabbed my hand with such a force that I almost stumbled into him. His eyes were bloodshot, and for the first time since we'd met I found him frightening. Lucky for me, Clarabelle was right next to us, munching like she did not know I was about to scream. I tried to push myself away from Jonny, and when he did not let me go, I guided his hand to Clarabelle's udder. There, I said to him, isn't this better? His face cringed but his hand cupped Clarabelle's udder greedily. I pulled my hand away slowly. Jonny was not really bad. If I were older I would not have minded marrying him.

That was the first time I had written something in my own words. Though to call them my words would be wrong. They were Fabienne's. The truth was, even before this trip, when Fabienne dictated her stories to me, sometimes I had a sense about what she was going to say next. Sometimes, before I went to bed, I would mimic Fabienne's voice and tell myself a few made-up things. It was better than praying, which my mother still hoped I would do.

"How old are you?" the man asked me after reading my words.

"Thirteen," I said. "I turn fourteen in July."

He nodded and lit another cigarette. I could tell he liked what he had read, because this time he was smoking not out of boredom, but to keep himself from showing any excitement.

"Why did you decide to write the stories?" he asked.

"I don't know," I said. It was close to the truth.

"Why did you decide that these stories should be printed as a book?"

"M. Devaux thought so," I said. Neither he nor Fabienne had told me what to say, but I did not need help when it was time to act baffled. Perhaps that was my intuition, acting sensibly and disarmingly baffled, as though the world were a mystery beyond my capacity, which I had accepted without protest, along with the fact that I, too, was part of that mystery, defying my own understanding.

There came a stretch of time—two or three weeks—during which life went on as usual. Jean was dying, though slowly. Joline died after only one day of misery in childbirth. Sometimes I wanted to pray to god to end Jean's suffering soon, but my mother was still praying for his recovery. I knew god had already made up his mind, and even if I said nothing, he would take my side in the end. For that reason I pitied my mother.

Two of my sisters, Marcella and Rosemary, often came back to see him around this time. They were two years and a year younger than Jean, so they had known one another well before my birth. He let them stay around, and had a conversation with them when he felt able to. Sometimes he even said things that made them laugh. On those days my mother seemed more hopeful, even though she herself would never be able to bring life back into him.

I now understand it was my mother's lot to be already banished from Jean's world. The cruelty and the kindness of that banishment were one and same: he was saving her from the humiliation of defeat. Marcella and Rosemary were both married, and each had their own brood of children, but they were not Jean's mother. We forgive many people for what they cannot do for us, but not our mothers; we protect our mothers more than we protect others, too. Sometimes I think it may be just as well that I cannot have my own children: I can count more things I would not be able to do for them than what I could; and I would rather march through life without the futile protection from my children. People often forget that it is always a gamble to be a mother; I am not a gambler.

Gisele, my eldest sister, was often bedbound for a few days in those years, afflicted with something chronic, though no one had told me what the illness was. She was not dying, or perhaps it would take her a longer time to die than Jean. Before his deterioration turned him into a total invalid, my mother used to visit Gisele, but she had not done that for some time. I wondered if she would pray for both Jean and Gisele. Would she think herself too greedy, asking god to spare both of her children? Would she trade one for the other? If I were a fair god, I would take Jean; Gisele had five children, and they all needed her.

The days were getting longer. Fabienne's two older brothers started to join their father at the bar in the evenings. Her brothers, who used to treat me just as they did Fabienne, began to show me some respect and sometimes seemed eager to talk with me, telling an insipid joke or making some banal remark like real adults would do, but Fabienne was good at intercepting their attentions. As boys they were all right, but people could be all right, or all wrong, and either way they had nothing to do with Fabienne and me.

We had begun a new book, this time about a village postman. We did not show it to M. Devaux at first. It was not his story, in any case. The man in our book was younger, more handsome, and was madly in love with his sister's best friend. His sister and her friend were both excited about this development, and they made plans to encourage him, followed by schemes to make him suffer. Sometimes when Fabienne dictated the story, I could not stop laughing at all three of them. Such silly girls they were; such a silly man.

We went to M. Devaux's in the evenings regularly. He had installed a few brighter bulbs in his house, and he had better food in his cupboard than could be found in Fabienne's house or mine. But food was a secondary concern to us. We went there, as Fabienne said, as his equals. It was his duty to be hospitable; we were eating his food only to acknowledge this duty.

M. Devaux welcomed our visits. How could he not? He would have little else to do in the evenings but to write his poetry and then read to his pigeons, who would show him the same amount of curiosity if he leveled insults at them. Fabienne asked him about his school days, and about the cities and towns he had been to. Theaters and music halls and cinemas. Restaurants and dances. His friends. What people did to amuse themselves. How people got married, what kind of affairs they had outside their marriages, what fallouts happened between couples and friends. He told us what he had seen in his life, and also what he had read in his books.

I had always known Fabienne could make me tell her anything, but that was because I never wanted to keep a secret from her. I now saw that she could do the same to M. Devaux. She did not harass him, and she did not plead. She asked and he gave her what she wanted. The only difference between how she treated me and how she treated M. Devaux was that she did not often call him an idiot to his face. Perhaps they were two equals, and I was only half of what they were. That thought bothered me for a few days, until I found a way to convince myself that it was not true. M. Devaux might know more about the world than I did, but he did not know the secret of being Fabienne's true friend: to stay still in her shadow, to be as empty as the air around her, and to be everywhere with her. M. Devaux was always eager to prove himself as superior to Fabienne. I could see his days were numbered.

M. Devaux grew up near Paris, and in his youth had spent time in the city. How he had ended up in our village and married his wife he did not explain. Sometimes he would close his eyes when he described a public garden in Paris, or the river where he and his friends had fished. Sometimes he opened an atlas and showed us a lake or a town. Once, in the middle of describing a play, which he called a minor masterpiece, he paused and looked at us, and then wondered aloud if we thought him a bore. Fabienne said, Who do you think we are—idiots willing to be bored to death?

I did find M. Devaux's soliloquy tiresome, and I asked Fabienne later what about him she found interesting. "It's not him I find interesting, but what he knows," she said.

"Why?" I asked.

"We want to know how other people live."

"Why do we want to know that?"

"You and I haven't got enough experience," she said.

"Enough experience for what?"

"For writing our books, silly."

I could not wait for Fabienne to lose interest in our book-writing game, so we could stop visiting M. Devaux. I missed the days when we spoke endless nonsense or lay in the graveyard without moving or speaking.

ONE AFTERNOON, a man we had met in Paris, a M. Chastain, arrived in the village with M. Perret, the man who had taken us around to see the publishers. The men had gone to the post office first before coming to our house, accompanied by M. Devaux. My mother was in the garden, and my father was nailing down a loose plank at the side of the barn. I was changing out of my school uniform and putting on my overalls for my chores—cleaning out the rabbit hatch and the chicken coop—when the visitors arrived. It was a brilliant day in June, the sky cloudless after a night of rain. I had never paid attention to the sky until then, when the three men stood in a semicircle in front of me, their faces looking stern under their hats, behind which was the bright sky that was more white than blue. All my life, since that day on, I have paid special attention to the sky when something important happens. People close to you at one moment may disappear the next moment, but the sky is always there, whether you have a roof over your head or not.

I stuck my sweaty hands in my pockets. The Parisians were here to tell me that I had deceived them, I thought. I had always known M. Devaux could not be trusted.

"Do you remember me?" M. Chastain asked, as though I were a five-year-old.

I said yes. He was the man who had asked me to write while he smoked.

"M. Chastain is here to discuss something with your parents," M. Devaux said. "He would like to publish your book."

M. Chastain held out a hand to shake mine. I rubbed my palms on the side of my overalls before resigning it to his grasp. Where was Fabienne? I was always there when she needed me, but now, when I absolutely needed her by my side, she was nowhere to be seen. We had not discussed what we would do next if the publishers in Paris were interested in our book.

M. Devaux gave me a meaningful look, but I did not know what he was telling me.

"Agnès, you may be excited, but don't forget your manners," M. Devaux said.

I thanked M. Chastain and said I would get my parents for him.

"Your daughter has written a most astonishing book," M. Chastain said to my parents when all the grown-ups sat down in the house. I stood next to the door, ready to bolt if anything went wrong. "We would like to publish it and we would like to invite Agnès to Paris to meet the press in September."

In my parents' eyes I saw their effort to be courteous despite their unease. We had never had such well-dressed visitors to the farm, and my parents, like most people I knew, did not trust city dwellers. My father exchanged a look with my mother and asked me what I thought about the invitation.

My parents were never cruel to me. Perhaps they were too worn-out to feel much of anything. Of course they wanted the best for me, but they had wanted that for every one of their children. No one can stop you from wanting something for your children, but most of the time what you want will never be granted. Some people have to become parents themselves to truly understand that. Not me. I learned that by watching my parents.

I said I would love to go to Paris, and my parents did not seem to have much more to say. My mother must have been thinking of the weeding that still needed to be done. If the men stayed any longer, she might ask me to cook dinner while she finished in the garden. My father replied that they agreed to let M. Chastain arrange the trip, and M. Devaux said he would help me, and that he would certainly discuss anything with my parents regarding my future. They thanked him. Perhaps they would welcome anything that would make me different from Fabienne. They did not like her. They thought her crude and unruly. "The way Gaston lets Fabienne run wild"—I had overheard my mother say to my father of Fabienne's father once—"soon she will become another Joline." My father agreed, and said that had Joline stayed alive, she would have had a litter of bastards running wild now. At the mention of Joline's name my mother had whispered a prayer.

M. Chastain asked me what I was going to do in the summer. I hesitated, and said I was writing another book. He turned to M. Devaux with a questioning look. I was thrilled and amused that M. Devaux, who did not know anything about our new book, had to come up with something smart to say on the spot. He explained to M. Chastain that he had not revealed this to him earlier because he had wanted M. Chastain to hear the news from me.

~

"DID THEY SAY SEPTEMBER? Perfect. We can finish in the summer. When you go to Paris, you can drop a few hints about the new book," Fabienne said later that evening when I told her of the Parisians' visit. She did not seem to think much of the visit and the arrangements for me to meet the press. She was making a willow whistle, cutting precisely the right length of twig and then twisting it gently. She was good at that. My hands were clumsy, and I either broke the twigs or lost patience before the tender pith could be neatly separated from the green bark.

"Why don't you want to have your name on the book?" I asked. "We can tell M. Chastain we wrote the stories together. It's not too late."

"A book should just bear one name," Fabienne said.

"Why not two?"

Fabienne did not reply. Was this finally a question she could not answer? "Why can't it be just your name?" I asked.

"You wrote the stories down," she said.

"You made them up."

"I'm not interested in being an author."

"Why not?"

"I'm fine being who I am."

That couldn't possibly be true, I thought, and yet who else could Fabienne be? The girls at school were uninteresting: swap one girl's clothes with another's, switch one girl's parents with another's, what difference would it really make? All the girls, other than me, wanted the same things: to own a pair of stockings so their legs would not look bare and childish in their humiliating ankle socks; to have the best notebooks to record song lyrics, those sickeningly sweet words of dreams and loves and hearts; to be praised by the teachers, but more importantly, to be admired and envied by one another; to catch the attention of the right boys. I would have been one of them had Fabienne not been in my life. What a tragedy that would have been, living an interchangeable life, looking for interchangeable excitements.

"Why, you look like a sad potato," Fabienne said. "What's wrong?"

"I'm only thinking it's a pity that you don't want your name on a book."

"It would be a pity if I did want that," Fabienne said. "Don't you see?"

"No."

"Oh, you imbecile. Say I wanted to be an author. I would have my name on the book. I could tell people I have several more books in my head. Where would that leave you?"

"What do you mean?"

"I'm making this a two-person game. You're saying that one person—me, Fabienne—could play the game alone. What would you do then?"

"I can still write your stories down for you," I said.

"You really don't understand, do you?" Fabienne said. "How hard is it to write things down when you already have them in your head? I could do it myself. Then what?"

I hesitated. "I would watch you being an author and I would be happy."

"No, you would be sad," Fabienne said.

"I would?"

"Yes," Fabienne said. "Because you would have no part in the game. The books would have nothing to do with you. And what happened to me would have nothing to do with you. Don't you see?"

I saw it then. I truly was an idiot, for not seeing all the losses I would have to endure, for not knowing that Fabienne minded how I would feel.

"So, you see, I'll write the books and your name will be on them. We're equally essential. What we need to do is to make you look believable," Fabienne said. "I don't see why people won't find you so."

"Believable in what way?" I asked. I remembered M. Chastain puffing on his cigarette and waiting for me to tackle a blank page. Would there be more tests like that? I had not told Fabienne about that page I had written for M. Chastain.

Fabienne sighed. "When will you stop needing me to explain everything to you?"

"When I get to Paris," I replied.

Fabienne studied me with an amused look. I asked her questions all the time, and depending on her mood, she answered them or ignored them, but her questions to me were never meant for me to answer. She gave the willow twig one more tender twist—the whistle was perfectly finished. She put it in my hand. "Here, for you to charm Paris."

I wanted to put it in my mouth to try, but she stopped me. "Don't move. I better make sure you're ready." She held my face in both hands and looked from different angles. I tried not to follow her face with my eyes. I wondered if she would kiss me. It would not be our first kiss. When we were younger, we used to stick our tongues out and let them touch for as long as we could stand it, and then dissolve into hysterical laughter. But that was before Fabienne's mother died. After her death, Fabienne and I stopped playing some of our silliest and wildest games, and she no longer laughed like she used to.

"You see—" Fabienne said, not letting go of my face. "But of course you cannot see what I see. You have the perfect face."

"I do?"

"Yes, it can make you pass as a genius or an imbecile, and people don't often know which is which. They need others to tell them, and when you go to Paris, someone is going to tell them that you're a genius. You were born with that face. And you're good at putting on the perfect kind of look."

"What kind?"

"When people first see you, they think they know what's on your mind. Then they look again, and wonder if they know anything," Fabienne said. "I've seen my brothers look at you that way. Even M. Devaux."

I smiled. Fabienne squeezed my cheeks. "Stop grinning," she said. "What's so funny?"

"Half the time I don't even know what's on my mind," I said.

"But I do. I always know what you're thinking about."

I wished this were true.

"You see, I don't have your face, and I can't fake that look you're so good at," she said. "People don't find my face agreeable."

Fabienne had a narrow head and a sharp chin. My face was rounder, and my eyes did not protrude as hers did. Her hair was hay-colored, thin, and dry, mine was dark and smooth. I never wondered what Fabienne and I could do to improve our looks. She did not care, so I did not.

"Is my face agreeable?" I asked.

"Terribly so," she said. "Besides, you have the patience to carry something out. I have too many animals to look after. I have too many stories on my mind. I have too little time and patience."

That was true. Fabienne's day was lived as though from one squall to another. In comparison I felt like an idle cloud hanging in the sky all day long, not loftily high, not heavily low.

"When you go to Paris, think of what people want from you, and give them exactly that, no more, no less," Fabienne said. "Do you know how to do that? Well, I have the whole summer to prepare you."

I was surprised. Didn't Fabienne already know that was exactly what I did the best? I gave Fabienne what she wanted: *her* Agnès. I did not give this Agnès to others, but what they asked of me I did my best to accommodate. I was quiet and hardworking at school, though I was never any teacher's favorite; I was unobtrusive with the adults in the village; I obeyed my parents. My only flaw was that I was Fabienne's friend, but that my parents had accepted, with the hope that we might drift apart when I advanced in my schooling.

~

SOMETIMES YOU HEAR PEOPLE say so-and-so has lived well, and so-and-so has had a dull life. They are missing a key point when they say that. Any experience is experience, any life a life. A day in a cloister can be as dramatic and fatal as a day on a battlefield.

Some people count only what they seek as life: fame, wealth, adventure, happiness. What they make happen, to others and to themselves, and what they make impossible, for others and for themselves. To me, anything that happens is life. A fly dropped dead in the soup is as strange and laughable as a marriage proposal from a mere acquaintance—both happened to me, neither sought by me.

Am I passive? I have noticed that Americans are quick to call a person passive, which is never meant as a compliment. Some of my husband's family think of me as passive. I am not what they thought a Frenchwoman should be like. As far as I can see, people handing out this verdict freely are those for whom any external movement is a sign of decisiveness, personal strength, virtue. But my chickens, with their small brains, never seem to tire of walking around, pecking, cooing, clawing. The geese are much more tranquil. They do not flap their wings at the slightest disturbance, and when they float in the pond, they stay still for so long that you know they would not mind spending the rest of their lives suspended in their watery dreams. Yet geese are never called passive.

Two people who are constantly seeking experience rarely settle for each other.

Two people enduring experience rarely meet in life.

That's why Fabienne and I were meant for each other. We were the perfect pair, one seeking all that the other could experience.

The summer of 1953 was the happiest of my life. I don't know if Fabienne would agree with me. It is too late to ask her. Though even if her ghost were next to me, what would I get out of questioning her? Happy—Fabienne's ghost might say: How have you made yourself more of an imbecile now, Agnès? Happy days, unhappy days: they are only days, one not longer than the other.

We once thought of growing happiness, I would remind her ghost. Your happiness and my happiness, two crops, remember?

The ghost might dismiss that as a child's game. What's happiness? she might ask me.

Happiness, I would tell her, is to spend every day without craning one's neck to look forward to tomorrow, next month, next year, and without holding out one's hands to stop every day from becoming yesterday.

Have you ever felt that kind of happiness? Fabienne's ghost would ask.

Yes, I would say.

That was how I felt the summer of 1953. Like the summers before, Fabienne and I spent our days together, even though half of the time we were just lying in the graveyard or under a tree, not saying much. When we did talk we talked about our book: the village postman and the two friends who were to make his life miserable. We visited M. Devaux when we felt like it, but he was no more than a branch floating on the surface of the pond of our days together.

The only time I was worried was when the railway workers went on strike. "What if the trains are still not running when I am supposed to go to Paris in the fall?" I asked Fabienne.

"It's weeks away. Why do you even think about something so far in the future?"

"But writing a book, is it not all about the future?" I asked.

"All about the future?" Fabienne said. "Don't speak nonsense."

I did not argue with her, though secretly I was listening to the news on the radio about the general strike. When it ended I was relieved.

During the general strike, M. Devaux, not going to the post office, kept badgering us about the book we were to show him. When he finally read the first half, we could not tell if he thought we were making fun of him. He did not say much, but he commented that we were both improving, and that he thought we would have a finished book by September.

~

IN SEPTEMBER I WENT TO PARIS alone, as M. Chastain requested that M. Devaux not accompany me this time.

Nobody in Paris knew about Fabienne, but everyone from the press had been told about M. Devaux. They asked me how, under his tutorage, I had learned to write, how he had shaped my way of comprehending the world, whether I planned to write more books, and whether I would still seek his guidance in my future endeavors as a writer. They all seemed to know the book well, even better than I did.

Did you know an American Negro executed as you described in your book? someone asked. Did you know a young woman who suffocated her newborn and left it in a pig trough? another person wanted to know. Are you yourself a pigherd? Did you ever watch a madman having sex with a cow? Or another madman cutting off the head of a chicken to show the children how a headless chicken would dance? Did you truly promise the children before they died that you would write them into a book so the world would know their stories? Did you change their names? How did M. Devaux discover you? Did you seek his help or did he convince you to show your writing to him?

I answered the questions with what the press later called *équilibre et confiance.* Me, Agnès? What confidence did I have? But I was lucky to have come up with how best to present myself as a child author: I was imagining a person who was half Fabienne and half Agnès, and I had no trouble stepping into the shoes of that person. A mysterious girl who had made up for her lack of education with good intuition—that was what the press needed to see.

I could detect the satisfaction in M. Chastain's face. I had a sense that I did not do too badly, though the journalists kept returning to the fantastic morbidity, which, they told me, was a trademark of my stories. How does an amiable girl, as we've seen you in this room, let yourself become transfixed by horrific images most adults look away from? someone wanted to know. There must be pretty sceneries in the countryside, no?—why are you not interested in writing about them? How much of the stories came from your life, how much from your fabrication? Does it give you pleasure to tell ghastly tales? Have your parents read what you've written? How about your teachers? What are your friendships with your schoolmates like? Did they know you were writing a book? Did they find the stories in your book familiar, or utterly strange?

I learned, on this trip, to talk slowly, as though I had to form and re-form the sentences before speaking. I might look like an imbecile, but I also learned, on this trip, that a simple girl from the countryside could be transformed into something else. *A girl in a secret communion with herself* was how one of the journalists characterized the pauses between my sentences. Had I been auditioning for a role as a child author in a play, I would have failed, but this was not an audition. The good thing about life is that most of the time you do not have to audition to be yourself—or, in this case, Fabienne and myself combined into one person. If the press felt there was something unfathomable about me, that was because they could never tell that I was not one girl. It was Fabienne who was unfathomable. All I did was display that mystery to strangers, adding a dose of pleasantness and sweetness when necessary.

A man asked if there was an author in Paris whom I would love to meet. I could see M. Chastain wanted me to give a nice reply to impress the audience. When I did not say anything right away, he cut in and said of course he would arrange for me to meet authors who could guide me, and the press would be invited to document those meetings, too. The man who asked the question nodded, and then turned to me and insisted on hearing my opinion. Surely there were many authors in Paris. Unfortunately their names would not find their own ways to my lips. "Do I want to meet other authors? But of course, yes!" I said. "Our cows and goats are sometimes unfriendly to newcomers, but our rabbits are often curious if other rabbits stop by for a visit."

The men all laughed. "Are you saying," the persistent journalist said, "that some authors are like cows and goats, and others are like rabbits?"

"Quite the contrary," I exclaimed. "I think rabbits are like authors. They are curious and inoffensive animals."

More laughter from the men. "Mademoiselle, wait until you know more about writers," a journalist said.

For a moment I could not decide if this meant I had blundered, but M. Chastain nodded at me approvingly.

~

IN PARIS people decided that I had given them a glimpse of the countryside that was fantastical and horrendous. Later, in London, a similar group of people would decide that I had given them a glimpse of the France under American occupation, which was mad and foul beyond imagination. People must have reasoned that a girl like me, innocent, ignorant, could not possibly make the world a mad and foul place. That world must have been mad and foul already, and all she did was tell the truth in her own words. Unflinchingly, they said. They must have thought that a girl like me knew too little about civilization to flinch. They were not entirely wrong. I did not know then, for instance, that at the sight of a spider or a toad some girls my age would scream like pigs about to be butchered.

But the world I—no, not I, Fabienne and I—had given them: Was it real? How much of it was real? We cannot measure a world with a ruler or a scale, and conclude that it is two inches, or two ounces, short of being real. All worlds, fabricated or not, are equally real. And so they are equally unreal. If I told my parents that in Paris I was posing for the press to photograph, they would say I was making up stories no one would believe. Paris was not real to them. Neither was my fame.

The world Fabienne and I made together: it was as real as our nonsense.

~

AFTER THE MEETING with the press, M. Chastain asked an assistant, Mlle Boverat, to take me out and buy me a new outfit. I was wearing my rose-plaid frock, as I had been on my first trip to Paris.

Nothing exorbitant, M. Chastain said. Mlle Boverat asked if he wanted her to make a hair appointment for me, too. They both studied me, and I felt a tingling sensation on my face. A few years earlier Fabienne and I had loved a game, tickling each other's neck and face not with our fingers but with lightly blown air. I had felt the same tingling sensation when she did that, her mouth an inch away from my skin.

"A new hairdo would be nice," M. Chastain said.

My mother used to cut my hair, short and shapeless. But one summer Fabienne had said that instead of being turned into a walking bird nest by my mother, I should entrust my head to her. I did, and Fabienne did a better job. My parents, who did not like Fabienne, had to agree that the haircut she gave me was better. She also cut her own hair, without a mirror but with my help. The left side is longer by two fingertips, I would say, and she would chop more.

"I don't want a haircut," I said.

"Don't you want to have a new look when the photographer comes tomorrow?" Mlle Boverat asked.

"Another one?" I asked.

Mlle Boverat exchanged a look with M. Chastain. "Perhaps we ought to have explained to you, though we didn't want to overwhelm you before you met the press," Mlle Boverat said. "M. Bazin, a well-known photographer, will come to photograph you tomorrow. He is also planning to visit your home village and document your life there."

"He was there with the press earlier," M. Chastain said. "He wanted to take a look at you. We didn't introduce him to you, as that can be done tomorrow."

I did not mind doing anything in Paris—that, according to Fabienne, was my responsibility to the book. To have a photographer coming to our village? "But there's nothing to photograph in my village," I said.

"Quite the contrary," M. Chastain said. "Based on my brief visit there, I can guarantee you that there is a lot for him to work with." He then came close and tousled my hair this and that way. "All right, let's not change the hairdo," he said. "I like this, more authentic."

Mlle Boverat bought me a white blouse, a black woolen pinafore, white stockings, and a pair of black leather shoes. When I was assembled in the new outfit, I felt discouraged. I looked rather like a cow! She debated whether I needed a hat and decided against it, but added to the purchase a pair of dark blue barrettes, each in the shape of a dragonfly. They were startlingly beautiful, and I decided that for their sake alone I would endure the new silly outfit. I asked if I could hold the barrettes myself.

"Do you want me to put them in your hair?" Mlle Boverat asked. "They'll make your hair look even darker."

"No, not now," I said. I changed back to my old frock and put the barrettes in my pocket. I wanted Fabienne to have one of them, and the other one I would keep for myself.

Mlle Boverat looked at her wristwatch. The tiny watch face, cream-colored and oval, looked like something I could eat in one bite. "We have some time," she said. "What would you like to do?"

"Do I get to see Paris a little?" I asked.

"But yes, of course," Mlle Boverat said. "What do you want to see?"

What do you want to see? What do you want to eat? What do you want to know? These questions, seemingly innocuous, are more unreasonable than people realize. If you asked a cow, or a pig, or a chicken what it wanted to do with its life, it would have no idea how to answer, even if by some miracle it could understand and speak our language. If you asked a cow, or a pig, or a chicken how it would like to die, it would not fare any better.

Few of us would make a fool of ourselves in pressing the animals to give us serious answers about their lives, but we do that all the time to other people. What do you want to be when you grow up? my husband's parents and siblings have made it a family hobby to grill the young members at holiday gatherings. Which American cities would you like to visit? they like to ask me; or, What do you think makes America the best country in the world? Who gives people the permission to ask unanswerable questions, I often wonder, but this must have never occurred to those interrogators: they ask questions and they demand answers, not knowing that they have only said some brainless words, and only the brainless would satisfy them by answering.

What's there for me to see in Paris? Had I asked Mlle Boverat that question, she would have thought me impertinent or difficult. Yet that was the only honest question I could ask. No one knows how to want something that does not yet exist. Paris had so far only been the glimpses I caught from the car: boulevards and cafés and storefronts. The department store Mlle Boverat had brought me to was astonishing. Wherever I turned I could see myself in mirrors and in shining brass, yet even I knew there was more in Paris.

"Some places people come to Paris to see?" I said to Mlle Boverat, though I began to regret the request to be shown around. What was Paris if I did not have Fabienne next to me? I should have saved the city for her.

Mlle Boverat took me to see the Eiffel Tower, which cheered me up. We strolled by the river, and went to a garden, and then another garden. She bought an ice cream for me, which I had heard about but had never had. I took as long as possible to eat it, but it melted fast.

At the end of the afternoon, Mlle Boverat escorted me back to the hotel. "I arranged for your dinner to be sent up to your room," she said. "I thought it would be easier for you."

I thanked her, and when she asked me if I needed anything else, I summoned up my courage and asked her if I could use the writing paper and envelope in the drawer in my room. Mlle Boverat smiled and said of course. "Are you going to write your parents about Paris?" she asked.

I nodded. She told me that I could ask the hotel desk to post the letter for me. I was relieved. I was worried that she would offer to do that, and then she would see the letter would not be for my parents.

THE NIGHT BEFORE, when I had looked around my hotel room, I had found a stack of writing paper and some envelopes, printed with the hotel's name in a way that you could touch and read with your fingertips. This was like nothing I had ever seen at home.

Dinner arrived on a tray, white plates covered by a silver dome. So many beautiful things in this hotel, and the only ones I could show Fabienne were the paper and the envelope.

"Ma chère Fabienne, Paris is a better place than Saint Rémy. When we are older, we should move here together."

I then wrote about meeting the press, about being given a new outfit and taken around for sightseeing. I described the hotel room, the golden wallpaper with flowers and birds, the thick curtain made of fabric finer than the best clothes we had ever seen, the tall bed, so soft that if Fabienne were there, we would have been jumping up and down on it, the way we used to imagine jumping on a cloud. There were things I did not recognize in the bathroom. I wished I could draw them for her, but I was not as good at drawing as I was at penmanship.

From my window I could see a café across the street, where patrons started to fill the tables on the pavement. A couple walked past the café, and the woman turned to look at her reflection in the window. Perhaps they were going to the cinema, or the theater, as M. Devaux had described to us.

I touched the dragonfly barrettes in my pocket. I wondered if I could put one in the envelope with the letter, but decided against it.

The next morning I would give the letter to the hotel desk to post. I wondered how long it would take to arrive at Saint Rémy. What if I got home before the letter? Still, it would be the first letter I had sent, and I was certain it would be the first one Fabienne had ever received.

It then occurred to me that M. Devaux would lay his eyes on the letter before Fabienne. Would he open it first and read it? The thought of his holding the slender envelope in his hands, with the hair on his knuckles and his fingers stained brown and black by cigarettes and ink, made me nauseous. Until then I had tolerated him. It was true that he had helped us write the book and get it published. He had even told Fabienne and me that we would receive some money. He suggested that the money should be divided equally between us. What about you? Fabienne asked with suspicion, and he said he would not take our money. I would happily have given all the money to Fabienne, but M. Devaux told me that I should bring half home to my parents, so they would not suspect anything unusual. "And you," he said to Fabienne, "I can give you some advice about the money."

"Does anyone need advice on how to spend money?" Fabienne said.

"If you want to spend it wisely," M. Devaux said.

"On some poetry or philosophy books, so I can become civilized like you?" Fabienne said.

M. Devaux did not reply. He was a pitiful man, but in his own way he was concerned with our futures—though this I did not understand then. How could Fabienne and I have been fair to him when we were young? How could we have been fair to anyone but ourselves?

I put the letter in my bag. I would give it to Fabienne when I returned home. She would certainly call me an imbecile—a letter was supposed to be posted.

~

M. BAZIN, THE PHOTOGRAPHER, had a funny habit of tilting his head to the right when he looked at me, and before long I started to tilt my head to the left, our heads pointing in the same direction. No, he instructed, don't move your head. With every shot he came over and rearranged my hands and shoulders, sometimes turning my face, touching me ever so lightly that you would think he was adjusting a butterfly's wings. A litter of three-day-old piglets would have no trouble trampling him, I thought. "No, don't laugh," he said. "Smile."

His voice was as gentle as his fingertips. Had he ever pushed a wife to the wall or boxed a child's ears? I began to worry about his visit to Saint Rémy. Men in our village were made of coarser material. Women, too. Children, if they did not die young, turned into brutes in no time. I wondered if there was a way to dissuade M. Bazin from visiting.

I was in my new outfit, stiff as a cardboard cutout. The dragonfly barrettes, against my wishes, were clipped to my hair. Mlle Boverat had arranged them in an asymmetric way, which bothered me even more, but she must have had her reasons. Everyone had a reason to do something to me in Paris. I thought that Fabienne and M. Devaux should be happy that I never protested. And I began to see Fabienne's point: she would never be able to put up with all these instructions and maneuvers from the world.

The photo shoot began in M. Chastain's office. One at a time a prop was introduced by M. Bazin's assistant. First they placed me in front of a typewriter, and Mlle Boverat arranged a cushion on the chair so I could sit at the right height. Type something, M. Bazin told me. I was not sure what to do—I had never seen a typewriter before. All the same, type something, M. Bazin encouraged, and I moved a finger across the keyboard, until I found the letter *f* and pushed it down. A long metal bar reared itself up, but it did nothing to the paper. Harder, Mlle Boverat said, and came over to show me how to hit the keys, and in the blink of an eye the title of my—our—book was on the page. I did as she showed me. Soon there was a line of *f*s on the paper.

Next I was handed a telephone and told to imitate having a conversation, and I amused everyone by putting the mouthpiece to my ear and the earpiece under my chin. Behind M. Chastain's desk, there were shelves of books stacked to the ceiling. M. Bazin directed me to look at the books, taking one out and then putting it back, taking another out and flipping through it.

I would be lying if I said I had suffered. The truth was, I was thrilled, touching things that I was sure someone like me was never allowed to touch—a desk lamp with a green lampshade, a knife with a carved owl as a handle (the owl even had two glass eyes), a stool made to look like a giant book.

Even more thrilling was to know that everyone was watching me with some kind of delight.

"Mademoiselle is a natural model," M. Bazin said.

"Mademoiselle has many surprises for us," M. Chastain said.

After that, we went out into the street, and M. Bazin photographed me walking down a narrow lane, looking at a shop window, standing in the doorframe of a stationery, and later comparing two fragrant soaps in a chemist shop. Mlle Boverat, without my saying anything, bought both for me. I would give one to my mother, and the other to Fabienne. And I decided that I would always love Mlle Boverat.

"Do you want to photograph me in front of the Eiffel Tower?" I asked M. Bazin. I liked his soft voice so much. Sometimes when he adjusted his camera he mumbled a series of numbers to himself.

"Oh no," he said. "That would not be interesting."

I felt deflated. I had thought that he had become a good friend. He had chatted with me while his assistant arranged the lighting, asking questions about my schooling, my family, and the other children in the village. In response to the last question I did not say much. In my world, the girls were shallow and dramatic, and the boys were dirty and rude. I did not say a word about Fabienne.

AM I MAKING EVERYTHING on this trip sound easy? Am I painting myself as, in M. Bazin's words, a natural—impersonating a child prodigy? But here is an explanation, maybe, for the success of my trip. Life is most difficult for those who know what they want and also know what makes it impossible for them to get what they want. Life is still difficult, but less so, for those who know what they want but have not realized that they will never get it. It is the least difficult for people who do not know what they want.

I did not know what I wanted on this trip to Paris. Perhaps it would not be an exaggeration to say that most of my life I have benefited from not knowing. Some people have to figure out what they want from a life before they commit to that life. Some, like me, can commit to anything, which is like committing to nothing. Perhaps that is why my American relatives call me passive.

Often I imagine that living is a game of rock-paper-scissors: fate beats hope, hope beats ignorance, and ignorance beats fate. Or, in a version that has preoccupied me: the fatalistic attracts the hopeful, the hopeful attracts the ignorant, and the ignorant, the fatalistic.

~

SOME PEOPLE MIGHT WONDER WHY Fabienne alone took up all my attention, as there must have been other schoolmates who would have made better friends. Some people might wonder why she chose me, when I seemed to offer her little other than obedient companionship. Surely there were other children, endowed with stronger personalities, who would have been better matches for her. But people asking these questions do not understand children. Either they have had an insipid childhood, or, worse, they are determined to make childhood insipid in retrospect, so they become people who talk about children as if they were larvae or pupae. And if you are one of those people, I can assure you that many children you dismiss are more interesting than you are. And they despise you, rightly so.

Nothing is more inexplicable than friendship in childhood. It is not companionship, though the two are often confused.

Childhood companionship is forced upon the children: two playmates whose parents like to share a drink on the weekend, a boy and a girl assigned to sit next to each other at school, families renting the neighboring holiday cabins every summer. Childhood friendship, though it has to meet the same geographical and temporal prerequisites, is something rarer: a child does not seek to bond with another child. The bond, defying knowledge and understanding, either is there, or is not; once a bond comes into existence, no child knows how to break from it until the setting is changed. It baffles me that often songs and poems are written about love at first sight: those who claim to experience the phenomena have preened themselves, ready for love. There is nothing extraordinary about that. Childhood friendship, much more fatal, simply happens.

Take, for example, Geneviève, who sat next to me at school for several years because we were the same height. She had a pretty face, clean and gentle. Her handwriting was as neat as mine, and she excelled in spelling and arithmetic. Her parents were the grocers in the village and they did not drink. Above all, she always wanted to be my friend, and she expressed her affection by bringing me food from their house. They ate better than our family did.

I accepted her offerings. To deny her the hope of transforming me into a friend, with the help of a piece of cheese or a box of raisins, would have been cruel. I was never cold nor rude to her. At school we talked about trivial things to pass the time—a schoolmate's hair band, a new song we had learned for the end-of-school celebration, the miller's daughter who was set to marry the brewer's son, and other gossip she picked up from her parents' shop. In short, I liked her, yet how could she expect me to give her more of myself when, the moment school ended, I had to rush off to Fabienne to make up for a whole day of separation? I brought the food Geneviève gave me to Fabienne, who was hungrier than I was. She never asked where I got it. She knew my parents did not have anything to spare.

Why couldn't I have settled for Geneviève in her sweet innocence, walking home with her, our hands clasped, our shoulders touching, our footsteps matching each other's? Or, for that matter, Anne, who was meek and who had the best singing voice in the whole school? Or Berthe, the tallest girl in the class, whose friendship was sought-after by many of my classmates? These are good questions, but we may as well ask a plane tree, Why can't you keep your leaves in winter? or ask a wasp, Why weren't you born more useful, like a honeybee?

I WAS AWAY IN PARIS for two days. On the train back to Saint Rémy, I watched the scenery outside the window, already familiar to me, and the whole time I was touching the barrettes in my pockets. The dragonflies would not fly away or die after the summer ended. They were more beautiful than real.

Jean was dead. I did not need anyone to tell me the news when I arrived home. I saw my three sisters, who had returned and brought with them the younger children they could not leave behind. One of my nieces ran toward me and I caught both her wrists before she could leave sticky handprints on my new outfit, which I had worn to surprise my family. No one noticed.

"Go on, say a prayer for him," my mother told me.

I went to Jean's room and made a sign of the cross. He had been laid out on his bed, now freshly made with white sheets.

A fly circled near his head and I shooed it away, but when no one was around the fly would get its way. I wished I had thought of bringing Jean something from Paris, not to show my family that I had been thinking of him, but to convince myself that he had meant something to me. I wished I could shed a few tears so that later my parents would not call me stonehearted. But it was of no use. I could not find anything but impatience in my heart.

It took me a while to find Fabienne. She was not at one of our usual spots, but had taken her cows and goats to the far side of the barley field. Right away I prepared myself for her mood. To the world she was the sulky girl all the time, but I knew her well. A change of routine was never just the result of a whim.

She studied me from where she was sitting on a tree stump. "You can't wear those things on a farm, you know," she said. They were the exact words I had expected her to say, but there was a strange gentleness in her voice, as though she were amiably introducing a newcomer to the ways of the countryside.

"I . . . I want you to see them," I said.

"They fit you nicely," she said. "I like how you look."

When you are used to the sharpness of a knife, you can safely run your finger along the edge or press your palm onto it with just the right pressure. You can even keep the blade between your teeth without cutting your lips or tongue. But what if you touched the blade and felt the soft silkiness of a rabbit pelt? I knelt down next to Fabienne and put a hand on her forehead. It was clammy but not warm. "Are you all right?" I asked.

"Why shouldn't I be?"

"You sound strange," I said. "I thought you might be ill."

"Some people never get ill," she said. "I'm one of them."

"Yes, of course."

"Yes, of course," she mimicked my assent. "You are, too, don't you know?"

I did know, but I did not want to say anything, in case evil spirits caught me boasting. That was the difference between us. Fabienne did not believe that anything, real or unreal, could hurt her. I wanted to believe so, too, but I was more cautious. "Jean died," I said.

"So I heard," she said.

I waited for her to say more. She did not. I took out the barrettes from my pocket and said they were from Paris, and I thought we could each have one. She took the dragonfly and looked at me through its half opaque torso and then turned it toward the sun. I lifted mine and looked in the same direction. The sky turned dark, the sun softened and paled, looking like a full moon.

"I think I know what it means not to be a virgin," Fabienne said slowly, still looking at the sun.

"What? Do you mean you're not a virgin anymore?"

"That's not what I said," she replied. "I said: I think I know what it means not to be a virgin."

"You mean you've learned how to lose virginity?"

She turned to me with that mocking look in her eyes. "Don't be an imbecile," she said.

That was a relief—we had not changed. I had often felt that I was related to my siblings and to my parents only by accident, and I had often believed that had I been born in another family, it would have been no more than a different accident. But Fabienne was not an accident. If Paris made us strangers to each other, I would never set foot there again.

"Do you mean," I said, "you've learned something new?"

If I had learned something new from Paris, I thought, it was only fair that Fabienne had, too.

"What's new to be learned?"

She was right. We had acquainted ourselves with things nobody would teach us, by watching the farm animals, by listening to the crude words of drunken men, and, when we were much younger, by spying on Joline and her American boyfriend. We were not prudes, but we were not impressed by the mania people and animals had to put themselves through in having sex.

"What I mean to say . . ." She turned to me and then shook her head. "No, there's no point. So, how did you like the trip?"

There was so much I had wanted to tell her about, but I could not come up with anything to say.

"Did you lose your tongue in Paris?"

"I wrote you a letter," I said, sitting down next to her.

"I didn't get any letter," she said.

"Here, I didn't post it."

Fabienne looked at the sealed envelope. "Am I supposed to read it?"

"If you want."

She folded the letter carelessly and stuck it into her pocket. "Good thing you didn't post it," she said. "M. Devaux might have stolen it from me."

"That's exactly what I was worried about!"

"You know what we must do from now on? We'll write our books without his help."

"All right," I said, keeping my face neutral. She might change her mind if she knew how happy I was to hear the news.

"You should know by now how to write books," Fabienne said. "We must rely on ourselves."

"All right," I said.

"Do you not want to know why I don't want his help anymore?"

"Do you want me to ask?"

Fabienne sighed. "Normally you would ask," she said, "even when you know I won't tell you. You used to be full of questions. You never stopped asking them. But I can see Paris has changed you."

I could have protested. I could have crossed my heart and sworn that I had not changed a bit. But something about Fabienne made her different today. "What did M. Devaux do?" I asked. "Are we hating him now?"

"There, you're more like yourself now," she said. "No, he didn't do anything. He can't possibly do me any harm, you know?"

"I know," I said.

"But he can harm you," she said. "That's what concerns me."

"How?"

"He could say that you didn't write the book but that he did. People would believe him."

I thought about M. Bazin, who was planning to visit in a week's time. I did not want the world to know that I was not the real author of my book, even though I had not wanted to be its author in the first place. "What do we do, then?"

"I know exactly how to keep him quiet," Fabienne said. "But I haven't decided how necessary it is."

A shiver ran through my body. "You don't mean it?"

"I don't mean what?"

If she did mean it I had better not say it out loud. I looked at Fabienne, willing her to read my mind. I did not want to put the horror into words.

"Oh," she said. "You thought I wanted to kill him? That's certainly one way to keep someone quiet, but no, I don't plan to murder anyone."

I sighed. M. Devaux was a pitiful man, but he did not deserve a terrible ending like that.

"He asked me to be his lover," Fabienne said.

"But . . . but . . . he's an old man! And a widower!"

"Funny, isn't it?" Fabienne said slowly. "I told you widowers can be strange. They need something to occupy themselves."

Fabienne's father was not the worst kind of widower, then. Perhaps if M. Devaux took to drinking, he would feel better.

"I thought that was why we had asked him to help us write a book," I said. "To give him something to occupy himself."

"But now he wants more."

"We can give him the money the publisher paid for the book."

Fabienne turned to me and touched my cheek with the back of her hand. "Agnès, poor you, I can see Paris hasn't made you smarter."

The gentleness in her gesture made me mad. What was wrong with her?

"You see," she said, "money isn't what M. Devaux wants. He said he and I could be lovers and together we could produce more books to publish under your name. He said it was a good deal for all three of us, and nobody else needed to know."

"But you don't want him as a lover, do you?" I asked.

"That's the part I haven't figured out," Fabienne said. "I can't decide. I wonder if he has a point."

"He's revolting. If you want someone, it has to be someone younger and more handsome," I said, though I was being dishonest. A younger and more handsome man, like the desirable postman we made up in our second book, was a more absurd idea than M. Devaux. We had no need for any man, old or young, ugly or good-looking.

"I don't need a lover," Fabienne said. "But I wonder if it hurts to give it a try."

"You're an imbecile," I said, all of a sudden enraged.

She laughed. "Why, I never am. You are. Think about it. M. Devaux is harmless. What can he really do to me?"

"But don't you want to have a boyfriend, a real one, instead of an old man?"

"I don't. Do you?"

"Of course not."

"There, then," she said. "He's not too bad a choice to try something new, you know? It may be handy when we write more books."

I wished M. Devaux were dead. It was not fair that Jean, who had never had a girlfriend, would have to die so young, while an old man like him lived on and on. I hurled a pebble at a pair of birds chirruping in a tree, but the pebble did not fly high enough. Fabienne chose a bigger rock and aimed at the birds. They flew away in two directions.

"I told him I'd let him know my decision after you got back," she said.

"Tell him to go to hell," I said.

She shook her head. "Aren't you wondering what I'm wondering about?"

"That M. Devaux is not worried about being found out that he wants you to be his lover?"

"Not that," Fabienne said. "But that he asked me, not you."

"Me? He hates me," I said.

"A man like him doesn't hate any girl."

"Then why wouldn't he ask another girl?" As long as it was not Fabienne or me, I would not care what girl or woman M. Devaux wanted.

"If he asked you, and if your parents found out, they would make his life difficult. Most girls' parents would, but not my papa. He doesn't care. If others found out, they would say I was half to blame. No one would feel bad for me."

"That's not true," I said, only to comfort her.

"It's true. Nobody felt bad for Joline, remember? But don't worry, I have no use for anyone's feelings."

"Why don't we move to Paris?" I said.

"To Paris? You think that's possible?"

I could not decide if Fabienne was teasing me or testing me.

"Yes," I said. "A photographer is coming next week. Maybe we can ask him about it."

"A photographer? Why does he want to come here?"

"I don't know," I said. "Do you think we should tell M. Devaux?"

"We must," she said. "It's better he learns it from me than from others."

I noticed that she didn't say "from us." Was she planning to go to M. Devaux's without me?

"You see, before I make up my mind, we need him to be our friend so he can stay quiet."

"Or we can stop writing books," I said. "If he tells people the truth, so what? We can forget about him and the photographer."

"Then how do we get to Paris?" Fabienne said.

"There must be other ways."

"Like what, Agnès?"

I shook my head. It was not my job to solve any problem. "Is there another way to keep him quiet?" I asked.

"He can die. Maybe he'll die soon. He's an old man, you know?"

I looked at Fabienne, who was leaning back on the grass and looking at the sky, which offered not a wisp of cloud for her to study. I wished I hadn't given her the idea of killing M. Devaux.

~

I REMEMBER, A LONG TIME AGO, before Fabienne had the idea of writing a book together, we talked about fears. We were lying on the riverbank, one of those summer days when we lived entirely in a world made by the two of us.

"What is the thing that people fear and we also fear?" Fabienne asked me.

"Most of them fear death," I said.

"Not us," she said.

"Not us," I agreed. "Some of the girls at school fear scorpions."

"Who?" Fabienne asked. "I can catch a few scorpions and you can put them in their satchels."

That, I thought, would get me into trouble. "I know one thing everyone fears," I said. "Being blind."

Fabienne did not speak for a moment, then she closed her

eyes. I looked at the dappled sunlight on her pale eyelids. "It might not be as bad as you think," she said.

I put my hands over her eyes and blocked out the sun. "Being blind would be even darker than this," I said.

"How do you know? You've never been blind."

"Well, I hear people say the world is dark when you are blind."

"I think you're stupid to believe people. They say all sorts of things without knowing anything," Fabienne said. She pulled my hands closer and pressed them down on her eyes hard. "This is not too bad. We would get used to it after a while."

"It would make the whole world feel like a minefield," I said. "And I would never be able to take a step."

"No, the opposite," she said. "It should make you feel that whether you put down your foot here or there doesn't make a difference. In a minefield a blind person is not more likely to be killed than a person who can see."

I thought about it, and realized that she was right. Still, I told her, I would not want us to be blind.

But were we not, in a sense, two blind girls? One would walk everywhere as though not a single mine were buried in the field. The other would not find the courage to take a step because the whole world was a minefield. Had they not been placed side by side by fate, they would have lived out their different lots. But that was not the case for us. Fabienne and I were in this world together, and we had only each other's hands to hold on to. She had her will. I, my willingness to be led by her will.

WE WENT TO M. DEVAUX'S AFTER DINNER. I was still wearing my new outfit from Paris, but he did not seem to notice it. He asked me if the trip was successful, and I said yes. A cause to celebrate, he said, and asked us if we would like to have a drink with him. I was about to decline when Fabienne squeezed my hand and said we would love that. He poured a little gin in one glass for us to share, and a bigger one for himself. Fabienne took a sip and made a hissing sound. "I don't understand why anyone likes to drink," she said.

"You'll get used to it," M. Devaux said. "Try again."

Fabienne tilted the glass just so that she could lick the rim.

"Can I try?" I asked.

"No, you're too young," she said.

"I'm a month older than you," I said.

"Still, you're young," Fabienne said, winking at me and

then turning to M. Devaux. "Don't you agree, M. Devaux, that Agnès is terribly young, and we should protect her innocence?"

He did not reply.

"Well," Fabienne said, placing the glass on a nearby shelf. "Agnès promised her parents she'd be home early. It's Jean's funeral tomorrow."

"I forgot to say how sorry I am for your family's loss," M. Devaux said to me. I did not think he felt anything at all.

"I'll walk her out," Fabienne said.

"She knows how to get home," M. Devaux said. "You can stay."

I did not like how that sounded, but Fabienne ignored him, and made me walk with her out the door. "I'll be right back, M. Devaux," she said, and held my elbow tightly until we turned a corner down the lane.

"Listen," she said, "I've got an idea for how to deal with him. It'll keep him quiet."

"How?"

"Do you know he drinks?"

I shook my head. M. Devaux was a cultivated person and never went to the village bar. That evening was the first time I had seen him with a drink.

"While you were away I saw him get drunk. He gets useless and weak when he's drunk."

In my mind's eye I saw M. Devaux slumped by the table, his head lolling on his extended arms, and behind him Fabienne lifting a poker. I shuddered. "Don't," I said.

"Don't what?"

"Don't kill him."

"Kill him? Who said we were killing him? Do you want to kill him?"

"No," I said. "But I don't want you to do anything that could get us into trouble."

"He's the one who'll get into trouble," Fabienne said. "This is what I'm going to do. I'll pretend to drink with him, and make him drink more. Then I'll run out and scream for help, saying he's trying to take off my clothes."

"What if people don't believe you?"

"They will," Fabienne said. "Besides, I'm not lying entirely. He did try to touch me the other day."

"Where?"

"Here." Fabienne pointed to her chest.

The thought of M. Devaux touching any part of Fabienne's body made me nauseous. "What if he corners you so you can't escape?"

"How likely is that?" Fabienne said. "I have sharp elbows and knees. He's an old man."

I turned to look at M. Devaux's house. He had not followed us. "Let's both go," I said. "Let's forget him."

"No, we can't. He'd make trouble for us unless we set a trap for him first."

"Let him," I said. "We can quit this book-writing game. We can find something else to do without his help."

"But you forget that it's up to us to say when we stop. We can't let him blackmail us," Fabienne said. "This is what you're going to do. You go home, wait for half an hour, maybe an hour, and then you come back here. By then he'll be drunk and silly. I'll run out and scream for help. Wait until you hear me scream, and then you scream. I'll tell people what's happening. You won't have to say anything. Just cry. It's us two against him."

"What if people don't believe us?"

"If I scream loudly enough and you put on a good performance, they'll have no choice but to believe us."

~

I DID NOT GO HOME, but hid in a nearby hedge. Soon it was dark. Waiting for Fabienne to scream felt like waiting for death. I told myself there was no reason for me to doubt her. She had always been right about everything. But that was like telling myself that there was no reason to fear death because I was still young. Young people die; children, too. I thought of Jean, who would be buried the next day. A year from now nobody would remember him. If the same thing happened to Fabienne, I would be the only person to remember her. The thought made my legs shake. Of course she might die. Even if we decided to be nice to M. Devaux and not to kill him, what would stop him from killing us? Perhaps he had sent me away so he could kill Fabienne. Why had this never occurred to me?

I stepped out of the hedge. Two men were coming down the road, one of them holding a torch, its circle of light bobbing on the ground. I walked toward them, and bade them good evening, and then began to run. When I got to M. Devaux's door, it was locked. It was never locked when we came to visit. I pushed, and then knocked, harder each time.

No one answered. I put my ear on the door but there was no sound from inside the house. Perhaps the deed had been done. I turned and looked at the two men, already far, the torchlight weak, though still visible. The house next to M. Devaux's was dark, but maybe people had just turned off the lights to save money. Farther down, two orange windows floated in the darkness.

Help, I said, in a low voice through my clattering teeth, as though I were only practicing saying the word. Then I raised my voice. Its shrillness startled me. A hare was once caught by the rat trap behind our barn—you would never imagine how a small animal like that could make such a horrendous noise. I was no different from the hare. The two men were running back, and someone opened a window in a nearby house. Soon, people gathered outside M. Devaux's door.

Was I so hysterical that I could not answer their questions, or was I only pretending so that I did not have to answer them? To this day I can believe in either possibility, but the truth is, some people can pretend so well that they cannot, in the end, tell the difference between pretending and being. Fabienne schemed, she told lies, but there was never a moment of pretense in her life. She was always and forever being herself. I adapted. There is not that much of a difference between adapting and pretending.

The door opened. Fabienne, her blouse ripped open at the neck and reeking of alcohol, pushed people away and threw herself into my arms. She was screaming, too, but I could not tell if she was imitating me to make fun of me, or if she was truly, like me, getting carried away by blind hysteria. Someone brought a blanket for her. She pulled me close and wrapped the blanket around our shoulders. And then, underneath the blanket, she poked me hard in my side. So, I thought, she must think I was an idiot. I had arrived too early.

M. Devaux did not appear at once, but when someone shouted that someone was on the way to get M. Meinen, the village gendarme, M. Devaux emerged. People drew back when he came through the doorway. He was a respected man in the village. He was courteous with everyone. He did not go to the bar in the evenings and get drunk like many men did. That he turned out to be like a woman, drinking secretly in his own house—that alone people might forgive, but not for two screaming girls, one with her clothes torn.

M. Devaux appeared neither ashamed nor afraid, but when he saw us, his bloodshot eyes turned still. He reminded me of a trapped animal, after fighting for its life in vain, slouching at the corner of a cage, not because it all of a sudden ceased to be afraid, but because fear made no difference. He did not deserve this, I thought, looking at the bald top of his head, surrounded by thinned gray hair. I had not even had time to share with him my experience of meeting the press and being photographed. If anyone in the village was truly interested in my trip, it would be M. Devaux.

Fabienne and I did not have to tell too many lies to M. Meinen. That she and I had made friends with M. Devaux was no secret. He had himself told people that I had more potential than the village could foresee, which my trips to Paris had confirmed. He had also said that he would take it on as his own responsibility to educate Fabienne, and to help me, so that we could both proceed in the world as allowed by our aptitudes. We were often seen to visit him together after nightfall, and usually we would leave together. That evening,

I explained to M. Meinen, M. Devaux found an excuse to dismiss me first. But it felt wrong for me to leave Fabienne behind, all by herself, so I returned to look for her.

M. Devaux had given her gin, Fabienne said, and afterward she had felt weak and nauseous, so he asked her to rest on a couch. No, she couldn't remember what had happened, she said. She either fell asleep or lost consciousness, and she was having a nightmare with demonic noises in her head, until she heard me scream. Where was M. Devaux when she woke up? M. Meinen asked, and she said she didn't know. It was dark in the house, and she thought M. Devaux was dead.

While we were talking with M. Meinen, M. Devaux, out of earshot, sat down on a rickety chair that had, for as long as I remembered, always stood next to the wall. And when M. Meinen asked him to go to the station, he obeyed, and left without looking back at us.

What now? I tapped Fabienne's hand, hoping she would have an answer to my unasked question. "Can we leave now?" she raised her face to the adults around us and asked. "I'm dead tired."

How old are you, Fabienne? someone asked, and she said fourteen. Someone sighed and said that the world was going crazy. It would be better, they decided, to tell Fabienne's father in the morning, when he was less drunk and less likely to do something silly. Two women volunteered to accompany us back to my house.

My sisters shushed their children, who had crowded to the front room to see the unexpected visitors. There was some ferocious whispering among the adults. Afterward, even my father was gentle with Fabienne. My mother put down some straw and old blankets in a corner of the kitchen for us. I could see that she was resentful of this disturbance on the eve of Jean's funeral, but she did not say anything to either of us.

"What happened?" I asked Fabienne when we were finally left alone. "Did you really drink a lot?"

"He gave me a lot to drink," Fabienne said. "But he didn't see I spilled it all on my shirt. His eyesight is not that good, you know. Poor old man."

"Did he really make you do it with him?"

"Oh, Agnès, I'm not an imbecile," Fabienne said. "No, I said I wanted to hear him talk first, so he went on about what he was like when he was a young man."

"What was he like?"

"Silly."

"Sillier than he is now?"

"He said he had many dreams. He wanted to be a poet. He wanted to travel. He wanted to marry a beautiful girl, who could sing and dance and write poetry. And then he started to get really sappy. I've seen him like that before. I think that's why he doesn't go to the bar. He cries when he drinks."

"And then?"

"And then you came to knock the door down. I told you to wait until you heard me first."

"So you didn't really do it with him?" I lay back on the straw, feeling relieved.

"What if I had wanted to and you ruined my chance? What if he's the only man who really cares enough about me to want me to be his lover?"

I lifted my head, but it was too dark to see her face. I traced the top of her head and then her jaw with a finger like a blind person. For the first time I could imagine what she looked like to other people who did not love her.

"What?" she said. "You're tickling me."

"I wish we had never got involved with M. Devaux," I said. "I wish we had never written a book."

She gave me a hard knock on my head. "Don't you see we can write this into our next book?"

"This—you mean tonight?"

"Yes, why not? Think of it this way: whatever happens in our lives is not real until we write it down."

"What do you think will happen to M. Devaux?" I asked. "What if he tells a different story from ours?"

"It doesn't matter," Fabienne said. "Nothing went as planned, but everything turned out just fine."

JEAN WAS BURIED THE NEXT DAY. M. Devaux was released before lunch. M. Meinen visited Fabienne's house and talked with her father, but did not tell him what had happened or might have happened. No one wanted Fabienne's father going to M. Devaux's house with an ax after a night in the bar. Instead, M. Meinen asked if they had some female relatives with whom Fabienne could stay.

"He said some influence from an older female might be good for me," Fabienne told me that night, when we went to the cemetery. I showed her Jean's grave, and we lay down next to the raw patch of dirt, on a stone carved with my grandparents' names, his on top, bigger than hers.

"What did your papa say?"

"He has no one to send me to," Fabienne said. "He can't afford to lose me. Who'd cook for him and my brothers if I were gone?"

"Did your father ask why M. Meinen talked with him?"

"If someone speaks with him before he gets his hand on his drink, all he thinks about is the drink. After, well, you know how he is like after."

"But do you have any relatives? Like, an aunt or a cousin?" I asked. I wanted to make sure that there was nowhere for her to be sent to.

"There must be some if we dig around, but who wants to do that? I take good care of myself," Fabienne said. "What? Why do you look like that? Are you hoping they will send me away?"

"No," I said. "But we have to come up with a way to stop them. Like having one of your cousins or aunts to come stay here for some time."

Fabienne touched my face with the back of her hand.

"What?" I said.

"I often wonder what adults' faces feel like when they speak nonsense," she said. "Now I know."

"I'm not speaking nonsense."

"You speak like an adult," Fabienne said. "It makes your skin feel leathery."

I touched my cheek, and felt the smooth coolness. "The letter I wrote you from Paris," I said. "Did you read it?"

"What's in there that I don't already know? We see each other every day."

That was what I had feared. It was the first letter I had written in my life. Perhaps it is bad luck when a letter is not posted. A letter, written to remind the recipient of the sender, should arrive while the sender is at a distance. Words in a letter, unlike words said, do not vanish into the air. But my letter to Fabienne did none of those things. She had not even bothered to read it.

Fabienne leaned over me. "Look how your eyebrows are knitted," she said. "I was teasing you. I did read it."

"Really?"

"If you want to believe it. Or maybe the cooking fire read it for me. Don't you think M. Devaux should make a pupil out of fire? It would devour any poetry or philosophy he wants to teach."

I was miserable. I would never know the true fate of my letter. "What do you think of our moving to Paris together?"

"Do you think that is a possibility?"

"Why not? I've already met a few people there. I like them. And I like Paris."

An owl hooted somewhere, and Fabienne hooted back. She was good at imitating birds and other animals. I could not make the sound of a lamb or a cow. I could not even make a convincing barking sound to attract another dog.

"Where would we live?" Fabienne said after the owl hooted back. "What would we do there? I don't think there are cows and goats to herd in the city, are there? What would you tell your parents—that you're off to Paris to make a living by your pen? What would I tell my papa, that I'm going to work in a factory?"

"Maybe you could be a zookeeper?"

"How many zoos are there in Paris?"

"I don't know," I said. "But maybe we can start in Paris with the money M. Chastain pays us. We'll sort out the rest of it later."

"You're beginning to sound like me," Fabienne said. "Except when I say I'll sort something out, I have a plan. You've only learned to use my words, but you don't really know how to make things happen for real."

WHEN M. BAZIN, THE PHOTOGRAPHER, ARRIVED a week later, he seemed disappointed that I had put on the full outfit Mlle Boverat had bought for me in Paris. No, he said, that's not what we want. He told me to change into my school uniform, and asked me to show him the school. Mme Loisel, the headmistress, received M. Bazin warmly. She considered it a great honor that her school had produced a child author, she told M. Bazin. She was warm to me these days, even though she had not paid much attention to me before. I never fawned over the teachers, nor made any trouble for them. Now I was no longer bland and forgettable. In my heart I lapped up the attention I received, though my eyes still turned downward, my smile humble.

At the school, M. Bazin made me pose for a few pictures: standing near the school gate with a few books clutched to my chest; sitting at my desk, with my chin rested on my hands; hanging upside down on the parallel bars; walking on the school grounds with an open book—my own book. It was the first time I had seen a copy of the book, but before I had more time to study it, M. Bazin took it away, and told me that we would go back to the farm for a more native setting.

By then the word had already got out, and a band of younger children had gathered, asking M. Bazin questions and pestering him to take their pictures. When Joline's American boyfriend visited, he had always come prepared, with chewing gum and chocolates. M. Bazin had to seek help from the adults watching us, and one of them summoned M. Meinen to keep the children in order.

My mother gave M. Bazin a pair of gum boots to walk in the manure and mud, and placed his leather shoes, already dusty from walking around the school grounds with me, in a cleaner corner of the house. I changed out of my school uniform into my work clothes, dark gray overalls that used to belong to my mother, and a pair of gum boots too big for me. I felt ugly, and asked M. Bazin why I had to dress up in this way.

"We want to give your readers a taste of what you look like in your life," he replied.

"A peasant girl?"

"A peasant girl with an enormous gift and a bright future," he said.

"Do you really think I have a bright future, M. Bazin?"

"That depends on how you make use of your new fame. But yes, you will have a future better than all those kids."

"If I move to Paris," I said, "do you think I can find a way to make a living there?"

"But you are, how old are you, only fourteen, no?"

"Yes," I said.

"Don't you think you're too young to think of moving to Paris for work?"

"How do I make use of my fame if I stay here?" I said. "Tomorrow everyone will forget that you've come to make me into a star. People care about cows and goats and beets and cabbages. No one will read my book here."

M. Bazin shook his head and said he was not in a position to give me any career advice. He suggested that I consult M. Chastain.

On M. Bazin's instructions, I fed the chicken, throwing handfuls of bran while smiling at his lenses. Then I sat on the barn floor and held two young goats, much closer than they were used to, but their protests did not move M. Bazin, who kept telling me to embrace them tighter, and smile, and talk to them, and smile again. I poured buckets of feed into the trough, even though it was not mealtime for the pigs yet. I pulled one of our rabbits out of the hutch and put my face into its fur. I pumped water from the well. I hung up some sheets on the clothesline. I weeded the vegetable garden and collected the last of the season's beans in a basket. I did more chores in those two hours than I usually did in a day. I felt like an idiot.

When M. Bazin spotted my father's bicycle, he asked me if I could ride it down the road. But my father did not allow me to touch the bicycle. It was his treasure, and on less busy days he liked to turn the bicycle upside down and clean every part of it with a rag dipped in oil, including all the spokes, until it looked shiny and new.

I said I did not know how to ride a bicycle. M. Bazin told me to push the bicycle to the back of the barn. He followed intrepidly, stepping into the muddy manure. Exactly what he needed, he said while he scraped off some of the mud under his soles onto the wheels and the spokes of the bicycle, which now looked a beggar version of itself. I hoped my father would not be outraged. Perhaps my new stature would help. He, like my mother and the other adults, had shown respect when M. Bazin had arrived.

As instructed by M. Bazin, I stood astride the bicycle, one foot on the pedal and the other on the ground. I was not good at balancing, and a couple of times I nearly fell, and M. Bazin steadied me with one hand while holding on to his camera with the other. His grasp was firmer than I imagined his soft-looking hands would manage, though he did not show a trace of meanness.

When he was finally satisfied with his results, we returned the bicycle to its place near the house. I pulled a handful of leaves from a tree, trying to wipe the mud off as well as I could. M. Bazin watched with an amused look. After waiting for a few minutes, he said we should carry on. "What else can you show me?" he asked. "Are there other things that reflect your daily life here?"

"Do you want to photograph cows?" I asked.

"Yes, but I don't see any cows."

"We don't keep any," I said. "My parents are busy enough in the fields, but my friend, she has cows. We can go find her."

The night before, I had reminded Fabienne that the Parisian photographer would arrive the next day. I had been disappointed that she had not asked to accompany me. "Don't you want to take a look at him when he's here?" I asked. "You said we need all the experience we can to write books."

"What about my cows and goats?" she said.

Whenever Fabienne did not want to do something I suggested, she would say she was busy taking care of her animals. I knew she did no more than herd them to the meadow and lie next to the river for hours at a time. What was she thinking about when I was not around? It surprised me that it had never occurred to me to ask the question. My life was, up till then, separated into two parts: when I was with Fabienne, and the rest of the time—what happened then did not feel important to me. School and home were just for me to endure. They kept me away from Fabienne. But her life was continuous, unless she considered time spent with me and time spent without me as two distinct parts, and that she, too, had to endure our separation. Dared I hope for that? Not in a million years.

"Wouldn't it be good if you could meet this man?" I had asked. "Maybe he can help us find a way to move to Paris?"

"Nobody can help us," Fabienne said. "And I don't need anyone's help to get what I want."

She was wrong. Whatever she wanted, I was there, and I always helped her. But this I did not say. Nor did I point out that M. Devaux, more than having helped us, had made many things happen. After that night, Fabienne and I had not talked about him, and in the evenings, when we were out together, we avoided the path leading to his house. My parents told me that M. Meinen could not decide if M. Devaux had committed a crime. All the same, he had caused enough of a scandal for the village. He would move away soon, my parents said. To where? I asked, and they said they did not know. When I shared the news with Fabienne, she simply nodded and said she had thought that would happen.

HAVE YOU READ THE BOOK?" Fabienne asked M. Bazin when I brought him to meet her. She was sitting on a rock and did not get up when we approached her. It struck me that M. Bazin might find her rude, but if he did, he did not show it.

M. Bazin said that indeed he had, and that was why he had traveled to the village to photograph me.

"Because you wanted to see if everything is as the book says?" Fabienne asked.

"It'll do Agnès a great service when the photographs are published," he said.

"But not the book?"

"Of course they'll help the book," M. Bazin said. "The photographs will offer a context to the stories."

"Do you like the book?"

M. Bazin glanced at me and said yes.

Fabienne asked M. Bazin if he had a copy, and he handed her the one he had brought with him as a prop. I had not received copies of the book, even though M. Chastain had promised that he would send some. I wondered if I should talk with Fabienne, to see if she thought M. Devaux had burned the parcel sent to me from Paris.

She looked at the cover closely. "Why did they print M. Devaux's name on the cover, too?" she asked.

I looked over her shoulder. The title of the book, *Les Enfants Heureux*, and my name, Agnès Moreau, were framed together by a blue rectangle. Underneath, in smaller print, was a line: *"Récit recueilli par Maurice Devaux."* When I was posing with the book earlier, I had not even thought of looking closely at the cover.

"I suppose M. Devaux has played an instrumental role," M. Bazin said.

"He makes himself sound more important," Fabienne said. "Men always do that."

M. Bazin looked at Fabienne, but did not speak. He beckoned me to follow him. I could see that he did not like Fabienne. Not many people did. Adults in the village thought she was ill-mannered and violent, though they avoided confronting her. She was known to play heartless tricks on chickens and young children, even dogs that seemed capable of fending for themselves. I was hoping someone from Paris would see Fabienne differently. But I could tell that in M. Bazin's eyes, she was only an insolent girl from the countryside, and she was not even pretty. I knew she did not care what he thought of her, but it occurred to me that she had made the right decision not to put her name on the book cover. She would not have been able to do half as well as I had in Paris.

The cows were indifferent, and M. Bazin had a smooth time photographing me with them. When we returned to Fabienne, he thanked her for her help. "Can you tell me what this introduction means?" Fabienne asked him. She had been reading the book while we were doing the photo shoot.

"Just a note from M. Chastain about how he discovered Agnès," M. Bazin said. "With M. Devaux's help."

"Yes, that's what's said in here," Fabienne said. "I can read. What I'm asking is: Does every book have an introduction about how its author was discovered?"

"No," M. Bazin said. "But this is a unique case, and naturally people have questions. Not that anyone is doubting that Agnès wrote the book, but to explain how M. Devaux assisted only makes the situation more believable."

"Believable?" Fabienne said. "What is there not to believe?"

"People like explanations and assurances when something extraordinary happens," M. Bazin said. "And your friend Agnès wrote an extraordinary book."

I was worried that Fabienne's questions would trouble M. Bazin. It occurred to me then that people I decided to like might not see anything likable in Fabienne.

"For instance," M. Bazin continued, "people might wonder how the idea of writing and publishing a book could have occurred to a young peasant girl, and the introduction answers that. It was M. Devaux who recognized Agnès's potential. Or people might wonder how much of the writing credit goes to M. Devaux, and the introduction explains that, while he assisted with grammar, the words and sentences are Agnès's own. You see these are all good measures to ensure the book's success?"

Fabienne did not reply right away. She looked at the introduction for a moment and said to me, "You didn't tell me they gave you a test to see how well you could write."

I grabbed the book from Fabienne, and she pointed to the last page of the introduction. It was the paragraph I had written for M. Chastain when I was in his office. Underneath he had written that after personally testing my writing aptitude, he was satisfied, and he trusted that the paragraph I had written, in less than twenty minutes, offered solid evidence to readers that they would be embracing a literary wonder.

"Oh," I said. "I forgot to tell you about it."

"You forgot?"

I feared that she would say something nasty in front of M. Bazin, but he had moved a few steps away and was taking pictures of a cluster of bellflowers.

Fabienne turned to M. Bazin and asked if he could take a picture of us together.

"Why?" I asked. I wondered if she had changed her mind about something.

"We've never had our picture taken," she said.

M. Bazin arranged us to lean on a linden tree, my arms folded across my chest, her two hands placed on my two shoulders as though she were in the middle of turning my face toward her.

~

THE BOOK WAS PUBLISHED in October. M. Chastain arranged for another trip to Paris so I would meet more press. I came to realize, during that trip, that living in Paris with Fabienne was not going to be as simple as I had thought, at least not until we were a little older. I asked Mlle Boverat, M. Chastain's assistant, how she had found the position in the publishing house. What she said was discouraging to me, as we did not have any connections who could recommend us for any kind of position, as Mlle Boverat had had in her uncle.

M. Chastain was a little surprised when he learned that M. Devaux had moved away from Saint Rémy. He said he had received no letter from M. Devaux informing him of this move.

"Why do you need him? You can write to me," I said.

"The question," M. Chastain said, "is whether you need him."

"Need him for more books? No, not at all."

"The book you talked about when we met you in the summer, did you finish it?"

"Yes," I said.

"You wrote it all by yourself? Did M. Devaux read it?"

I thought about how to answer. "He read parts of it, but not the entire book," I said, which was not quite a lie. Fabienne still had not given the book an ending.

"Did he say anything about the parts he read? Did he express any opinions?"

"He said I was improving," I said.

"And?"

"Nothing more. You see, M. Chastain, the book is about a village postmaster."

I could see his interest was piqued. I promised to send it to him the moment I copied it into a clean workbook.

"M. Devaux helped us with other things. We would still like to have an adult to supervise and assist you with any business decisions. Do you have any idea who else can help you with these things? Your parents, for instance," M. Chastain said, but I thought he only said that to be nice. He had met them; I suspected that he did not think of them as useful.

"Can M. Bazin supervise me?"

"You mean the photographer? Oh no, of course not!" M. Chastain said.

"How old do I have to be before I can handle my own affairs?" I asked.

"We can discuss this further. We don't have to make a decision right at this moment."

When I returned home, I told Fabienne that M. Chastain

was keen to see our next book. Truth be told, I could not tell if the love story between the young postmaster and his best friend's sister was interesting, but Fabienne seemed to have faith in what we had written.

"When do you think we'll finish with writing books?" I asked Fabienne.

"Next week. I have to figure out one more thing and then the book is done."

"What I mean is, is this going to be it? After this book we won't be writing another one, right?"

"Why, you don't want to?"

"I can't see how this will help us move to Paris," I said.

"Of course you can't."

"But you can see?"

"This is what I know: if we stopped writing now, we would never make it to Paris," Fabienne said. "You see, it's like a game. We don't know when the game is going to be over, but since we've already begun, and since we don't have another game to play just now, we may as well stick with this one."

This was the longest game we had played. Normally it was Fabienne who ran out of patience.

The money from *Les Enfants Heureux*—my half after M. Devaux had divided the payment between Fabienne and me—I had given to my parents. They were happy, that I could tell, but this happiness was not enough to make a difference. Some people became loud and grumpy when they grew old. My parents, who aged overnight into their older selves after Jean's death, looked shriveled, more subdued and slower in everything they did.

At school, the teachers seemed to respect me a little more. Some of the girls had asked about my book and my trips to

Paris. Had I been a different person, I would have used this opportunity to make some friends and secure a more favorable position for myself in the small society of school life, but I did not see the point in changing anything. Geneviève, ever so loyal to me even though I was only lukewarmly friendly with her, informed me that some of the girls talked about how I had become arrogant and aloof now that I was an author.

~

A LETTER ARRIVED from M. Chastain a week later. *Les Enfants Heureux* would be translated into English, and it would be published in Britain and the United States in the coming spring. I showed the letter to Fabienne. "Do you think this will help us?" I asked.

"Anything will help us," Fabienne said.

"Maybe we can go to America one day."

"For what?"

"We can find work there," I said. "And we can live together."

"Just the two of us?"

"Yes," I said. "We don't need anyone else, do we?"

Fabienne looked at me strangely. It was not one of her usual looks, teasing, or contemptuous, or mockingly affectionate. I knew every expression on her face as she knew every thought on my mind. But now her eyes betrayed something else. Alarm. Incredulity. Even hostility.

"I mean it," I said. "I don't think we want husbands or children, right?"

"You dream big," she said.

I shook my head. I told her that the book-writing game was dreamed up by her, and I was only following her, and I would do what she wanted me to.

"That's not what I mean," she said. "You think everything is done for a reason, and whatever we do will make a difference later. And you think everything that happens now will lead to something good in the future."

"Is that what I think?" I said. Oftentimes I needed her to tell me what I was thinking.

"Most people think that way," she said. The lack of malice in her words was unfamiliar. Fabienne did not get sick. She rarely felt tired. But there was something in her voice that reminded me of a tired or sick person.

"I'm like most people?"

"There's nothing wrong with being like most people. But myself," she said, "I don't do things with any grand purpose in mind."

"For what, then?"

Fabienne looked at me the way she would look at an injured bird before wringing its neck. All my life, no one else has looked at me with such tender pity. "I don't think you understand," she said.

"Then tell me," I begged. "What don't I understand?"

"The problem with you," she said, "is that you don't think much and you don't feel much, so you're easily amused and satisfied."

"I don't think much because you're doing the thinking for me," I said.

"Exactly," Fabienne said. "I don't mind thinking for both of us, but what can you do for me?"

Have I not, I thought, done everything she's told me to? She took out a folding knife from her pocket. "Close your eyes," she said. I did, and felt her take my left arm and push the sleeve up to my elbow. "Don't open your eyes," she said.

I felt something sharp poking into my forearm, and even before I made a sound she shushed me. I wondered if she was planning to slice my vein open. "What do you feel?" she said.

"A knife."

She pressed the tip of the knife harder and drew it along my arm. "And now? Does this hurt?"

"A little."

She let go of my arm and told me to keep my eyes closed. "What do you feel now?"

"Nothing."

She told me to open my eyes. Next to my intact arm lay hers, a red cut traveling down to her wrist, oozing drops of blood. There was a strange neatness with the cut.

"You can't feel it, can you?" she asked. "I can think for both of us, yes, but can you do the other part, feeling for both of us? No, this—" She wiped the cut with a thumb and then pulled down her sleeve. "This proves that you cannot do the feeling part for us."

If she sliced my arm she would not feel my pain, either, but I did not say that.

Fabienne folded the knife and returned it to her pocket. In a changed tone, as though nothing unusual had happened, she told me that she had the ending of the love story all figured out.

From what we had written so far, I was certain that the postman would finally win his lover's heart. But no, that was not Fabienne's plan. The girl rejected the young man, saying that she had never felt anything for him. But that couldn't be, he said; he thought there was something special between them. There was always something between two people, the girl replied. But whatever that was for them, she explained to him, it was only his sister's doing. What do you mean? he asked, and she said, You should ask your sister.

When the postman approached his sister, she told him that a man should have his heart broken into a thousand pieces, but only once. She thought it was best that his heart be broken by someone she trusted. From then on, she said, he could go out into the world to be a heartbreaker. That was all she and her best friend could do for him.

"What a bizarre ending," I said.

"Bizarre only because most people want them to fall in love," Fabienne said. "What we must remember is never to give people what they want."

"Does that also mean we shouldn't give each other what we want?"

She made a gesture as though she were about to box my ear. "You're an absolute imbecile. Of course we're different. You and I are like . . ."

"Twins?" I said when she did not finish her sentence. "One person?"

"No. You and I are like day and night."

"What do you mean?"

"Is there an hour that is neither day nor night?" she said. "No. So you see, you and I together, we cover all the time, we have everything between us."

SOMETHING STRANGE HAPPENED even before *Les Enfants Heureux* was published in England. A Mrs. Townsend wrote from London, telling me that she was an admirer of my work and suggesting that she pay me a visit in early December. The letter had been sent to M. Chastain, and he had forwarded it to me, accompanied by his own letter. He explained that Mrs. Townsend had been in touch with him when the French edition was published, and subsequently she had met him in Paris. They had discussed my future, M. Chastain wrote, for which Mrs. Townsend had made an ingenious proposal. He would leave her to work out the details with my family, as he was not in a position to reveal her plan or to make a decision for me. However, he wrote, he very much endorsed Mrs. Townsend's proposal. At the end of the letter he asked if I had finished the novel I had promised to send him.

"Have you not sent the novel to him?" Fabienne said, after reading the two letters. "I thought you did yesterday."

I had finished copying the book in my best handwriting, which Fabienne had given the strange title *Le Cœur Dans la Poste—The Heart in the Post.* I did not understand the title. Whose heart was she thinking of—the young postman's, or one of the two girls'? Fabienne had told me to send the book off, and she had begun to talk about what we would write next. But I had found excuses not to go to the post office the day before. The new postman, a man younger than M. Devaux (but not as young or handsome as the one we had made up in our book), was friendly enough, but the thought of going to the post office made me tired. I would need to engage in a conversation with him. Even if he did not question me extensively, he would look at the address and in no time the villagers would know the contents of the parcel. If this book-writing was a game, I would rather keep it between Fabienne and me. Yet, just like a game in the schoolyard, sooner or later others decided they could be part of it.

"I'll do it today," I said. "I'll reply to M. Chastain's letter, too."

"Why? You sound odd. What's wrong with you?"

"When will this be over?"

"Don't worry," she said. "We won't be doing this forever, but at least for a while. We haven't found something better, have we?"

MRS. TOWNSEND WAS NOT TALL, but she gave the impression of towering over anyone she encountered. Her permed hair, inelastic and steely, made me wonder how she could sleep comfortably without hurting her neck. Her tailored suit and stern heels would not be out of place in Paris, but here in Saint Rémy they made her look like one of those courtiers we were taught about in history—the only reason you take them seriously is because they put on such an impeccable air. She wore a strand of pearls, and later, when I knew her better, I often thought that those pearls, with their soft hue, looked harsh and cold on her. Anything would make her look harsh and cold. Mrs. Townsend was the kind of person whose approval you feel you must win, even though you cannot understand why you feel this way. She was not benevolent, but fair. Maybe god is like that too.

She arrived in the early afternoon, and I was not informed

until the end of the school day, when the teacher told me that my mother had stopped by and asked me to go home straightaway after class was dismissed. By then Mrs. Townsend had already persuaded my parents to accept her proposal. I was to go to England and attend her school, which was, according to her, a highly selective place for the education of the best young female minds from around the world. My attending the school was on the condition that I was to stay strictly under her supervision for a whole year, and I was not to return home for a visit. This, Mrs. Townsend explained, would be to ensure that I would gain maximum benefits from the school. "You will be our youngest student," she said to me, and explained that most of the girls spent a year there before entering society. "But that will be good for you, as you will have the older girls to look up to. I expect, of course, that you will be behind in all coursework except for French, another reason for you to be placed under the right tutelage as soon as possible."

We were sitting at our dinner table, I on one side, and my parents and Mrs. Townsend on the other. When Mrs. Townsend talked, my father seemed to be studying the wood grains of the table, but he nodded in agreement at the appropriate moments. My mother's eyes appeared unfocused.

"But we can't afford it," I said when my parents did not protest.

"That," Mrs. Townsend said, "shall not be your concern." As she had told my parents, she explained, she had secured some patrons for me.

"But why?"

"Why do the patrons invest in your education? Because you've proved yourself an exceptional girl."

That praise in her stern voice sounded more like an indictment. I had nothing to say to defend myself. "When do you want me to go to the school?" I asked.

"Straight after the new year. I don't suppose you see any reason to dawdle here, Agnès. You of all people should know what to do when opportunities arise," she said. She had the full support of my publisher in Paris, she continued, adding that M. Chastain and she had discussed that I would need some adult supervision where my business was concerned. "I understand M. Devaux is no longer available for such a task. Naturally, I offered my service to M. Chastain, who agreed that I could serve you well in more than one way. Why, you don't look convinced."

"Do you mean I will go to the school in January?"

"There is no reason for delay, is there?" Mrs. Townsend said. She told me that she would arrange for my trip to Paris, where she would meet me, and after that we would travel to London. "You need not pack many things," she said. "When we get to London, the first thing we will do is to shop for you, and"—she looked at my hair—"we will visit a hairdresser before going to Woodsway."

Soon I would look nothing like myself, I thought.

"You will thank me later," Mrs. Townsend said. "I'm not sure you understand how lucky you are."

~

SUPPOSE I DON'T WANT TO GO to England?" I asked Fabienne that evening.

"Then everyone will think you're an idiot," she said.

But why would I care about what everyone thought? There was only one person's opinion that mattered to me, and I never hid my idiocy in front of Fabienne. "I don't see why I have to go," I said. "I don't even speak English."

"Sure you do," Fabienne said. "*Hello. How are you? By god, you're lovely. Smoke gets into your eyes, babe.*" Those were a few phrases we remembered from having Joline's boyfriend around.

"*Gimme une Lucky Strike!*"

"*Gimme a Lucky Strike!*" Fabienne corrected me. "If you want to go to America, you have to learn English."

"We can go to America first and then learn English there," I said.

"But why not now? I don't see what's so bad about going to that English school."

"I won't be allowed to come back even for a visit," I said.

"Maybe that woman doesn't want to spend extra money on your traveling."

I thought for a moment. "I know," I said. "I will ask my parents for money. They should give some to me. I gave all my money from the book to them."

Fabienne shook her head. "Maybe she has other reasons."

"Like what?"

"How would I know? Let's go back. I'm cold."

It was not that late or that cold. The dark, moonless sky and the wind through the leafless branches used to be our friends. I caught up with Fabienne, half a step behind her because I was afraid of seeing her face.

"You know I don't want to go," I said in a pleading voice. If I could convince her to agree with me, then I would find the courage to say no to Mrs. Townsend.

"You must go," she said.

"Do you want me to?" I asked.

She stopped walking and took one of her shoes off, knocking it on a tree trunk. I wondered if there was a pebble that was bothering her. She did not speak.

"I'll go if you want me to," I said. "But you have to know that if I go, I'm doing it for both of us."

"How can that be?" she asked. "What would I get out of your schooling in England?"

"Then I'll write to Mrs. Townsend and tell her I've changed my mind."

"Oh, stop being an idiot," she said. "What would I get out of your *not* going to England?"

I did not know what to reply.

"Are you going to write a book when you go to that school?"

"By myself?" I said. I had an urge to pull her old scarf off and trample it underneath my feet. "It's all your doing. See what a mess you've got me into."

"A fun mess," Fabienne said. "That's what we do best, isn't it?"

"That's what you do best," I said. The situation, I thought, was not fun for me. M. Devaux, who had had to move away, would not think he was in a fun mess. Even his pigeons, who had always lived in this village, had to learn to think of a new place as their home. I had always known that Fabienne liked to make a game out of everything, but I had only wanted to be next to her, watching and cheering her on.

"Don't be so morose," she said, holding up my face with both hands. "This is bound to be a great adventure."

By myself? Nothing would be good if Fabienne was not there. But even as I said that to her, I felt a tinge of unease. I was not being entirely honest.

"We can write to each other," she said. "It'll be like us putting our hearts in the post."

I smiled. It was the first comforting thing she had said the whole evening.

"In fact, you must write to me about everything when you get there. We can make it into our next book."

"And you promise you'll write me?"

Fabienne made a gesture to hush me. She often did that when she wanted me to know that she was working something out in her head. "I'll write you," she said after a moment. "But you'll also receive letters from Jacques."

"Who's Jacques?"

"Your boyfriend," she said.

I must have looked more stupid than ever, as Fabienne broke into a dry guffaw. "Oh, Agnès, use your brain," she said. "I'll be Jacques."

"But you'll still write to me, as yourself?"

"As Fabienne, and as Jacques."

"Why do you want to write as two people?"

"Two is always better than one," Fabienne said. "It's more interesting. Fabienne and Jacques will both write you, about different things."

I imagined what Fabienne would write in her letters. I knew the village well, the people and the animals. I wondered how she would be able to write two sets of letters when nothing ever happened here. "How do I write to two people if they are both you?" I asked.

"You'll figure it out," Fabienne said. "Don't look like I'm asking you to jump into a fire. It's not going to be that difficult."

"But . . ." I hesitated. "I'll miss you."

"It's only for one year. It'll be like, poof, a night of sleep."

"Yes," I said bravely, not wanting her to see my disappointment. That she would not miss me I had already expected. Still, wouldn't it be nicer if she could just lie once, saying some soft and loving words to me?

MON CHER JACQUES,

I am writing to you from Paris. The moment I arrived at Paris-Austerlitz, I began to imagine that someday you will make the same journey, and will see the gray buildings with the high windows, smoke-blackened towers, and the glass dome of the station. Thinking of your trip made me feel less lonely.

Mrs. Townsend did not come to meet the train herself, but sent someone from the hotel. I am staying in a room next to hers, and there is a door between our rooms, which she told me not to lock. We will be in Paris for two days, and then we will go to London. Please keep me in your heart. I will write again when I settle down at the school.

Agnès

I wrote that short letter before leaving for London. I was afraid of saying too much because the letter was addressed to Jacques instead of Fabienne. I wanted to see whether it would feel different if I was writing to Jacques, whom I had not met, but who had begun to take shape in my head as I sat on the train to Paris. I had never spent much time thinking of anyone but Fabienne, and even a made-up boyfriend seemed to me an intrusion. On the other hand, I thought, Jacques would think more highly of me than Fabienne. He would never call me an imbecile, and he would be willing to listen to me a little more than she did. He might even love me.

And the best part, of course, was that he was really Fabienne.

Perhaps he would make it easy for me to say things that I had never said to her. Perhaps she would feel the same, too, saying to me things she would never say as Fabienne.

I could barely wait to receive a letter from Jacques, but that would not happen until I arrived at the school. There was no other address for Fabienne and Jacques to reach me. For the first time I looked forward to England, and to the school.

I asked the hotel clerk to please post the letter for me. On the envelope I had to put Fabienne's name. What was Jacques's family name? Fabienne had not told me, and it had not occurred to me to ask. The hotel clerk, a man with side whiskers and a soft voice, both of which I found fascinating, showed me a newspaper from a few days ago. There was my own picture, gazing out of the page, the street behind me blurred. Mademoiselle is a celebrity, he told me, and I had to remind myself not to giggle but smile. Later he phoned me in my room to say that the manager of the house wondered if I would mind signing a copy of my book for the hotel so they could put it on prominent display.

What an odd world. People who did not know me found it easy to like me.

~

THE NEXT DAY Mrs. Townsend dropped me off at M. Chastain's office and said she would pick me up later. I did not know if it was because she was foreign, or because I did not know her well, but when I saw M. Chastain and his assistant, Mlle Boverat, I felt I could breathe more easily.

M. Chastain handed me a thick package. "Letters from your readers," he said.

I did not know if I should open the package. People writing letters to someone whom they had never met—that was something new to me.

"Certainly you don't have to reply to them," he said. "In fact, I would recommend that you don't write to any one of them."

"But wouldn't they want a reply?" I asked.

"They can want," M. Chastain said. "But we don't want people to think they can have easy access to you."

"Should I read them?"

"You can sample the letters, but you don't need to read them all," M. Chastain said. "If you agree, we'll send a card as a reply on your behalf, saying you will spend the coming year in England, advancing your education, and asking them to respect your time and privacy."

I was amazed how M. Chastain's words made me into an important person. "All right," I said. I put the package down on my lap. I would bring the letters back to the hotel and read them before I went to bed.

M. Chastain looked at me closely. "You don't sound too excited about England."

"Do you know," I said, "I will be there for a long time without seeing my family?"

"Yes," M. Chastain said. "And I agree with Madame Townsend that it is for your own good."

"Oh," I said. I wondered if Mlle Boverat would offer me some sympathetic words.

He pointed to a stack of papers at the center of his desk. "Here," he said, "it's your next book, all typed up. We've noticed a shift with this book. It's a little different from *Les Enfants Heureux*, don't you agree?"

I studied his face, half hoping that he would say that the book was no good, half fearing it would be the case.

"It's a good shift," M. Chastain said. "At least we think so, and we hope the critics and the general public will concur. It's a less morbid book than the last one, a natural development of your intellect, one might argue. And yet it has your signature. The characters are uniquely yours."

"So you will publish it?"

"But yes, of course, there is no doubt about that," M. Chastain said. "Though it has become obvious, if you don't mind my saying this, Agnès, that this book should be the last one set in your home village. The readers will have learned enough about the place, and there is little more to be gained from revisiting it. This relocation to England is a good move. A French peasant girl going to an English finishing school as a child prodigy. That would make a good story, newsworthy and rich with potential."

"What's a finishing school?" I asked.

"I suppose Madame Townsend will give you a fuller explanation when you get there," M. Chastain said. "You will be an unusual student there, of course, but that will be all the more interesting for you and your readers."

"Do you mean I am to write a book about going to school in England?"

"There's no hurry," M. Chastain said. "And there's no pressure. We agree with Madame Townsend that we will moderate the publicity you will be exposed to while you're at her school. The goal is to strike a balance. Fear not, we won't be hiding you away entirely in the English countryside. We want to give the public some tantalizing glimpses of your life there."

I nodded as though I understood what he meant.

"It's Madame Townsend's belief that you need some proper training to better prepare you for the next stage of your career. And she might have mentioned this to you, but we both feel that you need someone capable to replace M. Devaux, whose assistance is no longer available to us. Do you trust that Madame Townsend and I can help you with that?"

I said yes. Fabienne would have said yes, too. She was never much interested in all this business talk, so I did not see why I needed to bother myself further.

"Perfect," M. Chastain said. "And, can I give you some advice? Keep a detailed journal when you are at Madame Townsend's school. Everything there will be of interest and can be used in the future. Do you see what I mean, Agnès?"

~

"AU REVOIR, PARIS," Mrs. Townsend said when the train left Gare du Nord. She asked me if I wanted to bid farewell to the city. Paris did not belong to me, and seeing the city outside the train window going backward, I felt neither joyful nor sad. But when Mrs. Townsend did not avert her scrutinizing eyes, I put a palm on the windowpane, as though my hand were too heavy for a wave.

On the boat leaving Calais, Mrs. Townsend said, "*Au revoir*, France." I held on to the rail with both hands, and put my chin on top of them. I had never been on a boat before. The water that expanded between me and the land, swirl after swirl, made me nauseous. Three days earlier I was in Saint Rémy, feeding the chickens and the pigs, sleeping on a makeshift mattress on the dirt floor. In Paris I was the young peasant girl who had written a book and who had slept in a hotel bed with fabrics softer than my own skin. What would I be in England?

Your fame has traveled ahead of us across the Channel, Mrs. Townsend had said at breakfast before we left, showing me an English newspaper. All I could read was my own name next to my photo, and Saint Rémy. In the photo I was hugging an unwilling baby goat.

By the time I was allowed to go home, I thought, the baby goat might be old enough to have had her own kids.

"Has M. Chastain arranged a press clipping service for you?" Mrs. Townsend said.

I looked at her blankly.

"I'll write to him about that. I saved some of the news cuttings, but they may not be comprehensive."

One day I would learn that Mrs. Townsend was a good record keeper. Of her own life and, for the duration when I was under her supervision, my life. People like Mrs. Townsend, who are obsessed with keeping a full account of their lives, are like artists who create optical illusions. A year is a year anywhere, a day is a day for everyone, and yet with a few tricks these archivists make others believe that they have packed something into their days, something precious, enviable, everlasting, that is not available to everyone.

~

DUSK FELL EARLIER IN LONDON than in Saint Rémy. By the time Mrs. Townsend and I exited the department store, the streets were all lit up, and people hurried along as though they could not leave this dim and wet world behind fast enough. A doorman hailed a cab for us, and arranged the parcels and boxes expertly at our feet. Apart from a pair of suede gloves for Mrs. Townsend, the purchases were all for me: dresses, jackets, blouses, skirts, stockings, shoes, hats, gloves, nightshirts, a hairbrush with a bouquet of peonies painted on the back, a light blue box with a toothbrush inside, of the matching color. There was even a gown, dreamily white. Trying it on, I felt as though I had stepped into a cloud. In June the school would hold its summer dance, Mrs. Townsend told me, as she watched the sales assistant adjust the shoulders of the gown for me. They talked between themselves in English, and then Mrs. Townsend told me in French that they had decided the extra half inch might not be a problem, considering that I was a growing girl.

I felt I ought to say something to express my gratitude or excitement, but I could not find the right words. As we sat in the cab I thought once again that I should say something. Still no words came. I touched the dragonfly barrette in my pocket. I had been carrying it since I left home, stroking its smooth and slender body whenever I could. It was comforting to think that Fabienne owned its twin, even though I knew she would not carry it around as I did.

In the cab I looked at the streetlamps through the rain. I had never watched waterdrops elongating on a glass pane from inside a car. When it moved forward the water streaks changed direction. Back at home rain was simply rain. In this new life, raindrops and streetlamps and the dark shapes of bare-limbed trees all seemed to have something to say to me, but if they were to speak, it would be in English, a language that was still foreign. I wished that I had listened to the rain speaking French to me when I was at home.

"What's on your mind?" Mrs. Townsend asked.

"Nothing," I said. "Nothing really."

"London in January is not the gayest place," she said. "But we'll be back before long. I assure you, once spring comes, you will become enamored with the city."

I nodded.

"But know your first loyalty is to Woodsway," she said. "I expect that you will love the school as you have never loved anywhere else."

Mrs. Townsend often carried on a conversation without needing a response from me. Even so, I dared not let my attention slip for a second. In Paris, M. Chastain had given me a thick leather-bound journal as a farewell gift. Write everything down, he had said several times, though I already knew that not everything in my life would go into that book. Some of Mrs. Townsend's words, for instance, would be better left out.

Mrs. Townsend started to talk about Woodsway. In every conversation it was never merely the school, but a future—my future—she so avidly foresaw. Upon my arrival, I was to learn English, and then Italian and German. "And, of course, all the other subjects we so proudly provide our students. You will not leave the school until we transform you. You see, an educator works like a sculptor. Whatever material comes my way, I'll ensure that something is made out of it. And it has to be something beautiful and perfect. That's my standard. Not merely useful or ornamental, but something of enduring quality."

When we entered the department store earlier, a few people had glanced at me, and looked at me more closely when they took in the sight of Mrs. Townsend, who was as sleek and inviolable as her fur coat. What stories people had made up about me, I could not fathom. A mute and deaf orphan she had picked up at a street corner? At the hotel lobby, the men in uniforms seemed always to look at the top of my head, or the space beyond it, even though they all greeted Mrs. Townsend with impeccable manners. At the restaurant that evening, when the food Mrs. Townsend had ordered for me arrived (tasteless, I decided), she instructed me on how to position my arms and how to use the fork and the knife. "You should observe the girls when you get to Woodsway. It'll save both of us some embarrassment," she said. "I cannot possibly teach you every single thing, but I trust that if you're smart enough to write a book, you should be able to learn many things by watching the world around you."

The next day we had luncheon with a man named Mr. Thorpe, who was to publish my book in the UK. He was very tall, and had to stoop when he shook my hand. Very tall men, to my mind, were like very short men. You could not possibly take them seriously. To keep a straight face, I spent much of the time watching a Miss West, whom Mr. Thorpe called his deputy. Her lips were perfectly painted in a shade of red that I had never seen before.

Mr. Thorpe and Miss West talked mostly to Mrs. Townsend. At the end of the luncheon, Mr. Thorpe turned to me and said in French, "We've heard about your second book. M. Chastain has planned to publish it this coming summer."

"Yes," I said.

"Will you write more books set in your home village?"

"No," I said.

"Why not?" Miss West asked. "Do you think you will return there after your time at Mrs. Townsend's school?"

I did not know which of her questions to answer, so I looked up at Mrs. Townsend. "Go on," she said. "Tell us your plan."

I said I did not have any specific plan, but that I would like to improve myself while attending Mrs. Townsend's school. "There are many new things for me to learn," I said.

"Will you write a book about your time in England?" Mr. Thorpe asked.

"Do you mean my time at the school?" I asked.

"I suppose it's a bit too early for Agnès to decide," Mrs. Townsend said.

"Yes," I said. "I'm afraid this is not the time for me to think about what to write next."

"We agree," Mr. Thorpe said. "Though can I point out one thing to you, mademoiselle? The world is eager to hear what you have to say, but don't keep people waiting for too long."

A waiter, walking past us at that moment, looked over the top of a tray at my face and then at my hands. I wondered if the world was waiting for me to make a mistake, to dip a spoon in the soup the wrong way, to snag my new dress on an unseen nail. Sooner or later I would break down, like a criminal unable to stand an interrogation.

Sooner, I decided. Fabienne would have approved of this kind of resolve. She was the one to say that we must surprise the world all the time.

"I may not write another book ever again," I said.

I could tell, from all three adults' faces, that I said a perfectly wrong and horrible thing. Mr. Thorpe and Mrs. Townsend exchanged some words in English, nodding, and I looked at the glass in front of me, trying to decide what kind of flower was etched on it. When I looked up I met Miss West's gaze. I smiled at her, as though I did not care what she thought of my first blunder in England.

WHAT DID YOU MEAN, that you might not write another book?" Mrs. Townsend asked that afternoon, while she was showing me how to pack for our trip to Woodsway. Along with the outfits for different occasions, Mrs. Townsend had also bought two leather suitcases for me. She had asked me to pick a color I liked. I had chosen a pink one, but she had disapproved. She had selected another color—powder-blue, she called it, and said it was more elegant and suitable.

"I don't know if I want to write more books," I said.

"*Rubbish*," Mrs. Townsend said. Later, I would know that was the English word she would use when I said something that displeased her. "*Rubbish*," she said. "You're too ignorant to understand your good fortune. And you're too young to decide what you want."

I did not know if I should apologize to her but did so all the same.

She looked at me and sighed. That heavy sigh, I would also learn, came about when she found me crude or primitive or beyond reasoning. *Beyond reasoning* were Mrs. Townsend's words, even though she never really reasoned with me.

"Agnès, here's something you need to remember," she said. "There are millions of girls out there, and many of them are prettier than you, and many are smarter than you. Many come from better backgrounds. But why is it that you alone are so fortunate?"

I was fortunate because Fabienne did not want to be me.

"All those girls, any one of them would be dying to be you. What makes you so special? Are you truly the prodigy the press makes you out to be?"

I did not know what to say, so I only looked at her. Soon I would learn that her questions were rarely for me to answer.

"You have something in you. That I don't doubt," Mrs. Townsend said. "Or else you wouldn't have written a book at all. Perhaps you didn't know what you were doing. You only stumbled into being an author. But if you give up your effort and stop writing, you will be just like the others, which means you will become nothing, do you understand?"

"Yes, madame," I said.

"You don't need to call me madame," she said. "All the girls at Woodsway call me by a special name, Kazumi. It's a Japanese name. Go on, give it a try."

I had never imagined Mrs. Townsend as anyone but Mrs. Townsend. Kazumi was the wrong name for her, anyone could tell. Kazumi should be willowy, with long, supple limbs and a faint sweet fragrance. Mrs. Townsend, square and harsh, was the wrong person to be called Kazumi.

"I was given the name when I lived in Japan," Mrs. Townsend said. "Do you know where Japan is?"

"Yes, madame."

"Yes, Kazumi," she corrected me.

"Yes, Kazumi," I said. It was a horror to think that I would have to use this name for her. It gave me an itchy feeling all over, but I could not scratch it in front of her.

"Japan is a beautiful country," Mrs. Townsend said. "Have you ever thought of traveling?"

I looked at her blankly.

"Naturally, you don't yet understand the importance of traveling," she said. "There are many places in the world worth visiting."

"I would like to go to America someday," I said.

"For what?" Mrs. Townsend frowned. "That's hardly what I'd call a worthy ambition for you."

For the chocolates that Joline's boyfriend used to distribute to us generously, I thought. For the fragrant soaps and chewing gum and the easy laughter of those long-legged soldiers I remembered from my childhood. For the oranges they had brought us. It was the first time we had ever seen the fruit, and to this day, I have always loved oranges, an inexpensive fruit that always makes life feel luxurious. When I mentioned America to Fabienne, she had been dismissive, and had said sharply that I dreamed big, but it was also the first time she had looked at me with alarm and respect in her eyes. Why? Because I had come up with the idea of America before she did. How could Mrs. Townsend tell what was a worthy ambition for me? She thought writing a book was such a tremendous accomplishment. Perhaps it was, for her. Fabienne had only sat up from the gravestone and said: Let's begin a new game; let's write a book. A game was never an ambition.

"There are other places to visit," Mrs. Townsend said. "Places with history and culture and beauty."

~

Before I went to bed that night, I wrote a letter to Fabienne. I would get up first thing in the morning and ask the hotel clerk to post it for me before we went to the train station.

The letter was short, more or less like this:

Ma chère Fabienne,
I am writing you from London. It is a city as big as Paris, but I am not sure if I like it as much as Paris. I am told that I will find more reasons to like it when spring comes. Once the weather is nice, Mrs. Townsend said, we will have school trips to London, to visit the museums and to attend the theaters and concerts. She bought me more clothes than I can ever imagine needing. I will look like a doll at my new school. We also went to see a Mr. Thorpe, who will publish the book in

London. He is very tall. I wonder if he needs a bed specially made for him. Maybe he will also need a coffin specially made for him when he dies.

I miss you, ma chère Fabienne. In fact, I feel terribly unhappy. Mrs. Townsend asks me to call her by a silly name, Kazumi. It is like an old sow deciding its name should be Mignonette.

I wish I could get on a different train and travel home tomorrow.

Agnès

After I sealed the letter, I went to bed and cried into my blankets. It was the first time I had cried since I left home. Perhaps this was what people called *le mal du pays*. But my homesickness was not about home. I was missing not a place, but a person.

~

THE NEXT DAY, at Waterloo Station, a man approached me and asked me in French if I was Agnès Moreau. Mrs. Townsend was talking to a porter, and when she turned and saw the man, her face became icy.

"What is it that you want?" she asked.

The man said he was a photographer, working for a Parisian agency. He had heard that Mlle Moreau was going to an English school, and he wanted to know if she would mind being photographed there.

"It's not up to her," Mrs. Townsend said. She introduced herself as the headmistress of Woodsway and my legal guardian in England. "We don't believe in exposing any of our students to unnecessary public attention," she said. "Surely you understand?"

"I do," the man said. "All the same, these moments in Mlle Moreau's journey would be worth recording."

Mrs. Townsend shook her head and asked him coldly but courteously to excuse us, as we had to catch our train. She hurried me into the carriage. When I sat down by the window, I saw the man on the platform. I wished I could smile to convey that I was not rude and unfriendly. After all, he was the first of my countrymen I had met in London. Unlike M. Bazin, who had come to our village to photograph me, this man was tall, handsome, with beautiful eyes and a clean-shaven jaw, and he was not as awkward as M. Bazin.

"That man," Mrs. Townsend said, "won't give up so easily." Sitting across from me, she, too, was watching as he turned away.

I did not speak. I had spent only a few days with Mrs. Townsend, but already I knew that we disagreed about almost everything. I was not in a place to express my disapproval of her, but at least I had the option of staying quiet. It occurred to me that was one reason I preferred the photographers to the journalists: the former rarely expected me to speak; the latter asked me questions all the time.

"It's my job to protect you from frivolity," Mrs. Townsend said.

"A photographer once came to our village . . ." I said.

"Yes, we've all seen his work," Mrs. Townsend said. "Don't misunderstand me, Agnès. I don't disagree with that man. It is worth recording your time in England, but I don't approve of his sneaking up on you. He should've known to approach me first."

"Yes, Kazumi."

"The French," she said. I must have flinched, as she smiled. "I don't mean to offend you. My father is English, but my mother is French. I have the right to criticize France, just as you do, too."

Why would I want to criticize France, or any country? But that I did not say. "Were you born in France?" I asked.

"Ah, this is more like you," Mrs. Townsend said. "I know things feel overwhelming at the moment. But you're an author, and it's your job to be curious about all things and ask questions."

So that was another thing I would need to do. Ask questions, whether I was curious or not.

The train gave a long whistle. The whistle of an English train was the first thing I had liked about this new country. French trains sounded shrill, like someone screeching. This train we sat on—its whistling sounded like a greeting. I wished Fabienne were here with me. She was good at mimicking birds and animals. She could easily have whistled like this old and even-tempered train.

Mrs. Townsend asked if I was comfortable. I nodded. "So, yes, Agnès, as I told you earlier, my father is English, and my mother is French, but they met in Switzerland, and that was where I was born. My father was a headmaster of a boarding school there, so you can almost say I was born into my profession."

I smiled and nodded.

"Switzerland is a beautiful country, and someday you should visit it."

"Yes, Kazumi," I said.

"And Surrey, which is where Woodsway is, is a beautiful place, too. The Switzerland of England, some people call it."

Had I been given a map at that time, I would not have been able to locate on it either Surrey or Switzerland. Much later, when I traveled from France to the United States, a woman on the ship had told me that she was from Sacramento, *the Paris of the Delta*. What delta is that? I wondered.

To call a place by another place's name was a stupid trick that people never tired of.

The two women sitting on the other side of the aisle, one middle-aged and one older, both looked at us and then returned to their almost inaudible conversation. I wondered if they understood French. Mrs. Townsend did not look concerned about being overheard.

"I've lived in several countries," Mrs. Townsend said. "But Switzerland and Japan are my favorites. Austria, well, that's a complicated place. China and Singapore and Malaysia, good for a visit, but I don't see anyone feeling at home there except the natives. England is an incomparable place. You're lucky to be able to spend some time here."

"You've not lived in France?" I asked.

"I've only visited," she said. "I don't find the idea of living in France appealing."

To that I had nothing to say.

"When I was your age, no, even from a much younger age, I wanted to be an author," Mrs. Townsend said. "I've kept a journal since I turned nine. I've written poetry and stories and stage plays."

"Oh," I said.

"I suppose in a way I've always been a writer, as I've never stopped writing," she said, looking wistful for a moment. "But I haven't achieved anything professionally with it, as you have."

I wished I could tell Mrs. Townsend that I would not mind *not* being an author. I wished I could say: Here, take my accomplishment, take anything you want from me, and let me go back home.

She told me a few other things about her life, mostly about her traveling, her enduring dreams of becoming a writer, and her dedication to her teaching. "I do believe in making a difference by being an educator," she said. "Of all my students, Agnès, you are the one who will allow me to maximize my influence."

"Yes, Kazumi," I said, heavy with apprehension.

Thinking about that trip now, I marvel that a slow girl like me could have a rare moment of seeing the future all too well: in that train carriage, sitting across from Mrs. Townsend, I felt an urge to scream, to break free before the train reached its destiny. Yet in retrospect, with the present to vindicate the past, everyone can claim the illusory status of being a seer.

We saw the French photographer again on the platform when we arrived at the station at Easthumble. He had boarded our train, and had known our destination. It did not occur to me that someone might have tipped him off about our journey. I was only worried that Mrs. Townsend would be annoyed with him. She was. Tersely she told me to take a seat on a bench and not to speak to anyone, then she walked with the photographer farther away on the platform. How could I talk to anyone? Other than the photographer and us, only two more people disembarked, and there was a man walking down the platform, back and forth, deep in his thoughts, his hat in his hand. I suspected none of them would walk up to me and say, *Bonjour.*

The train wheezed and then left, slowly, as though it were almost sorry to leave me behind. I looked at the broad back of the stationmaster and admired his uniform. I wiggled my toes in my new boots. I studied my hands, the suede gloves, soft like the underbelly of a young lamb. My tears from the previous night felt as far away and unreal as my childhood, as France. My life was not that bad. Perhaps I would find more good things when we arrived at Woodsway. Perhaps I could even turn myself into Fabienne, seeing in everything a game to amuse myself.

Mrs. Townsend and the photographer walked back. She told me that she and M. Lambert had come to an agreement. They both thought it was a worthwhile endeavor to record my stay at Woodsway, and M. Lambert would take a few photos of me at the train station. As the term had not begun, Mrs. Townsend said, M. Lambert would not accompany us there that day, but he would visit soon, once I had settled in.

Being a famous girl author could be a game. Smiling brightly at M. Lambert's lens, looking wistfully at the January mist hanging low over the treetops, studying the timetable posted at the station (in English, which I could not read), listening to Mrs. Townsend while looking obediently engrossed—they could all be part of the game. This was different than writing a book. I would not be able to write anything without Fabienne, but I could make up my own games. I looked straight into M. Lambert's eyes when he wished me good luck and bade me farewell. "Bring news of France to me soon, monsieur," I said. I had never been so forward with a stranger.

A man named Meaker met us at the station. He had already transferred our luggage into his car while M. Lambert was taking my photos. I greeted Meaker, but he did not speak French. It's time for you to use English now, Mrs. Townsend said, and taught me to say "How do you do?" to him. His red hair seemed in need of a good combing, and right away I imagined standing on tiptoes and touching that mess on top of his head. Meaker was the kind of man who made you want to do something for him, or to him, instead of shaking his hand and saying an insipid how-do-you-do.

Meaker was the only man who lived at Woodsway. He chauffeured, and also worked as a gardener and maintenance man. Soon he entered my journal—the first assignment I had received in my new school. For an hour after dinner, I was kept at a writing desk in Mrs. Townsend's sitting room, where I was to write in the thick leather-bound notebook M. Chastain had given me.

I did not know what to write about, but Meaker seemed a good topic, as he was as harmless as a tree—not an old and stately tree, nor a sapling, but a tree that looked like any other tree. But to be cautious, I did not write his name in my journal. I wrote that the first man to welcome me in England, upon my arrival, was a man with a bird nest on top of his head. A day later I decided to put a few skylark eggs in that nest. Then I turned him into an acrobat who moved around on a pair of stilts so he did not have to use a ladder when he was working in the orchard. He was good at keeping his balance, as the eggs never rolled out of the nest. He was kind to the mother bird who roosted on top of his head, and he slept sitting up in a chair when the mother was hatching the eggs. And then, when the chicks pecked out of their eggs, he would feed them when the mother bird had not returned in time for their hungry mouths. In this way he made friends with the chicks, and even when they were old enough to fly away, they never left, as he always offered them a feast of worms and grubs from his garden.

~

THERE WERE FIFTEEN GIRLS at Woodsway, and I would be the sixteenth. The other girls, away at their homes or their friends' homes or at ski resorts, had not yet returned from their winter holiday.

The house, Shelbrooke Manor, had been built not too long ago, Mrs. Townsend told me. Tudor-style, but not as old, she said, and then added that of course the house guaranteed modern convenience that would not be available in older houses. There used to be a mill nearby, the Shelbrooke Mill, and an industrialist had built the house for his family, but he had died before the house was finished. Then the two sons of the family both died in the Great War. The industrialist's widow and her three daughters once lived here, and for the past seven years the Woodsway Finishing School for Girls had made Shelbrooke Manor its home. It's the perfect house for a girls' school, Mrs. Townsend had told me when she showed me around on the day of my arrival.

The house was unoccupied but for the cook, her assistant, and the two maids, who seemed to have their mysterious ways of moving about. They were heard—felt—more often than seen, like one's own stomach. For the past few days I had been eating alone in the dining room. The younger one of the two maids, Essie, brought in my tray, but she did not speak French, and when I spoke my broken English, she seemed embarrassed on my behalf. She was not much older than I, but already she was making a living. I wondered if there were finishing schools in France. Fabienne and I could work at a place like that, moving in the underworld of a mansion. Nobody would truly know who we were, and precisely for that reason we would be happy and free.

Twice a day, in the morning and in the afternoon, Mrs. Townsend gave me English lessons. Her sitting room was furnished with many Oriental-looking objects, whose names I learned and have since forgotten. This room was not where lessons usually took place. But as the girls hadn't returned, she explained, we might as well make ourselves cozy.

"I see you're trying something new," Mrs. Townsend said to me one afternoon. "Are you working on a different approach?"

I did not know what she was talking about.

"I mean in your writing," she said. "Are you trying new things?"

"My writing?"

"I took a look at what you've written in your journal in the past week. You've done some excellent work."

My journal. I felt not alarmed but vindicated. Mrs. Townsend had not asked to read my journal at the end of my writing hour in the evening, but I had suspected that she would come into my room when I was not around. It was a pretty room, really very pretty. The window overlooked the orchard, and the white lace curtain was so fine that I sometimes sat on the windowsill with it wrapped around me like a costume. Rows of pale roses blossomed on the light blue wallpaper, each as beautiful and perfect as the next, all of them looking the same. The bed, the chest of drawers, and the desk—none of them was new, I could tell, but they were nicer than anything people in Saint Rémy had seen. That Mrs. Townsend would enter my room and read my journal was a price I must pay. I was smart not to have written about a sorceress who looked like Mrs. Townsend, with permed hair like steel strings and a necklace of pearls that looked like a congregation of cooked fish eyes.

"This man with a bird nest in his hair, is he Meaker?"

"Oh no," I said. "Not at all."

"So he's a man you made up."

"Yes, Kazumi."

"How did the idea occur to you?"

I shook my head as though I were baffled by myself. In Paris the journalists had asked how this or that idea of a story had occurred to me, and I had always behaved as though they had asked a question too complicated for me to answer, and also too absurd. "I don't know," I said to Mrs. Townsend. "I can never explain how an idea occurs. Some of our hens are good layers, but they cannot explain how they lay the eggs."

"*Rubbish,*" Mrs. Townsend said. "Writers are not hens."

"No, of course not," I said. "What I mean—"

"I know exactly what you mean. You were quoted to have said that in the press before. I don't know if you came up with the analogy yourself or someone taught you to say so. But I must warn you: You're doing yourself a disservice with that kind of language. A hen can be replaced by another hen, and all eggs look the same to us. Do you understand?"

"Yes, Kazumi," I said, trying to look grave. Mrs. Townsend could not be helped if she did not know that the eggs from different hens did not look the same.

She nodded, and leaned back on the sofa, as though to have a fuller view of me and the chair I was sitting in. "I don't think," she said, "it is my place to rein in your imagination, so my advice is that you keep doing what feels most natural to you. However, a fantasy like the one you're writing is, to my mind, not up to your standard."

"I will stop writing it," I said.

"No, that's not what I meant," Mrs. Townsend said. "Carry on what you are doing. Any new development with your writing is bound to be of interest to me and the public."

"Why?" I asked.

"You must understand, Agnès, that you've offered a rare opportunity to the world to observe how an underformed mind changes when subjected to a different environment. I need not be circumspect with you. You've written a book set in your home village, and it's done well. My understanding is that M. Chastain will publish a second one, set in the same place, and no doubt it'll receive all the attention it deserves. But how much more do you think the public wants to hear from a peasant girl about a wretched place like Saint Rémy? Next month, they'll find new pleasures in a street urchin's tales about the back alleys, or an account of a young candle-maker's life in her workshop. Do you follow?"

I did not. "Yes, Kazumi," I said.

"Your coming to Woodsway is like a new chapter in a book," Mrs. Townsend said. "Whatever you write in your journal—fantasies or epic poems or a realistic record of your life—anything you write has potential, do you understand?"

"Yes, Kazumi," I said. Those two words, I realized, were sufficient.

"So my advice is that you write, at this beginning of your new chapter, anything that feels natural to you. However, you must always keep in mind that there is a gap between potential and one's ability to realize it."

If anyone had potential, it was Fabienne, yet I was the one trapped in this house by that potential.

That evening, in my journal, I let the man with the bird nest on his head feed the birds a feast of worms. Now it's your time to fly away and find your life in the woods, he said to them. It's not, it's not, it's not, they chirped. But the man would not listen. He was not unkind, but he did not think it natural for him to stay friends with the birds forever. You see, he said to them, I am getting tired of sleeping upright.

Somewhere there must be another man who does not mind having birds sitting on top of his head and who will never get tired of staying upright in his sleep—the birds said so among themselves, and did not feel sad at all when they bade farewell to the red-haired man. Maybe they will find a statue in a public garden, the man said to himself. He knew he would miss the birds, but another mother bird might come the next spring, building a new nest in his hair.

The next evening, when I opened my journal, I regretted, for a moment, sending the birds away. Now that I could no longer write about the man, it felt as though I had lost my first friend at Woodsway. I looked around, trying to find something else to write about, and just then Mrs. Townsend's dogs followed her into the sitting room. They were an odd pair: a giant named Ajax, and a little one named Willow. Ajax, she had told me, was a Great Dane, and Willow was a Pomeranian. Harmony, she explained, resides in finding the perfect balance between opposites. I did not know what she was talking about. Her nonsense, unlike the nonsense Fabienne and I used to make up, made me drowsy.

Mrs. Townsend's dogs, living in harmony and not having to fight for food, might have an easier life than the dogs in my village, but I pitied them. If she noticed that they were not by her side, she would blow a whistle, which she kept in her pocket at all times. The whistle, she explained to me, made a sound that only the dogs could hear. And when she blew on it, the wretched beasts would appear right away, their tails tucked between their hind legs, their eyes not meeting hers. *What's the matter with you?* Mrs. Townsend would say in a reprimanding tone. Or, *What's wrong with you?*

Pity did not bring me closer to the pitiable. I did not like the dogs, but they were good enough to give me some inspiration. That evening I wrote about a tiger and a fox living in a manor house, with dark framed windows looking over a fountain and a wide lawn like many shrewd eyes. The tiger was not fierce but coy, the fox vain but not pretty. They complimented each other's good looks and intelligence. They called themselves the most fortunate animals in the kingdom. They lived in harmony, eating from two porcelain bowls side by side, and sleeping under woolen blankets softer than their own fur. Someday, I thought, a disaster would befall them, and one of them would have to eat the other so as not to starve.

~

NEXT WEEK THE GIRLS WILL RETURN," Mrs. Townsend said one afternoon, after we'd finished my English lesson. "Shortly after they settle in, the photographer will visit."

"Yes, Kazumi."

"Tell me, how do you like Woodsway so far?"

"It's a nice place," I said. "I like it here."

"What do you like about the school? Not that you've had a taste of the real school life yet, of course."

"I like everything here," I said, looking around for a better answer. "I like that there are many books in the house, and I like the rugs and the lamps. I like Mrs. Fisher's cooking. And that I have my own room, and I can take a bath."

Mrs. Townsend nodded. "So you do like baths now?"

"Very much," I said. On the day of my arrival, Mrs. Townsend had told me to take a bath, but I had resisted. In the hotel rooms in Paris and London, I had seen bathtubs, but I had found them as suspicious as the toilet that could flush and rumble with a mysterious force. At Woodsway Mrs. Townsend was the one to draw the bath and add bubbles, and watch me undress and encourage me to immerse myself entirely into the water. She said I would get used to it soon. She was right. I liked how warm and smooth and fragrant I felt after a bath.

"Good," Mrs. Townsend said. "And you're brushing your teeth twice a day, as I instructed you?"

I nodded. Toothbrushing was another thing I had learned upon my arrival. It did not give me the same pleasure a bath did, though. I gagged when I tasted the toothpaste.

"Have you written your parents and friends?"

"Yes, Kazumi."

"Where are the letters? Show me before I post them for you."

I paused before speaking. "I asked Clara to post them for me."

"Clara!" Mrs. Townsend said. "She's Mrs. Fisher's assistant. It's not her duty to post your letters."

I felt my face turn warm. In Paris and in London, people at the hotel desks were always ready to post a letter for me. I had thought that in this new life, all I needed was to ask for assistance.

"In the future you will always come to me when you need to post a letter," Mrs. Townsend said. She then brought a stack of letters out of the drawer, saying they had arrived in the previous two days. "Who's Fabienne Martin?" she asked.

I tried to keep my face smooth. "A friend," I said. "We grew up together."

"And Jacques Martin? Her brother?"

"Oh yes," I said. A clever solution, I thought. This was easier than imagining a Jacques whose life I knew nothing of.

"Why are they both writing you? Do you write them both?"

"Fabienne doesn't go to school anymore," I said. "She asked me to write her and tell her what it was like to travel to Paris and to go to school in England. She's curious."

"That is understandable," Mrs. Townsend said. "And Jacques?"

"He . . . he is . . ." I stammered. "Jacques . . . he is my boyfriend."

"Just as I thought," Mrs. Townsend said. "How old is Jacques?"

"Sixteen," I said. "Actually, seventeen. He turned seventeen last week."

Mrs. Townsend studied the envelope. I wondered if Fabienne had made Jacques's handwriting convincingly different from her own.

"In my opinion, you're too young to have a boyfriend," Mrs. Townsend said. "Besides, this Jacques's penmanship doesn't reveal him to be a good match for you. It might not hurt to call him your *petit ami* in your village, but it's now time for you to look ahead. You can certainly write to your friend Fabienne and your parents, but I would recommend that you stop this childish love game with Jacques."

I did not speak right away. If Fabienne wanted to write to me as two people, it was my job to hold up my end of the bargain.

Mrs. Townsend studied my face. "Why, do you disagree?"

"I don't see why I cannot write to Jacques."

"What do you gain by doing so?"

The question was: What do I lose? The answer: A lot. In the past two weeks I had written to Jacques and to Fabienne separately. In my letters to Fabienne I described everything in my new life without saying much about myself: the buildings and streets in Paris and London were other people's; the furniture and curtains and the rug in my room belonged to Woodsway; the new clothes in my wardrobe were like arrogant strangers, looking down upon me from their hangers. In my letters to Jacques I was chattier and less worried about being called an idiot: I tried on the soft slippers I was supposed to wear only in my room; I drank tea from gold-rimmed cups, the handles looking so dainty that I sometimes imagined taking a bite at them; the sweet-scented soap, a half-opaque oval, golden as honey, had left my face and hands soft and fragrant, unlike the dung-colored, hard-edged soap bars we used at home, which made our skin burn. Jacques was better than any boy I had known: he had all the qualities of Fabienne, and he loved me more than Fabienne did.

I glanced at the letters. These were the first ones from Fabienne and Jacques. I wondered how different they sounded. "I like to get letters," I said. "I like to receive news from home."

"You get them from your parents. And this friend, Fabienne."

"Jacques tells me different things."

Mrs. Townsend looked at me, and in her eyes I read surprise and distaste. It was the first time I had replied to her not with my standard, Yes, Kazumi; No, Kazumi; Thank you, Kazumi. Someone hearing her pet parrot saying some lewd words would feel a similar shock.

"All right, let's take a look at their letters. Let's see what news Jacques is telling you that his sister can't."

I did not know what Mrs. Townsend meant by that, but before I could respond, she ripped open the letters from

Jacques and Fabienne. She had once shown me a thin blade, its handle a carved jade fish. It was the first time I had seen a letter opener. I hated the uneven tears left by her rude fingers. No, I hated her.

She handed both letters to me. "Why don't you read them aloud, so I can judge their merits."

I recognized the writing paper Fabienne had used—pages from a student's workbook, the kind in which I had written out our stories. If I sniffed the letters I might catch the fresh scent of the meadow or the muddy smell of the barnyard. How on earth had I gotten myself into this strange country and strange school, being ordered around by someone who called herself Kazumi, even though she looked nothing like a Kazumi? There was only one person in the world whose wishes were my wishes, whose life was as important to me as mine. I put the letters in my pocket. "I'll read them later," I said.

"That's not the instruction I gave you, Agnès."

I know, a voice said in my head, but nobody says I have to listen to you all the time. I slumped in the chair and studied the desk that separated me from Mrs. Townsend. I was not the kind of girl who sulked, but once in a while I let myself slip into what Fabienne called my "playing-dead" mode. I never did this in front of my teachers or my parents, but sometimes, when Fabienne was too rough with me or mocked me too ruthlessly, I would turn immobile, imagining myself as a tree trunk or a boulder. It infuriated Fabienne, but when I kept my body still, my breath shallow, and my eyes half-closed so that I could see only blurry shapes, her escalating anger, her threats, even her hard punches could not harm me. The only way to reel me back from that state, Fabienne knew, was for her to soften up. She never apologized, but I could sense when her anger was replaced by something else—respect or resignation, or simply a wish to see me come back to life. Sometimes she found a few wild berries and rubbed them on my lips, or she would place a pair of leaves on my eyelids and then suddenly remove them as though she were a magician, showing a new world to me. Those were her ways to wake me up. I always did.

"Agnès," Mrs. Townsend said. She was insistent in drawing my attention back to her, and yet I knew that as I kept my mind unfocused, I could remain far from her. I wondered if I had been smiling with my eyes half closed. A moment earlier I had nearly tasted the sweetly tart flavor of the berries, which Fabienne had sometimes squeezed through my shut lips in her effort to bring me back to life. Once, only once, I had bitten her fingers, catching her unprepared. That had not angered her. In fact, she had broken into a wild laugh.

"Agnès," Mrs. Townsend said again, her voice less hard this time.

I opened my eyes and looked at her the way I might look at one of those women in the train carriage from London to Surrey.

"What were you doing?"

"Did you say something?" I asked. I could feel her scrutiny, and I kept my face flat and my eyes unfocused. Perhaps she would think I was a mad girl, but many geniuses, I remembered M. Devaux had told us, were mad people.

"We'd been discussing your correspondence," Mrs. Townsend said.

"Oh yes." I put a hand in my pocket, feeling the two letters.

"And I asked you to share them with me," Mrs. Townsend said, with a coaxing tone, which was new to me.

"But they're letters addressed to me," I said.

"Is that a good reason you cannot share them?"

Would Fabienne have foreseen that her letters to me might not be safe from Mrs. Townsend's eyes? I could not decide. If Fabienne had written about our books in her letters, Mrs. Townsend might have grown suspicious. I looked at her blankly.

"Agnès?"

"But they're letters to me," I said again.

Mrs. Townsend took a deep breath. She was about to say something, but then paused. She pointed to a pile of letters on the desk. "In fact, these are the letters I really would like to discuss with you. They're from your readers. Your French publisher forwarded them to me. Do you want to read them?"

I had read the readers' letters M. Chastain had given me in Paris. Several people asked for my autograph; others asked to be my correspondents. A man queried how long—how long exactly, a few seconds, a few minutes?—it took the pigs to devour a dead baby. He wondered if I had foreseen that I was supplying murderers with a new way to destroy criminal evidence—rather an ingenious way, wouldn't I agree?

That Mrs. Townsend no longer pressed me to read aloud to her the letters from Fabienne and Jacques made me think I had won a round in this game, so I decided to give her something in return. "I'll do what you think is the best," I said.

"Very sensible," Mrs. Townsend said. "I don't see why you'd want to waste your time reading these things. I'll put them away for now. When I have a free moment, I'll go over them. I don't expect to find any treasures here, but I'll share anything interesting."

I thanked her. I was eager to return to my room to read the letters from Fabienne and Jacques. I wondered if Mrs.

Townsend had already opened and read them and then resealed them. But even if not, I would not be able to stop her from entering my room and reading them later, just as I would not be able to stop her from reading the journal I was told to keep.

JANUARY 20, 1954

MA CHÈRE AGNÈS,

Fabienne came back from the post office yesterday, carrying the envelope with your letters to her and to me. When I asked her for my letter, she said I could wrestle her, and if I won, I could have it. I said she could give it to me another time, or she could read it and write a reply to you for me. She said, Are you afraid of losing? I said, I don't wrestle with girls. She said, Don't worry, you won't be able to hurt me.

But I wasn't worried about hurting her. If I lost a wrestling match to her, the whole village would know it and they would laugh at me. If I won, the village would still laugh at me for wrestling with a girl.

In the middle of the night, she rolled your letter into a

ball and threw it at my face. I pretended that it didn't wake me up, and when she left, I read it by the torchlight. I wish you could send the letter directly to me, but Fabienne said it was safer for her to receive our letters in the same envelope, addressed to her. She said if the journalists knew you were writing to a boy, they would make a big fuss about it. I don't see why they would. I think she arranged that with you so she can read your letters to me. She knows how I feel about you, and I think that's why she insists on being in the way between us.

There is not much happening in the village. Your life sounds busy and wonderful.

I miss you.

This is not a great letter, and I'm sorry I said the things above about Fabienne. She's your friend, so it's not honorable of me to complain about her. But you know how it is with her. I can never understand her. Still, she's the other person close to you, so I forgive her.

Jacques

JANUARY 20, 1954

Ma chère Agnès,

I read your letters to me and to my brother with great amusement. You sound like a perfect fool when you write to him, which is understandable. Most girls turn themselves into chirrupy birdies when they think they are in love. All I can say is that you should make sure that, after Jacques, you will not fall in love with another boy. Jacques—he is all right. He's not that smart but I like him better than most boys. You can be in love with him as long as you want.

But don't count on him. He is a boy and soon he will be a man. Men have very changeable hearts.

Many things have happened since you left. Père Gimlett died—maybe you have heard from your parents. It was a freezing day and he slipped when he was walking to the outhouse and bumped his head. Poor old man. He died with a full bladder.

Two weeks ago Louisa gave birth to a baby boy, so you lost your bet. They named him Pierre. The next person who will have a baby is Josephine, in March. I will still bet on a boy, so you have to bet that it's a girl.

Last week I went to your house and asked your parents if they could give me one of your rabbits. I told them that I wanted to have something of yours because I missed you. I could see that your mother did not believe me, but your father said yes. Maybe he misses you, too.

Guess which rabbit they gave me. And guess what happened after.

Write to me about everything. Remember, everything.

Fabienne

I just reread these two letters, along with the others I received from Fabienne that year, as herself and as Jacques. I wish I knew what happened to my letters to her. She might not have saved them. But perhaps that would be for the best. No one could rake through her things after her death and read my letters.

I used to name all our rabbits and chickens and pigs, but that never saved them from being butchered. I must have guessed which rabbit she was referring to when I first read her letter. I don't remember their names now. But I knew even then that Fabienne asked my parents for the rabbit not because she missed me, but because she was hungry.

I read those two letters several times on that day. The letters I had written Jacques were to an imaginary person, but Fabienne's response had made him real. I studied the two letters, in different handwriting, side by side. If Mrs. Townsend read them, would she suspect anything? I walked around my room until I found the perfect hiding place, in the inside pocket of the coat I had worn when I had left Saint Rémy. It hung at the innermost corner of my wardrobe. After I folded the letters and hid them in the coat pocket, I stuffed the coat into one of the suitcases Mrs. Townsend had purchased for me. There was a silver lock with two tiny silver keys, and it took me a few tries to successfully lock it. It had not occurred to me, until then, that I had a place to hide something away from Mrs. Townsend's eyes. I placed the unlocked suitcase on top of the locked one, and placed one key in the box that was holding my toothbrush, and the other key inside an old pair of winter socks in my chest of drawers.

~

THE HOUSE WAS A DIFFERENT PLACE when the girls returned. Mrs. Townsend had told me the night before that she would be helping the girls settle in, and that my study with her would be suspended for a day. She had not told me what I was expected to do, and I wondered if I should sit in the drawing room and greet the others when they arrived. I could sit with one of the French books Mrs. Townsend had asked me to read, a collection of poetry (but why would I need to read poetry?) or a collection of maxims of La Rochefoucauld (I looked at the first page, but my brain refused to absorb what my eyes read). Or I could pretend that I was writing in my journal. Surely there was no better way to introduce myself than to be found in the middle of school life, not having to explain myself.

In this new life as the author of *Les Enfants Heureux*, I faced the never-ceasing pressure to explain myself. I wondered if all authors faced the same demands. Any person who had written anything could explain himself better than I could. Perhaps I could just claim a spot on the sofa, with the two dogs Ajax and Willow sitting near me on the floor, all three of us as natural as the furniture in the drawing room.

But I lost the courage to carry out my plans, and I stayed in my room. I listened to the girls' voices, speaking different languages, laughing in a way that felt out of place on this gray, wet, and chilly winter day. Even with my door closed, I could feel that the air in the house was taking on a different quality. Warmer, thicker, with a whiff of camphor balls and fragrances unfamiliar to me. I sneezed twice, and was glad that I had not left my room. Imagine sneezing whenever a girl walked past me, shaking like an eager pup!

By teatime I had met all the girls. They were pleasant, some greeting me in French and others in English, which by then I had begun to understand, just a little. But soon they fell into conversations in twos and threes, eager to catch up with one another.

After tea, a girl named Catalina, who had thick wavy hair that was so black it looked almost blue, and large, plum-dark eyes, invited me to sit in the solarium with her and her two friends.

"You look even younger than in your press photos," she said. Her French was perfect, but with an unfamiliar twang. I smiled, not knowing whether to agree with her or not. "Isn't that so?" she asked her friends. They both studied me, and surprisingly I felt more at ease than I had earlier, when I had to sit among the girls pretending I was one of them. That I welcomed the girls' attention was a new discovery to myself. Can a zoo animal feel happier being observed in a cage than being allowed to roam among other animals in the forest?

"What does it feel like to be an author?" another girl, Margareta, asked. Her French sounded funny.

"Most days I don't think about being an author at all," I said honestly.

"Are you going to write another book?" Margareta asked.

"Everyone wants to know that!" the third girl, whose name was Rose, said.

"My second book will be published this year," I said. "But after that? I don't know. Maybe not."

"Why not?" all three girls asked in unison.

"Writing takes a lot of time," I said. "I have come to Woodsway to get a better education than I could get at home."

The girls laughed, though not in a mean way. "None of us is here for what you call an education," Catalina said.

"You're already famous," Margareta said. "Education is the last thing you need to think about."

"Is that so?"

"I think you should write another book," Margareta said. "You can put us in your book."

"Yes!" Rose said. "I saw an article in the evening paper the other day, saying people were guessing whether you would set your new novel in Woodsway. I'd say that's the perfect thing for you to do!"

Margareta and Catalina agreed. Everyone seemed to have an opinion about my future. I smiled without making a comment.

"You're too modest for a literary star," Margareta said.

"Perhaps Agnès is feeling shy," Catalina said, and then turned to me. "We don't mean to overwhelm you, but we've all been eager to meet you."

I asked them where they came from. Margareta was from Argentina, Rose was from Siam (though she did not look

Oriental at all to me). Catalina said her father was Italian and her mother was from the United States, and they lived in Rome.

"Are all the girls from abroad?" I asked. "Is there anyone from France?"

"You're the only one," Margareta said. "Wait until I write to my parents about this. My aunt keeps bothering them, saying they made a mistake not to send me to a Swiss school. Now my parents can tell her that no Swiss school could provide a world-famous French girl author!"

"Why did your aunt want you to go to a Swiss school?"

Margareta waved a hand. "Oh, don't let me bore you with that."

Catalina, who I could see was the leader of the three friends, explained that most of the girls were from England and other Commonwealth countries. The three of them, plus a couple girls from the United States, were the only ones who were not *Her Majesty's subjects*.

"What?" I asked. The English phrase was lost on me.

"*Les sujets de sa majesté*?" Rose said hesitatingly.

I did not know what they were talking about, but I nodded as though I understood. "But you all speak English?" I said.

They said yes.

Later, at dinner, Catalina asked me to sit next to her. "Kazumi told me to help you," she said. "Don't hesitate to ask if you need anything."

"Do you think you and your friends can speak English to me all the time?" I asked. Mrs. Townsend had told me earlier that the girls must converse in French on Mondays, Wednesdays, Fridays, and Sundays, and in English on the other days.

"Not all the time. We can't speak English to you on French days. Besides, we want to practice our French with you,"

Catalina said. She then looked at me closely. "Oh, forget about the rules. I can speak English with you if that's what you want. I'll simply risk not being understood! Shall I start now?"

"Yes, please," I answered in English.

But Catalina did not say anything right away. She was looking at Mrs. Townsend, who was sitting at the head of the table on a raised chair, her feet resting on a stool covered in a green-colored fabric. That way she could see all the girls and listen to our conversations, Catalina explained later.

Mrs. Townsend did not say anything, but her eyes opened wider than usual. Catalina nodded. In a lowered voice she told me to remove my elbows from the table and sit with a better posture, and then repeated the same request in English. I apologized, and Catalina said there was no reason to feel bad. "We all know how to look good and proper, we can arrange a perfect luncheon, but none of us has written a book," she said.

The girls, as Mrs. Townsend had told me, were all older than me. The youngest among them was Margareta, who was sixteen. The rest were seventeen and eighteen. By the summer, Catalina said, most of them would be ready to enter society. Or, in the case of some of the English girls, to enter a secretarial college and then work at the Foreign Office, where they would find the right husbands.

The girl sitting next to Catalina—an American whose name was Helen—put her knife and fork down and turned to me. "Tell us, Agnès," she said, and I knew right away that her French was not good at all. "Was it true that you minded"—here she used the English word—"pigs and goats before you came here?"

"Minded?" I said. I thought I knew the English word, but I did not understand her question.

Mrs. Townsend said, "Don't mix languages when you speak, Helen."

"Yes, Kazumi," Helen said in English, and then turned to me and asked me in French if it was true that, as it was said in the press, I was more comfortable with farm animals than most people my age.

"Do you not eat meat?" I asked, feigning curiosity.

"But I don't have to acquaint myself with the animals I eat," Helen said.

"Too bad," I said. "They all have pretty names. Some of them have good manners. Some not so good. We once had a pig named Hélène, and she was very rude."

I could feel Mrs. Townsend watching me, and the other girls, too. Catalina was exchanging a look with a girl across the table.

"How amusing," Helen said. "We're so lucky to have you here with us." She turned her face away midsentence.

I looked at the back of Helen's head. Fabienne could easily wring her beautiful neck. The thought calmed me down, but later that night the thought returned to startle me. Fabienne was not gentle, but she was not murderous. She would have said something blunt to Helen, she would have caught a handful of centipedes and released them in Helen's bed, but she would never have thought to solve anything by killing a person.

Was it possible that, between Fabienne and me, I was the truly morbid one?

THUS BEGAN MY NEW SCHOOL LIFE, which to this day I remember as one might a strange and vivid dream. In each retelling, the dream improves, offering fresh details, revealing forgotten twists.

Sunlight through the window traveling across the floor. Moonlight from the same window, grazing the framed watercolor of the Spanish cathedral. Can we say that sunlight moves with wings, and moonlight as if on the back of a snail? The wings of the rooks spread and folded, spread and folded, before blending into the dusk, when the girls, coming out of prep, yawned their elegant yawns—it was in these gestures that their bodies moved away from girlhood, waiting for real life to begin. On Fridays, we were served fish pies, a delicacy to me, which the others only picked at, remembering escargots, consumed with their parents, in a Parisian café or in a hotel in Menton. But you dainty girls—who among you ever questioned why the poor snails bothered to keep their shells, when the shells protected them from nothing?

The first syringas of the season, filling the air with a fragrance that grew stronger after nightfall. The flowering trees in the orchard: hawthorns and crabapples. The peony blossoms, splendid and short-lived. The mother wren darting about to feed her young. Three pianists seated at three pianos, playing different tunes. The dancing teacher's satin shoes, slung over her shoulder like a pair of skinny, lifeless dolls. French impressionist paintings and Roman sculptures projected on magic lantern slides. Nineteenth-century composers on the gramophone—their names, like their music, whirled in my brain and made me sleepy. We had the luxury of bathing as often as we wanted, unlike the girls at some other schools, we were often reminded by Mrs. Townsend. And there was the weekly visit of Mrs. Flask, who washed our hair with clinical precision. Morning and evening make a day. Days and nights make a week, a month, a life. Drop me into any moment, point me in any direction, and I could retrace my life. Details beget details. With all those details one might hope for the full picture. A full picture of what, though? The more we remember, the less we understand.

The days at Woodsway were organized around a gong, a bronze thing etched with inky Japanese characters, which at the beginning nearly always caught me off guard. Unlike the other girls, I did not own a wristwatch; Mrs. Townsend must have not considered that a necessary part of my wardrobe. The gong had a habit of ringing—announcing a meal, the lesson time, the departure for a field trip—right while I was tackling a task: washing my face and brushing my teeth, as instructed by Mrs. Townsend; choosing the right outfit for a class, a day trip, or for dinner—this Catalina often helped me with, as there were so many unwritten rules, known to all the girls but me.

Soon I learned to groom and dress myself satisfactorily, according to Mrs. Townsend's rules. But there were things in me that could not be scrubbed off or veiled over by a silky blouse. I first encountered wheat flakes at Woodsway, which, however long they were soaked in milk, tasted like sand to me. It was strange to watch the girls drink tea at breakfast. I had written about that in a letter to my parents, who I knew would be impressed. What kind of rich people, they would think, was I living with?

In the mornings we had classes with Mrs. Townsend: languages, art history, literature appreciation. After lunch we scattered around the house, reviewing our lessons or writing letters or doing nothing. Then we went to the garden for deportment lessons: I started with a book on the top of my head, but the other girls walked in a circle with a plate holding an apple on their heads. Tennis was popular—there was a racket in my room, though Mrs. Townsend did not think tennis a top priority for me. On rainy afternoons we gathered to arrange flowers—Mrs. Townsend was an expert since her years in Japan.

We were visited twice a week by Miss Griffin, the dance teacher. Mrs. Kopp, a music teacher from London, arrived with her violin case, and divided her time between the violinists, the pianists, and the singers. I was exempt from taking instrument lessons, and my voice would never make me a singer. Instead, when the girls practiced music from every corner of the house, I stayed at Mrs. Townsend's side, reading aloud to her in French and in English—elocution, she told me, was of the utmost importance for me. On Thursdays we traveled to London to visit museums and art galleries.

Mrs. Townsend was not a fan of motion pictures, which caused the girls to complain, though she did allow us to listen to popular music on the radio in the evenings. Bing Crosby was everyone's favorite; Archie Lewis was divisive. There were others whose names have since faded from my memory.

FEBRUARY 12, 1954

MA CHÈRE AGNÈS,

This time when your letter arrived, Fabienne gave it to me right away. She read it first, of course, but I think you may have expected that. I can tell from the way you write me that you're saving the words you don't want her to read. I like to imagine those words: it feels like we are holding our hands behind her back.

My life is a little boring without you, though this I don't tell people, not even Fabienne. I sometimes walk past the school gate or the village square to see if people are talking about you. Once I heard a girl, one of the three Maries, say to another girl: "What's so special about being an author? When I grow up I'll be a star of cinema." I laughed so loud that Marie was obliged to turn to me with a stare and tell me not to be rude.

Fabienne rarely talks about you with me. Well, you know she doesn't often talk with anyone. A few times I try to start a conversation about you, but she acts as though she's already forgotten you. She is heartless. I said this to her last night, but she said I got it all wrong. She said to me: You will soon get a new girlfriend because Agnès is not here, while we, Agnès and I, we will always be together no matter what. I told her that I would never love another girl as I love you. She laughed and said that no man should be trusted.

I think you should know that I will never have another girlfriend. I'm thinking of saving some money so I can make a trip to England. Do you think your school will allow me to visit you?

Jacques

FEBRUARY 12, 1954

Ma chère Agnès,

Your Mrs. Townsend sounds like a majestic cow made of cardboard, like one of those at the entrance of an agricultural fair. Are you sure she is worth your time? Do you think it's a mistake that you decided to go to England?

The school sounds like it would be a perfect place for M. Devaux. He could talk about philosophy and art and poetry, and then he could walk around the hallway after dark, catching sight of a girl bathing or changing. I wonder what that poor man is doing with himself these days. Do you think he might be writing about us?

You did not do a good job describing the girls. They all sound the same to me. If you need a better way to tell them apart from one another, here's something you can try: Go to the sunny part of the garden and look around for a snake. At this time of the year they like to stay warm in the sun, but mostly they are still lethargic. Grab the tail of the snake and whip it hard from head to tail. If you do this quick enough, no snake can stand a chance. Trust me: I have been doing this for a few days and now when I swing a dead snake like a whip, even boys like Étienne and Paul leave me alone.

Once you get a dead snake, show it to the girls one by one. Let me know which one of them screams and which one asks to touch the body.

No, if you are thinking what I know you are, you're wrong. I don't eat snakes. I don't even like killing snakes. But to perfect that skill is important.

Jacques is silly as always. He thinks he is in love with you, but I doubt that in six months he will remember you. I am thinking of looking for a little girlfriend for him. I don't think he'll remain faithful. Do you want to bet?

Fabienne

I was confused by the letters. When I wrote to Jacques, I was imagining someone who looked like Fabienne, but because he was a few years older than us and because he loved me, he was less volatile. Could it be that the boy I had imagined was different from the one Fabienne imagined? Why would she laugh at him in her letter, and why would he talk about her in a disapproving manner? When he wrote that he missed me and wanted to visit me in England, was he speaking for her, too?

Since the girls' return, Mrs. Townsend was busier, and I did not think she had had time to come into my room to read my journal. Rose, who waited for her parents' letters from Siam every day, was always near the hall table when the post came in, and that day she was the one to spot my letters and handed them to me. Mrs. Townsend might not have seen them yet. Still, I could not take any risks. One thing I was certain: they would get me into some trouble if Mrs. Townsend got hold of them; she might decide that not only was Jacques an inappropriate correspondent for me, but Fabienne was also a bad influence. I read the letters until I nearly memorized them, and locked them away.

I did not think that I could carry a dead snake into the house, though for the next few days, when I let my mind wander while Mrs. Townsend talked about art and literature, I tried to imagine the girls' reactions to a snake. None of them, I thought, would be curious enough to want to touch the cold, scaly body.

~

THREE WEEKS AFTER the girls' return, M. Lambert, the photographer who had accosted us on the day of my arrival at Woodsway, came for his visit. I posed everywhere as he requested. I even put on the clothes that I used to wear at home so he could take a few pictures that would reflect how I looked when I had first left the French countryside, stepping out of Meaker's car, carrying my suitcase down the walk to be met by a few girls. Inside the house, I was arranged on the rug next to the sofa, listening to Mrs. Townsend reading to me. Then the dogs were introduced, Ajax and Willow flanking me in front of the fireplace. In my room I laid out a gown and a pair of dancing shoes on the bed, my fingers touching the fabric, "with a desire tinged with awe," as directed by M. Lambert. He also took a few pictures of the girls walking in the garden or lolling next to the fountain.

Good press for Woodsway, or else the schoolmistress

would not have allowed me to do this, he explained to me in French when Mrs. Townsend and the girls returned to the house for a lesson. She had told Meaker to stay nearby and supervise us.

I felt the obligation to defend Mrs. Townsend, not because of M. Lambert's disparaging remarks, but because he had shown some solicitude toward Helen earlier. Given a choice, he would have made her the star of his photo shoot. "Mrs. Townsend gives me an education for free," I said.

"Your room would be empty otherwise. You're only one more mouth at her table, and one more girl in the classroom."

"But she bought me all those clothes. You saw them. You photographed them."

"I have no doubt that you've earned your crust," M. Lambert said.

I did not like his satirical tone, and said nothing.

M. Lambert changed his camera lens and asked me how I felt about being turned into a society girl. But I was not going to be a society girl, I said, and told him that I was at the school to get a better education than the one available to me at home. M. Lambert smiled. "Mademoiselle, you're too young to understand people's intentions," he said. He positioned me on a canvas chair next to the tennis court, and put a tennis ball in my left hand and a croquet ball in my right. I was asked to study the two balls, as though mesmerized by the difference between them. M. Lambert took a few shots and paused, telling me that it was reported in Paris and in London that I was Mrs. Townsend's experiment, how she planned to transform me from a pigherd into a debutante. "If only I had thought of bringing you a copy of one of the magazines," he said.

"Can I buy one here?" I asked him.

He shrugged and waved a hand at the garden. "Here?"

I wondered if Mrs. Townsend had seen those articles. "She talked about some sort of press-cutting service once," I said.

"Now hold that look and stay still," M. Lambert ordered, and snapped a few shots. He said he got something good.

"What?"

"That look in your eyes," he said.

I did not know what he was talking about. "Do you think I should ask Mrs. Townsend about those magazine articles?"

M. Lambert replaced the cap on the lens and looked around. Meaker was on the other side of the tennis court, cleaning and sharpening his gardening tools. M. Lambert grabbed a chair and set it next to mine, a little too close, but Meaker did not look up, and I did not think it necessary to inch away from M. Lambert. He sat down and offered me a cigarette. I shook my head, and he lit it for himself.

"Actually, if I were you," M. Lambert said, "I would not bother to read any of those things published about you."

"Why?"

"You don't look to me like a girl who can do this for a long time."

"This? What is this?"

"Posing as a child prodigy, clowning for the world."

"What do you mean?" I said, though I asked only because it felt like my duty in this conversation. Already I could sense what he was going to tell me. I did not know if I wanted to hear it.

"It means people think they can laugh at you. For them, you're a harmless amusement," he said. "If a headline says 'From Pigherd to Deb,' how would you expect the readers to think about you?"

I shook my head. Perhaps it was better not to know these things. I wondered if M. Bazin had read those articles, too, and if he, too, found me a harmless amusement.

"Have you thought of comparing what other people have gained from your story and what you've gained yourself?" M. Lambert asked.

I shook my head.

"Look here, I've got some really good pictures of you today, and I'll get paid for them. But what do you get out of this?"

I thought for a moment. "I can get out of going to the lessons today," I said.

"I thought you came here for a good education," he said. "Why, do you not like what you're learning here?"

"But yes, of course I do," I said, though I knew he did not believe me.

"Mademoiselle, no doubt you're a very clever girl, so let me speak frankly with you. What are you going to do after you're done with your education here?"

"Return to France."

"And what will you do then?"

What did a girl author do after a year in an English finishing school?

"What you're taught here—can you use the things you've learned here for your future?"

"Yes, I think so."

"Doing what? Being a debutante?"

I did not like how M. Lambert smiled, with one corner of his mouth lifted. But he was not alone in being a cruel person. Many people pounce at any opportunity of playing a cat who can fondle a mouse caught between its paws. Was M. Lambert any worse than Mrs. Townsend? At least he considered it his responsibility to destroy any delusion that I might have clung to till then. "Are you trying to tell me something I don't understand, monsieur?"

"You make a good story for many people, and everyone who writes about you or photographs you gets something in return. Your schoolmistress here probably benefits more than anyone else. I wouldn't be surprised if her enrollment goes up in the next few years. But these people—I include myself in that category—we are like bees. You're not the only flower for us. And how long can a flower stay in bloom? Do you see what I mean?"

I thought for a moment. "What should I do to become a bee instead of staying a flower?"

"That's not for me to say," M. Lambert said.

"Should I go back to France, then?" I asked, knowing that he would not answer that, either.

I SEE THAT JACQUES IS STILL WRITING TO YOU." One afternoon Mrs. Townsend called me into her sitting room, showing me two letters, one from Fabienne and one from Jacques. Rose must have been late that day to get to the post—I had dropped some hints to her that, like her, I was eagerly waiting for letters from home every day, and she had promised to keep an eye out for me.

I looked at the letters in Mrs. Townsend's hands. After she last talked with me about Jacques, she had acted as though she had forgotten the episode when I had played dead. I did not know how much I could trust her forgetfulness, though after the girls had returned, they had taken much of her attention. They were paid customers, as Helen had once explained to me, and paid customers, in any world, took priority over charity cases. Her French was not good, but you did not need to be fluent in a language to be unpleasant.

"Is there any new development between Jacques and you that I should know about?" Mrs. Townsend asked.

"Everything is fine between us," I said.

"So he's still your boyfriend."

I nodded.

"I thought I had made it clear that it wouldn't do to have a boyfriend when you're at Woodsway."

"The other girls talk about their boyfriends all the time."

"That's not true," Mrs. Townsend said. "You've misunderstood. The boys they talk about are not boyfriends, even if they make them sound like boyfriends. All the girls at Woodsway come from good families. You're much younger, and your parents have entrusted you to me. I have an obligation to make sure nothing goes awry. Do you see that?"

I did not reply. My life had already gone awry since the idea of writing a book had occurred to Fabienne. I could not possibly follow the wrong path and think I might one day arrive at the right place.

"Tell me, do you still consider yourself in love with him?"

I had never been in love. And now she was asking if I was in love with a made-up boy. Fabienne would have laughed. I would, too, if I were with her. But none of this was Mrs. Townsend's business. It was not up to her to say how long this game of having a boyfriend named Jacques would last.

"Agnès, I asked you a question."

"Yes," I said.

"So you're in love with him? Frankly, you're too young to be in love, and you're certainly in love with the wrong person."

"How do you know he's the wrong person?"

"The fact that you even ask shows me how inexperienced you are," Mrs. Townsend said. "I think it's high time you stop your correspondence with him."

"But I want to write him. And I like to get his letters. There aren't many people from home I keep in touch with."

"Your friend Fabienne writes you. Your parents do. Isn't that enough?"

"What's the harm in his writing me?" I said. "Why can't I have something I like?"

"You're uncultivated. If a person doesn't have a discerning palate, it's not up to her to say what kind of food is good. It's the same with people. You haven't developed the aptitude for evaluating people."

"You don't even know him. How do you know that he's wrong for me?"

"Do you know him well enough to be so certain that he's good for you?" Mrs. Townsend asked. "You've surprised me, Agnès. I thought your upbringing, deficient as it is, may at least have given you one advantage over many girls your age, but you've proven yourself to be as prone to hysteria as anyone."

I did not realize I had begun to cry until she said that. Even as I was wiping away my tears with my sleeve—Mrs. Townsend frowned at that, though she did not offer me a handkerchief—I thought how strange the tears felt on my face. I was not the crying type, and Fabienne despised girls who cried.

"Why don't you calm down and then we will speak," Mrs. Townsend said.

"You don't want me to write to Jacques—is this part of your experiment?" I asked.

"Excuse me?"

"The press called me your experiment," I said. "The photographer told me."

Mrs. Townsend opened a book on her desk, studied a few

lines, and then returned the book to another pile. She then looked up. "M. Lambert?" she said. "If he said that to you, he was extremely unprofessional."

"But is it true?"

"You're a clever girl, or else you wouldn't have written anything worth publishing," she said. "You can think yourself a child prodigy, but the world is never short of prodigies, and the world is always ready to move on to the next one. To your publishers, if I allow myself to be honest with you, you're no more than a monkey chained to a barrel organ. What are you going to do when you stop being a published author? Go back to your village to be a pigherd again? Marry and become a peasant's wife and give him a litter of children you can barely feed? Tell me, is that what you want? I can ship you home tomorrow if that's what you want."

I would hop onto the first train that would take me home, but Fabienne wanted me to stay here so we could go on writing books.

"Come, tell me, do you want me to ship you back to your village?"

I shook my head.

"Your ingratitude is as shocking as your ignorance. Though why am I surprised?" Mrs. Townsend said. "Now, back to this Jacques. Let's see what he has to say for himself."

I did not protest when Mrs. Townsend ripped open Jacques's letter. It was Fabienne's letters that I had to protect. For her I must sacrifice Jacques. The thought made me melancholy. It was like what was sung in those pop songs we listened to on the wireless: *I let you go because I love you. You can't see my tears behind my smile.*

Mrs. Townsend scanned the letter in a few seconds, and tossed it to me, along with Fabienne's letter, still safely sealed.

"Words of languishing and pining, all useless and sentimental," Mrs. Townsend said. "I don't see any merit in Jacques's letter. He's a weak man."

Yet he loved me as no other person in the world had. I refolded the letter and flattened it neatly.

"You must stop the correspondence with him right away," Mrs. Townsend said. "Why don't you explain to him that his letters are no longer welcome, and you will need to focus on your future instead? Better yet, write to his sister and ask her to explain it to him. I don't want to see any more letters from him, do you understand?"

"Yes, Kazumi."

~

THAT EVENING, MRS. TOWNSEND TOLD US that instead of listening to popular music, we should play some real music on the gramophone. Helen was the only one to make a face behind Mrs. Townsend's back. The other girls, despite their disappointment, gathered around the drawing room, some sitting on the rug, close to Mrs. Townsend's feet, taking turns to pet the dogs.

I found a chair in the corner. I did not know what to make of the music, a concerto by a German composer whose name I would fail to remember if Mrs. Townsend decided to quiz me. It was pleasant enough, but long, like one of those walks we took on weekends. What Mrs. Townsend and the girls called scenery was nothing but trees and flowers and an occasional creek, half as pretty as what we had at Saint Rémy.

I supposed the music was like the London museums and theaters, things that we were told would enhance our lives.

But to begin with, one had to have a life worth enhancing. I did not have any kind of life yet according to my schoolmates' standards. Things that came easily to the others did not to me. My penmanship might have been praised at our village school, but here the girls' dancing calligraphy made a mockery of my drunken-looking attempts. Though some of the girls spoke French in funny accents, they could all read and write French better than I did. There were magazines in different languages lying around the house, but I looked only at the pictures, and my eyes glossed over the printed words even if they were in French or English. Some of the girls—Catalina especially—genuinely wanted to help me, but others exchanged smiles whenever I did something wrong. And that happened almost every day. Inelegance and ignorance marked me.

Fabienne did not mind being different from other people. I did mind, here at Woodsway.

At the end of the concerto, Mrs. Townsend said we could enjoy ourselves for the rest of the evening and left the drawing room, Ajax and Willow following her. Someone turned on the radio. I decided not to stay. I wanted to be in my room, the only thing that I still loved about my life here.

Catalina followed me upstairs and into my room. "You look sad tonight," she said in English. She was as loyal a friend as I could find: as we agreed, she spoke to me in English all the time, and helped me out in French only when I could not make sense of her words at all.

I was not sad. I was bored. I missed that universe made complete by Fabienne and me. I would not have left that life (the happiest life I have ever known) if not for Fabienne's conviction that there might be something interesting out in the world. Something beyond our experience, which she deemed important to know. She had sent me to Paris, and then to

England, to take a look at the strangers and their lives. For a while I had tried to stay dedicated to the adventure, but the newness of this world—with the soft sheets, dainty clothes, abundant food, beautifully dressed schoolmates, and Mrs. Townsend, who, like the cuckoo clock in the drawing room, spoke the same instructions and in the same order throughout the day—faded fast. The girls, like angels, could look flawlessly beautiful, but that was because no maker of angels needed imagination—some fine material and a set of rules were all that were required. None of the girls would pause in the middle of a conversation about clothes or dances and listen to a faint hooting from a faraway owl; none of them would answer the owl, so real the hooting was that you knew somewhere a mother would look at her young child, worried about the omen that had been spelled out for the child. I wished Fabienne were right here so she could see what I saw: the world had no use for us; nor did we have any use for this world.

"Hello," Catalina said. "You're miles away tonight."

I closed my door. I had never known the importance of a door until I was at Woodsway. "I'm all right. Only these days I miss my Jacques very much," I said. It was easy to blame my mood on Jacques. None of the girls would suspect otherwise.

"You write to each other, no?"

"Yes," I said. "But Kazumi is not happy about it. She told me to stop."

"Kazumi must have your best interest in mind to make that decision for you," Catalina said.

"She doesn't know Jacques. Her reasons can't be good reasons."

"Don't say that," Catalina admonished me, and then softened her voice. "Do you have a picture of him?"

It had never occurred to me that someone might ask for

proof of Jacques's existence other than his letters. "We don't have our pictures taken at home," I said.

Catalina thought for a moment. "I do think you should know that you have a better future than he does," she said.

"Everyone keeps talking about my future, but nobody understands that I don't have a future."

"How can that be? You're an author!"

"Have you read my book?"

"Kazumi told us not to. She said she wanted us to know you only as a schoolmate. But of course once she said that, some girls right away got hold of a copy of your book."

"Has everyone here read my book?"

"Not everyone, not all the girls like reading, not to mention French books. Maybe some of them will read it when the English translation comes out," Catalina said. "But I hope you don't mind my saying this. Your book isn't what we had imagined. Margareta and Rose both thought the stories were repulsive."

"Did you think so, too?"

"I didn't read it," Catalina said. "You know me—I don't have a literary mind—but Rose told some of the stories to us. They were rather shocking! We were surprised how nice you were when we met you."

It occurred to me then that Catalina, Margareta, and Rose must either be true friends, or else they must be truly good performers.

"Forgive me for saying this, but your life back home sounded horrendous," Catalina said. "Not a life at all."

"It was a fine life for me and my Jacques."

"But you're here now," Catalina said. "You should know now that was a horrendous life."

"What's the point of knowing it? I'm not any one of you."

"You're better than all of us," Catalina said, with such sincerity that a month ago I would have believed her. "Oh, please don't look so crestfallen. You're an author."

I sighed.

"Do you want to write more books?" she asked.

"I wrote another book, and it is going to be published in the fall."

"And after that?"

"No," I said. "I don't ever want to write again."

"Really? What will you do if you don't write books?"

"When I go back to France, I want to find a job in Paris."

"What kind of job?"

"A secretary's position. Or a salesgirl."

Catalina laughed. "You must be joking!"

"What's wrong with having a job?" I said.

"You have to have the right job," Catalina said. "Let's see, Helen may work for her father for some time, until she marries. Margareta keeps saying she wants to establish a laboratory school for deaf and mute children. Rose will never work. Phillipa or Gillian"—she mentioned the two girls, one from Manchester and one from Newcastle—"they'll have jobs. They're both going to secretarial college after the summer."

"Do you think I can do that, too?"

"Why would you want to do that?"

If there were secretarial colleges in London, I thought, there must also be those places in Paris. "What are you going to do?" I asked.

"I'm not that ambitious. I want to get married and have children. But you, you should not rush. And you should certainly not marry Jacques."

I shook my head. "I don't want to marry anyone. I would rather have a job."

"You'll have to get married at some point. But it has to be to the right man. That's more important than having the right job."

"That's the problem. Whatever I have, any job, any husband, won't look right to you, don't you see?"

"I see that," Catalina said, her dark eyes looking especially sympathetic. "I see that perfectly. That's why I want you to listen to Kazumi. She must have great plans for you. She may look stern, but she's doing so much for you. More than she's done for any one of us."

"None of you needs her to do much," I said.

"That, too, of course," Catalina agreed. "More of a reason for you to trust Kazumi."

THE WEATHER TURNED WARMER, and Meaker spent more time working in the garden, sometimes mumbling to himself, sometimes speaking with a gentle look on his face, like he was talking with the seedlings and the buds. He lived in the gate lodge. A boy from the village came to help with heavy work, but most of the time he worked alone, busy on the school grounds or in the house, where he fixed loosened window frames, replaced broken bulbs, touched up the paint here and there, caulked the pipes. He greeted us with a nod and by moving his lips, but he never spoke to us, and he did not often talk with the cook or the maids. On the days when we went to London, he drove us to the train station, taking half of the girls on each run. I wondered if he could tell that I was different from the others.

"Why does Meaker never talk when we're around?" I asked Catalina one afternoon, when we were watching a tennis match. I did not play tennis. After giving me two lessons, Margareta and Catalina decided that they had taken on too big a task for themselves. They told me that I should ask Mrs. Townsend to hire a tennis coach for me. I then thought I could live without tennis.

"He keeps himself to himself," she said. "I think Kazumi likes it that way."

"Does he have a wife, or a family?"

Catalina laughed. "The questions you ask," she said. "We don't pry."

"We don't?" I said. The girls seemed to pry all the time. The previous day, a journalist had written from London to Mrs. Townsend, asking to interview me for the upcoming publication of *Les Enfants Heureux* in English. The moment I told Catalina, several other girls pestered me with questions.

"We do, but only in the right way," Catalina said. "And with the right people."

That I was to Catalina and the other girls one of the right people, I knew, was conditional. I could have easily slipped back into the opposite category, a nonentity like Meaker.

"Are we allowed to help Meaker with his gardening?" I asked.

"I don't think Kazumi would approve," Catalina said. Seeing my face, she added, "You do like gardening more than flower-arranging, don't you? Perhaps you could ask Kazumi if you could take care of one of the houseplants."

I was fond of Catalina, who was warm-blooded and warmhearted. All human beings, unless they are dead, are warmblooded and warmhearted, so I always find the descriptions laughable, though in Catalina's case she truly deserved them. But her personality, I now understand, was impaired by her desire to be good and to be right. To be good was in her nature.

She took genuine pleasure in being good. However, where does the desire to be right lead one, if not to the wrong place? Knowing Mrs. Townsend's mind and speaking on her behalf—these Catalina did with perfect ease and confidence, as she must have spoken on behalf of other authorities before Woodsway, and would continue to do so after Woodsway. I was too young then to dread a person like her. I have since encountered other versions of Catalina; each time I have to reeducate myself in avoiding people's good intentions.

The thought of spending some time alone in the garden—it did not matter if it was with Meaker or by myself—was an alluring one. In Saint Rémy Fabienne and I lived most of our lives outdoors, away from people. I had always thought that was because we held utmost contempt toward the villagers around us. But where does the line lie between contempt and fear? People coming too close can always do something to us. Fabienne and I had once had the good instinct to keep a distance, to save ourselves from dangers we could not articulate, but at Woodsway I no longer had that luxury. Fabienne was my only armor against this world, but even the sturdiest armor failed to protect from afar. The girls at Woodsway, beautiful and cultivated, were like marvelous seashells. I had learned on a field trip to a London museum that in the old days, shells of different shapes and sizes had been used as money. But I also remembered an illustration from an old book M. Devaux had once shown Fabienne and me: shells used for torturing a young female mathematician sentenced to death for practicing witchcraft. It was one of the rare incidences when Fabienne and I had not refuted his offering of knowledge. We had studied the illustration in awe, and had discussed afterward what happened to those shells used for the torture, after the young woman's death.

Mrs. Townsend was busy with enrollment for the following school year, and she spent many of her afternoons writing to potential parents and sometimes receiving visitors. My individual lessons with her grew less frequent. The schedule after lunch was also relaxed for the other girls. In June there would be a ball, attended by boys from a nearby boarding school, a tradition at Woodsway. The girls, looking forward to that night, to their summer travels, and to what awaited them at home, had much to talk about. I had little to contribute, and even the nosiest girls stopped asking me how it felt to be a published author. I was becoming a nobody, as Mrs. Townsend had warned me I would.

Perhaps I should have minded this, but mostly I felt a kind of lethargy. Woodsway was no longer new. Living with the same group of girls day and night had turned them into a herd of goats, or a flock of chickens. I could tune out their chattering whenever I wanted. I could look past them without registering each individual face. If they were hungry for anything they would not run to me. I had nothing to feed them. I would rather have my chickens around.

I missed Fabienne bitterly. Only in writing to her could I find the energy to focus. For some time I wrote about everything I could think of: Mrs. Fisher and the meals she cooked, the day trips to London, our weekend rambles, the journalists and photographers writing to Mrs. Townsend about visiting Woodsway. I wrote about every single girl in the school. I never said I missed her in my letters, but in my last letter to Jacques, in which I had had to inform him that Mrs. Townsend forbade us to write to each other in the future, I poured my heart out to him, and said things that I dared not speak to Fabienne.

Fabienne always replied promptly. "Nothing much has

changed," or "Nothing much is happening here"—every letter from Fabienne began that way, and she would list the births and the deaths in the village, the weddings and the illnesses. Once in a while she put in a sentence with a meaning only she and I knew. "The new postmaster, M. Laure, has a regular visitor now, a woman who looks older than he. They say she is his fiancée and a schoolteacher in Civray. They will get married as soon as the school year ends, and she will move to Saint Rémy after." In my reply, I wrote: "I wonder if M. Laure will settle in the village forever until he is widowed one day, like the postmaster before him." In another letter, she wrote that an older girl told her that the dark blue dragonfly barrette did not match Fabienne's hay-colored hair. "She's only jealous," Fabienne wrote. "But I told her if she wanted it, I could sell it to her for five hundred francs. She said I was crazy, and I only laughed in her face."

The thought of Fabienne wearing the barrette made me happy. (What was she thinking as she clipped the dragonfly in her thin hair?) I was not glad at all, however, that she would be willing to exchange it for money. (Though her asking for an exorbitant amount for the barrette might mean the opposite.) With Fabienne I could never be certain. If she told me in her next letter that she had hidden the barrette in a piece of sausage and fed it to a dog because she disliked its owner, I would not have been surprised.

Jacques no longer sent his letters separately to me, but Fabienne, he said, was generous enough to include his letter in the same envelope. Mrs. Townsend had not noticed the weight of my correspondence from Fabienne, though I wondered how long it would be before she discovered this new trick of Jacques's.

His letters continued to baffle me. He was Fabienne, and

yet he was not Fabienne. I knew her moods well, which were not different from the weather: for any kind of weather I could find a comfortable place for myself. But Jacques's moods seemed murkier. He criticized Fabienne, as though he were annoyed that I had her as my best friend. He talked about "our future" but I did not know what he meant by that. He complained about my long absence, and railed bitterly against the boring life in Saint Rémy. He kept saying he had saved enough money to visit me in England. I never knew how to reply to these requests. Fabienne could write as two people, but she had only one body. Would she be able to pass as a boy even if Mrs. Townsend allowed a French visitor?

~

IT WAS AROUND THIS TIME I wrote a little tale in my journal. I had not kept up with my journal for some time, and I suspected that one of these days Mrs. Townsend would ask me to present the notebook for inspection.

I decided to write a story about a gardener. She was an old woman, blind, wrinkled, who looked like a witch and was dreaded by her neighbors. But she was not a witch, she reasoned with herself. She did, though, have hands that could hear things just as well as her ears. She knew that on a warm day, the dirt buzzed, and on a cold day, the dirt shivered, heaving tiny sighing sounds. A healthy root could sing a song, a dead root cracked at the first note and could never find the right pitch again. Buds and petals and new leaves all had their own ways of talking, screaming, laughing, or groaning.

Once a day the villagers surrounded her shack and called out her name, asking her to leave because they did not want a witch among them. But what was so extraordinary about a blind person who could make a garden she could not see? People were strange, the old woman thought: If they wanted, they could pull me out of my shack, they could break my arms and ribs, they could put me in a cage and starve me, or drop me into a well, or burn me at the stake. An old woman with no sight and no way to protect herself would be easy to get rid of. But the villagers did not have the courage to go near her. All they did was raise their voices and hurl insults and threats at her. Couldn't they see that their words did nothing? Even her flowers, used to all this shouting, carried on their own conversations and slept their own closed-petal sleep.

~

ONE DAY, when Mrs. Townsend went to London for business, I found Meaker in the garden. He was pruning the rosebushes, and when I walked up to him, he nodded but did not stop his work.

I sat down on the ground, not far from the piece of tarp on which twigs and branches from the pruned roses, cut farther down to the same length, were kept in a neat pile. I had noticed that about Meaker. He arranged things carefully before carrying out his tasks. His painting brushes and rollers, his gardening tools, his hammers and wrenches—they were all lined up in a particular way that never changed from day to day.

"How do you do, Mr. Meaker?" I said. If Mrs. Townsend asked why I had talked to him, I could tell her that I was practicing my English and I wanted to talk with someone who spoke no French.

"How do you do?" Meaker said. "Did someone send for me?"

So he did talk, I thought. I liked his voice, not squeaky or raspy. He spoke slowly and clearly.

"No," I said. "But I wondered if you needed any help."

"Help?"

"I'm from the countryside," I said. "Do you know that?"

He nodded. "You grew up on a farm."

So he must have learned my story from the maids or even from Mrs. Townsend. "I can help you in the garden," I said, adding gestures in case he had trouble understanding my English. Mrs. Townsend would have frowned at my inelegance. "I did that kind of work at home."

"Thank you, but I'm doing fine by myself."

"Would it not be easier if you had some help?" I asked.

Meaker paused and thought carefully about his reply. "No, it wouldn't be easier for me."

"But why not?"

"I like to work alone," he said. "I'm like a one-man band."

I did not know what he meant by a one-man band. Neither of us spoke for a moment. He continued his pruning, wiping the shears with an old rag after every few cuttings.

"How long have you been here?" I asked.

Meaker wiped the shears once and placed them alongside the other tools. He then placed a ladder flat on the ground, invited me to sit down on one end, and took a seat on the other. "I cannot work and talk at the same time," he said.

I said I was sorry to interrupt his work, even though I did not feel sorry at all.

"I came with the house," he said. "When Mrs. Townsend rented the place, I stayed."

"So you were the gardener here before?"

"Yes."

"Who lived here?"

"Mrs. Brown."

That must have been the industrialist's widow. "What happened to her?"

"She died."

"How did she die?"

"She was an old woman."

"Then what happened?"

"The house went to her daughters. They talked about selling it and then decided to rent it to the school."

That seemed to be the end of the conversation. If I did not come up with something else to say, Meaker might go back to his work. He was already looking at his shears longingly.

"Have you always been a gardener?"

"For some time now," he said.

"Why did you decide to become a gardener?" I asked. People always asked me why I decided to become a writer, a question I could never answer. If I were a salesgirl in a department store, I could say it was because I loved seeing people and I loved being surrounded by pretty things. If I were a gardener, I could say I loved flowers and trees. I half expected Meaker to give me an answer like that. And then, if he had been taught how to have a good conversation, he would ask in turn why I had decided to come to Woodsway. Or why I had decided to write.

"Let's see," Meaker said. "When I came back from the war—"

"Which war?" I asked. He looked as old as my father.

"The Great War, the war before this last one," he said.

"When I came back from the war, I didn't know what to do. So I went to pray. I'm a Roman Catholic. I suppose you are, too, so you'll understand that."

I nodded as if I did.

"I prayed," Meaker said. "A few days later there were two openings—an apprenticeship to a gardener, or a job in a tin factory. I prayed again, and after I left the cathedral, I decided to become a gardener."

"Did god tell you to choose that?"

"I can't say. He didn't say that exactly."

"But do you love flowers and trees?"

Meaker thought about the question as though it were a difficult test he had to pass. "Love doesn't come into it," he said.

"Oh," I said. I did not know where a good conversation should go from there. I wished he would ask me some questions. He could ask me whether I had become a writer because I loved writing, and then I could say love hadn't come into that decision, just as it had not for him with gardening.

"I write books. Did you know?" I said when Meaker did not seem inclined to question me in turn.

"Yes, I heard."

"I don't love writing books, so I know what you mean."

Meaker nodded.

"Do you want to read my book?" I asked.

"I don't read French," he said, and then looked at his palms as though caught in an embarrassing moment. "I fought in France."

"Oh," I said. "But there will be an English translation. I can get you a copy."

He thanked me and said that he had too much work to

spare any time for books. He then picked up his shears. "I think you should go back to the house," he said.

"Mrs. Townsend is out today," I said.

"Don't you have your schoolwork?"

I could see that he wanted me to leave him alone, and I could not, for the moment, think of anything else to say.

~

I HEARD YOU WENT INTO THE GARDEN before the outdoor time," Mrs. Townsend said to me later that evening.

I wondered who had told her that. Meaker and I had sat and talked behind the hedge.

"I was getting some air," I said.

"By yourself?"

"I can't focus on my book when I'm in the house with the other girls," I said. "I can do my other work in the house, but to think about writing I need to be in the open air."

It was a lie, but right away I wondered how it had never occurred to me to use my writing as an excuse.

"So you've been thinking about your next book, after all," Mrs. Townsend said.

"A little, yes."

"And it makes sense to be wandering around when you compose. Isn't that how you used to write?"

"Yes," I said.

"Do you have a title in mind for this next book?"

"I'm thinking of calling it *La Forêt de la Sorcière,*" I said. *The Witch's Forest.* There were trees around Woodsway but there was not a forest here good enough for a witch, so if I gave a book that title, nobody could say I was writing about my life at the school.

Mrs. Townsend studied me, and I tried to erase what I imagined to be smugness from my face. Lies easily told could just as easily come true—how had I not understood this before?

"You look excited," Mrs. Townsend said.

"About the book?" I said. "I always feel excited when I think about writing."

"What has made you change your mind? A few weeks ago you seemed uncertain."

I had learned, from the trips to Paris the year before, that I did not have to answer every single question the press asked. Sometimes the best response was silence. I shook my head as though I were baffled myself.

"Perhaps you were getting used to life here," Mrs. Townsend said. "Now that you are settled in, you feel ready."

"Yes, you must be right, Kazumi."

"And you said you would prefer to have some time to yourself to be able to think," she said. "Is school life distracting to you?"

"No, not at all," I said. "I like learning things. Only I wasn't used to being around people all the time. At home I often wandered around by myself."

"Yes, of course. What if I gave you permission to go about freely in the afternoons? Do you think that would facilitate your writing? But I must point something out. That title is not quite right," Mrs. Townsend said. "It's a bit . . . childish and ordinary. Who is the witch?"

I did not know the answer to that question.

"Did you write something about the witch in your journal? Well, in fact, bring it to me in any case."

I could not come up with a quick lie, so I had to retrieve my journal. Mrs. Townsend flipped through it. "You've been irregular with your journal-keeping," she said.

"I'm sorry, Kazumi," I said.

"But you're learning from the girls when you're around them, no? And from me, of course."

"Yes, Kazumi."

She turned the journal again and read more closely, her lips pursed in disapproval. "I've been busy these days, and I can see that I've neglected to instruct you," she said. "I encouraged you to write anything in any way that felt natural to you when you first arrived, but now I can see you haven't outgrown that whimsical stage. In fact, I can tell you, you've taken a wrong turn. All these stories about birds and birdman, tiger and fox, twin owlets, talking flowers, witches and the forest—they're far below my expectation of you."

What would she do now, tell me that I had failed to earn my crust?

"What makes your first book remarkable is how you portrayed your village life with such brutal honesty. And I suppose people will say the same when your second book is published. Now that the setting has changed, perhaps you can give the same realism to your new life, rather than these fantastical nonsenses," Mrs. Townsend said. "It's your goal to use your eyes and ears, instead of your feeble and childish imagination."

I looked at her, not knowing what kind of expression would be appropriate.

"I have a better title for your new work," Mrs. Townsend said. "How about *Agnès in Paradise*?"

"Agnès—me?"

"Remember what your French publisher told you? People are curious about your experience in an English school, and this next book should be about Woodsway. Do you not agree?"

"Yes, Kazumi," I said. Already I regretted saying anything about writing another book.

"Still, I'm pleased with the progress you've made so far," Mrs. Townsend said.

It occurred to me that she was as good at lying as I was. I thanked her.

"And I think there's no better time to begin a new book. You've adjusted to the rhythm of life here, and yet your impressions are still fresh. What do you think? I would be more than happy to help you with your book. Your postmaster, what's his name, he did some work for your first book, did he not?"

"M. Devaux," I said. "Yes, he taught me a few things."

"Have you been in touch with him?" Mrs. Townsend asked, all of a sudden looking alarmed.

"No, he moved away last year."

"And he hasn't left you his new address?"

"No," I said.

"What a shame. He helped you start your career. Do you miss him?"

"Miss him? Oh no," I said.

Mrs. Townsend studied my face. The inconvenience of being able to lie easily was that when I said something truthful, it sounded like a lie. "You seem to have forgotten him despite all he did to help you," she said.

"I haven't," I said. "But you told me that I must look forward to the new life, Kazumi."

"Yes," she said. "Of course it doesn't do to forget people who've helped you, but we should welcome change." She reminded me that anytime I needed her help with the book, she would make herself available for me.

I felt like the country rat in the La Fontaine fable we had read at school. How immense the world is, the rat exclaims when he sets out for an adventure, congratulating himself that he is no longer a country rat but a creature of sophistication. And when he sees an oyster on the beach, he tells himself that a worldly eater will enjoy an oyster, so he sticks his head between the open shells. Like the rat, I was caught. I was doomed.

That night, I wrote to Fabienne: "I wonder if it is time for me to think about writing a new book. Everyone is telling me that my experience at the school would be interesting for my readers. How do you like the idea?"

~

MRS. TOWNSEND GAVE ME PERMISSION to be outdoors as long as there is no lesson," I said to Meaker a day later when he was weeding. It was early afternoon, and it would be another hour before the girls would come out into the garden.

"That's good," he said.

"I can help if you need me."

"I'm afraid I don't need anyone's help," he said, arranging the leaves of a dug-up dandelion as though combing a child's thin hair.

"But can I still be around and talk with you?" I said. "I can keep you company?"

He laid the trowel on the edge of the flower bed and looked up at me. I noticed that his eyes, up close, were the same greenish-gray color as Mrs. Townsend's.

"The thing is, I'm not good at talking," he said.

"Oh," I said. "But you're talking with me now."

"I have to stop working so as to talk with you."

I arranged the words in my head before speaking: "You'd be too kind by half if you oblige me."

Heaven knows what I sounded like to Meaker, as his face, often with a wooden look, broke into a childlike smile.

(*By half*—that expression, which I had learned from listening to the girls, has become one of my favorite phrases. By half, by half of that half—even now, I like to repeat it to myself when I am in a dividing mood. Halve life's pain, and we are not pain-free. Halve life's joy, there is still joy enough to be halved. Truly life can be a funny business, too prodigal by half, also too stingy by half. I have a habit of speaking to my geese as though to myself: You're too silly by half. You're too proud by half.)

I tried to think of another reason to prevent Meaker from turning me away. If I told him that my window was rattling too loud in a storm, he would have to offer his services. "Mrs. Townsend is encouraging me to write a book about my life here," I said. "Maybe you can help me."

"What can I do to help?" he asked, looking perplexed. I did not know what answers I could make up to convince him. I was not Fabienne. Her mind was like a bird. My mind was like a train, and someone had to lay the track down for me.

"I don't read or write French," Meaker said.

"I like to talk things over. It helps me think."

"Things? What kind of things? Can you not talk with the girls?" Meaker asked, looking genuinely curious. "Or Mrs. Townsend?"

"Mrs. Townsend is nice. And the girls are nice," I said. "But you see, I'm different. They call me a pig minder and a goatherd in the press. They call me the peasant girl writer. There are things Mrs. Townsend and the girls don't understand."

Meaker nodded gravely. He looked sympathetic, and I felt bad. I was trying to turn my brain into a bird, but it only thrashed about like a clumsy bumblebee.

"I understand how you feel," he said.

"You do?"

"I often find people strange."

"What kind of people?" I asked. "Strange how?"

"Most people. You're right that Mrs. Townsend and the girls are not from the same world as you. But I don't think that's the only reason people find one another strange. When I was growing up, in my hometown, I felt different from most people."

"Where did you grow up?"

He told me the name of his hometown. "It's near Brighton," he said.

I didn't know where Brighton was.

"I wouldn't know where your village is on the map, either," he said.

"But why do you feel you're different?" I asked. "How are you different?"

"I don't know why or how," he said. "God alone knows, and I don't question."

In Meaker's eyes, my journey from Saint Rémy to Woodsway was god's will, too. But it was Fabienne who had made it happen. "Back home I have a friend," I said. "We always feel we're different from other people."

"Is that the postmaster everybody was talking about?"

"You've heard of him?" I said. I wondered whether M. Devaux was more famous than I was.

Meaker looked abashed, as though I had caught him in

a petty crime. "I read newspapers," he said. "Before you came, the local newspaper ran a piece about you and the postmaster."

"What did the newspaper say about him?"

Meaker shook his head. "Nothing important. Some random conjecture."

I asked him to spell the word conjecture out for me so I could be certain it was the same word I had known in French. "What is the conjecture you saw in the newspaper?"

"That nobody knew if the postmaster might be the real author of the book you wrote."

I placed my chin on my knees. It was not untrue. All the same, I felt deflated.

"People like to judge what they don't understand," Meaker said.

"Like how I could write a book?"

"It makes people feel better when they can pretend to know everything."

"Nobody here really knows anything about me," I said glumly.

Meaker nodded. "It's all right. In fact, it's better that they don't know anything about you."

"Why?"

"It makes it easier to be alone."

"Do you like to be alone?"

"Yes."

"But I am alone, too," I said. "And I don't like it."

"You'll get used to it. You see, if one of the girls complains about something . . ." Meaker said, tilting his head toward the house. "If they complain about something, we can't simply say: You'll get used to it. But you're different. You know something they'll never know."

That was the longest speech Meaker had spoken to me. The kindest thing he had said to me, too, but it was unhelpful. I told him that my friend at home was not the postmaster, but a girl I had grown up with. "Her name is Fabienne," I said. I wanted to hear her name spoken aloud so she would be as real as I was, in this beautiful English garden. "She's smarter than I am," I said. "It's not fair that I'm here and she's not."

Meaker looked at me. It would have driven Fabienne mad to be pitied by an older man. She would have found a way to mock Meaker, just as she had M. Devaux. But Meaker was different—quiet and gentle, like a harmless tree or a shy animal. I thought about telling him that Fabienne was really the one who had written the books—a secret that I would not share with anyone else. Let others scratch their heads over the mysterious village postman. Only good people like Meaker would be awarded. "You see, Fabienne is the person who's made everything possible for me," I said.

Meaker nodded. He did not understand what I was trying to tell him. "I had a good friend, too, when I was your age," he said.

"What was his name?"

"Wilfred."

"So you did talk with him?"

"We didn't talk much," Meaker said. "We were both quiet types."

"Fabienne and I talk," I said. "All the time. Well, we used to talk all the time. Now we can only write to each other."

"You're lucky to be able to write each other. Wilfred died in the war."

"The Great War?"

"Yes."

I said I was sorry to hear that. "My brother died from this

last war," I said. "No, he didn't die in the war, but my parents still say the war killed him."

Meaker nodded.

"And my friend Fabienne, her sister also died," I said. I did not say that she had died for an entirely different reason. It would not be far from the truth to say that she had also died from the war.

"A war kills many people," Meaker said. "And young people, especially. You can say it's not fair they're dead and we're alive, but nobody is to be blamed for that."

"The girls here are luckier," I said, tilting my head toward the house as I had seen Meaker do. "They live in a paradise."

"We can't be certain about that."

"But Mrs. Townsend thinks this is a paradise. She wants me to write a book about my life here," I said. "She told me to call it *Agnès in Paradise*."

"Do you want to write the book?"

"I don't know," I said, and, remembering the good conversational skills we were taught, I asked him, "What's your opinion?"

He shook his head. "It's not for me to say, but if you do write a book about your life here, nobody can say that your postmaster is the real author."

~

MEAKER LIVED ALONE, and I wondered if he had had a wife. Perhaps he never married, or else, like M. Devaux, he had been widowed. I thought of finding an excuse to visit the gate lodge, to see if there were traces of a wife. In M. Devaux's house there had been plenty of evidence of a woman's existence. The lacy tablecloth had been mended with stitches so neat and minute that only by looking at it closely you could tell it had once been torn. On the bookshelf there was a small lily-shaped mold to collect melted candle wax, and, when I pointed it out to Fabienne, she had said that perhaps every time M. Devaux wanted to have sex with his wife, he would light up a lily-shaped candle to indicate his wish. I said that maybe she was the one to use it to let him know her wish, but Fabienne only scoffed at the possibility, saying no woman would be that stupid. Once, M. Devaux asked Fabienne and me to each pick a scarf that his wife had left behind. He had offered them as gifts, and Fabienne had replied that we had no use for an old man's gift. It occurred to me now that we had embarrassed and hurt him more than we had known. If M. Devaux, as Fabienne had made me and everyone believe, had expressed the desire to take her up as a lover, he could not have been that old. I wondered how old a man would have to be before he stopped thinking about women. Meaker would know, but I must get to know him a little better before asking him that question.

I decided to find an excuse to visit him at the gate lodge. I could say it was for my book.

I did not keep it secret from Mrs. Townsend or the girls that I was writing a new book. I did not come to the school as a paid customer. Rather, I was like a new rose Meaker had transplanted into his garden: I had to be watched until I bloomed. Mrs. Townsend would never be satisfied until I became a product of her design. Perhaps I should think of that as her form of caring for me, more than she cared for the other girls. They would leave soon, of course, and they brought her money. But I brought photographers and journalists.

Mrs. Townsend supplied me with five beautiful notebooks. They had soft leather covers, pale blue like the inside of eggshell, and pleasant to hold. She also gave me her own fountain pen; its body, smooth to the touch, was in a rich maroon color, with marbled swirls, lined with golden stripes. It was from her favorite Dutch fountain pen maker, she said, and unscrewed the cap to show me the nib, golden, carved with an intricate pattern. "I would have purchased you a new one," she said, "but a fountain pen is like a dog or a pair of shoes. It needs to be broken in. This one has accompanied me over ten years. It's perfect now."

I said I couldn't possibly accept the pen, but I only said that so she could insist on her generosity and overrule my will. I did not know when I had begun to understand this game I had to play with her. It was a game with clearly written rules and predictable outcomes, but all the same it was my responsibility to play my part.

When the weather was nice, I spent an hour or two in the garden while the other girls were practicing on the pianos and violins, writing letters, and studying the fashion magazines to improve their looks. I did not always seek Meaker out, but some days I would sit myself next to him as he worked. Soon he allowed me to complete a task here and there, separating the seedlings, pruning the hedge in a place where no one would really notice if I cut it at the wrong angle. I knew he preferred to be alone, but if I stayed quiet enough, unobtrusive enough, would that not make him feel that he was almost alone, as he used to be?

Mrs. Townsend stopped by sometimes, and appeared satisfied. Gardening, I told Mrs. Townsend, was a good way for me to think about my book. She did not offer the girls a gardening class, she explained, because of what awaited them in their future, for which flower-arranging was more suitable. "But for you, gardening seems a wise choice," she said. "Many writers are also good gardeners. Have you heard the saying that behind every great writer there is a great garden?"

As for the book I said I was writing, it was not hard for me to see what was asked of me. I had been given an opportunity to experience a life that I had never even dreamed of having, and the world wanted to see how that life unfolded. I did not have to make anything up. My life was already a fairy tale. If the world wanted that fairy tale from me, why not give it to them? Once the book was finished, I thought, perhaps Mrs. Townsend would no longer see the profit in keeping me at Woodsway, and she would send me home.

I was not the first trespasser in paradise, but unlike other violators, my punishment was not banishment. Rather, my sentence was to testify to its marvels. It soon became my belief that my only hope for escape was to write the book that everybody wanted. Only then would I be allowed to return home and resume my life with Fabienne.

I began my story with the day I left for Paris, and later crossed the Channel to London. It was not difficult to describe Harrods: the dresses and the hats, the patent-leather shoes and the long flimsy gloves, the women clad in fur coats, the doormen in green jackets. When the book followed my journey to Woodsway, I described every floor of the house, the pattern of the rugs, the orchard outside my window, the Japanese fans framed and displayed in the hallway. I did not change anyone's names, though in the book I did not call Mrs. Townsend Kazumi, simply Mrs. Townsend. The girls appeared just as they did in my life, fragrant like spring violets. They talked, laughed, danced, and they sang in the evening along with American pop singers on the wireless. I described their clothes, their hairdos, the conversations about the real life awaiting them, about to begin. I devoted more time to writing about Catalina: her dark eyes, her quick laugh, her round shoulders and strong limbs, her easy victories at the tennis tournament she herself organized often. I did not tell her that she was going to be in my book. Someday, I thought, she would open a copy and scream. She would read passages aloud to her husband, and she would keep the book for her children. Look, I'm famous, she would tell them. I once had a famous author as a school friend.

And of course Mrs. Townsend was on every page. I made her look a little younger (but not too young), less square-shaped, stylish like the Oriental orchids in the photographs she hung up in the classroom. She was never cross with anyone, and even the moodiest girls saw her as a confidante. I wrote about the hours she spent teaching me English and French, my gratitude for her boundless patience, and the pain of having to disappoint her with my inadequate scholarship, my clumsy penmanship, my inelegant body in the beautiful dresses she had bought me.

I wondered about writing Meaker into my book, not as the red-haired man with the bird nest on his head, but as my good friend. About him alone I could write passage after passage, but I had a feeling that Mrs. Townsend would not approve. Instead, I wrote about basking in the garden with my schoolmates, all of us feeling as beautiful as the new roses.

A week into the book, Mrs. Townsend asked me to show her what I had written thus far. I said I would make a clean copy for her. She rejected the idea right away, as I knew she would. It gave me pleasure to be able to anticipate her movements and to act accordingly, a pleasure similar to that when I watched Catalina on the tennis court, volleying with her opponent.

The next evening, just as the girls were settling down in the drawing room to listen to the radio program, Mrs. Townsend sent for me. The two dogs had taken their spots next to her feet, and she signaled for me to sit in a straight-backed chair facing the sofa. This was not a good sign. When she was in a better mood, she asked the girls to sit around her feet on the rug.

"So," she said, "tell me how you feel about what you've written so far."

I could not detect any apparent displeasure in her demeanor. Mrs. Townsend was not a patient person, and I had noticed that, with me, she made less effort to hide her irritation from her face or from her voice than when she was speaking with the other girls.

"I don't know," I said. "I'm still working on it."

"That I know," she said. "But do you like what you've written?"

I thought for a moment. "I think it has begun well," I said cautiously. "But there are things I'm hoping to make better."

"What kind of things?" she asked.

I let my eyes drift to the bookshelves behind her, hoping that I had taken on one of those looks that had been described in the press as mystified and lost for words. "I can't say," I replied. "I only feel them."

"Very well," Mrs. Townsend said. "This is what I think, Agnès. You've done a good job so far."

"I have?"

"I'm not saying it's perfect. There's much to improve, I agree with you, but so far you've exceeded my expectations."

I was so used to being criticized by Mrs. Townsend that I did not know, for a moment, how to respond.

"What strikes me the most is that you've outgrown the morbid childishness of your first two books. You've also outgrown your attachment to fairy tales. Remember, only very recently you were still writing those fantastic tales in your diary. They may be harmless for most girls your age, but I expect more from you, do you understand?"

"Yes, Kazumi."

"I'm glad to see that you've left that phase behind. You're more confident, and you've captured something precarious and scintillating, true to a girl in your shoes."

I looked down at my feet, the silver buckles of the leather shoes shining.

"But as I said, there are things we must revise. For one thing, despite your progress, your French grammar is far from perfect."

"I'm sorry," I said.

"No need to apologize. It's my job to improve you, and we're only four months into your education here. Besides, it is an easy problem to fix. That's what your postmaster did, is it not so? It would be no problem for me to polish a few things for you."

Everyone called M. Devaux "your postmaster" when they spoke about him. He was no more mine than my books.

"There's something else I find particularly interesting," Mrs. Townsend said. "You seem unwilling to write too much about yourself. Do you agree? Where does this reluctance come from?"

I was shocked. I thought everything I had written was about me. "Reluctance?" I said.

"How shall I put it? You of all the people appear most opaque in these chapters."

"Opaque?" I said. I did not remember that was a word the press and the critics had used to describe *Les Enfants Heureux*.

"Yes, opaque," Mrs. Townsend said. She picked up a copy of *Les Enfants Heureux*, which she had kept on her coffee table since my arrival, and turned to an earmarked page. "You see, if you read this paragraph here, about your watching the older girl giving birth, or the paragraph here, about your separating the pigs who were fighting with one another. Even though you did not say exactly how you felt in those moments, your prose was taut, and we can feel what you felt."

I did not know what she meant by taut.

"There are many savage moments in the book, but your writing has a kind of special clarity. Like a perfect C-major piece on the piano."

By then I was completely lost. I wondered if Mrs. Townsend forgot that I was exempt from music class.

She walked to the upright piano in the corner. There were three pianos in the house for the students to practice on, but this one, kept in Mrs. Townsend's sitting room, was a special instrument for her. She pressed some keys in succession. "How does that sound to you?"

"Loud?" I said.

"It sounds like your first two books. Clear and pure. Your first two books were written by a cloudless mind," she said. She then played some other notes. "How about these notes?"

They were equally loud, but I knew enough not to say that.

She played the notes again. "How do these notes sound to your ears?"

"Cloudy?" I said tentatively.

"Exactly," she said, and played an unfamiliar tune. "This sounds closer to what you've written in the past few weeks, a bit hazy, a big foggy, if you see what I mean."

I could not tell the difference. And I could feel my heart beating faster. Was this the moment that I would be revealed as an impersonator of an author?

Mrs. Townsend returned to the sofa. "You look pale," she said. "What's the matter?"

I said I felt bad that I had not done quite the right thing with my new book.

"But that's not what I meant," she said. "I was only making

some observations. Besides, as you yourself said, this is only the beginning." She signaled for me to sit next to her, and put an arm around my shoulder. "I think you misunderstood me," she said. "This is a good beginning, and we'll just work together to make it great."

~

A FEW DAYS LATER Mrs. Townsend handed an envelope to me. She made a show of double-checking the sender's name and address, and then pinched to indicate its thickness. "Your friend Fabienne has a lot to say to you," she said.

"Oh . . ." I said. "She often tells me everything that happens in our village."

"Is she also helping her brother to get his letters to you?"

"Jacques? No, that's impossible. They don't get along."

"And you wrote to Jacques and told him to stop writing to you, per my instruction?"

"Yes."

"Has he written you back?"

I shook my head. When Mrs. Townsend's eyes did not move away from my face, I explained to her that Fabienne and Jacques were from a poor family. "They would not have sent their letters separately to me if they were close," I said.

"Anyone would say they were wasting their money on separate stamps to write to me, but you see, they can't stand each other."

"And you feel all right, terminating your relationship with Jacques?"

For a split second I considered the option of playing dead again, freezing myself as though I had not heard her question. But Fabienne's letter was still clasped in Mrs. Townsend's hand, and I would risk losing it if I said something to provoke her. I nodded hesitantly, and said that I was trying to put Jacques behind me, and writing my new book helped me with that.

Mrs. Townsend nodded and handed me the envelope. "You may feel some pain for a few days, but what is life without a few little stings?"

MAY 5, 1954

Agnès,
What do you mean you started a new book? That is the most stupid thing I've ever heard from you. And you're not even that smart to begin with.

Fabienne

MAY 6, 1954

Ma chère Agnès,
It feels that we have been separated for years, but the calendar says only four months. I am bored. Not that I don't have some friends to go out with at night, but I don't think they are interesting. A few drinks are all they need to feel good about themselves, or feel tired enough to go to bed, like they have anything to feel happy about.

If luck strikes them, if they can find a girl for a stroll or a dance, then they behave as if they are kings of the world. What pathetic, hopeless lives they set themselves up for.

If not for you, I might have become one of them, going out with a girl who doesn't know much about life, and eventually marrying one who is not too repulsive.

Well, marriage is a stupid thing. Agnès, I hope you don't misunderstand me, but I don't think what you and I want is a marriage. There has to be something better than that.

Fabienne is in her usual dark mood. Maybe she also feels terribly bored. Too bad that when you put two bored people together they never come up with a way to amuse each other.

Jacques

MAY 7, 1954

Agnès,

I decided to waste a good sheet of paper on you again, but you should also know that I won't be a fool like this forever.

Last night I told Jacques that he is an idiot to think that his love means anything. I didn't give him the opportunity to repeat his usual words that he knows you and trusts you, that you two have already planned your grand future together. I pointed out to him that you never said yes to his proposal of visiting you in England. Doesn't that explain everything to you? I said to Jacques. Can't you see that Agnès has no use for you these days?

What should I do? he asked me.

I told him he should enlist.

Why? he asked.

Saint Rémy is not the only place in the world, I said. If he can't find any girl smart or interesting for his taste here, he should leave. Don't get stuck in Saint Rémy, I warned him. This is a place where only girls get stuck.

What about Agnès? Jacques asked. I promised to wait for her.

She's not coming back, I said. Do you want to bet on it? I asked him.

He said he would bet his life that you would come back.

My god, he's such a fool.

I told him he should go to the cemetery and start digging his own grave.

Fabienne

The letters, read and reread before the dinner bell, were like dark clouds over my head. Both Fabienne and Jacques were unhappy with me. I had explained to Fabienne in my letter that the reason I had to start writing a book now, instead of waiting until I returned home to her, was that I thought I would never be allowed to leave otherwise. Either she had refused to understand this, or she had her own reason for her fury.

What did Fabienne mean when she said Saint Rémy was a place where girls got stuck? Long ago, we had decided that the only part of life that mattered was what was made by the two of us. Saint Rémy, depending on Fabienne's moods, could be tedious, or stupid, or moderately entertaining. We had not known the world beyond Saint Rémy until we began to visit M. Devaux. And that was also why she had sent me out to

Paris and England. I had done that, and I knew now that the world she wanted me to take a look at was like the artwork Mrs. Townsend had brought us to see in museums and galleries: the landscapes had distinctive moods; the men and women in the portraits wore nice hats and beautiful jewelry; the sometimes naked and often twisted figures, supposed to represent Greek gods or people from the Bible, stayed naked and twisted no matter how you wished them a different fate. But the freshness of this world was going stale. It was during those few months when I was away from Saint Rémy that I began to realize something: I did not care much about what kind of future I had, as long as I was with Fabienne.

Fabienne was bored. I was, too. I did not know if we felt bored for the same reasons. When she felt listless she invented games for us to play, and she was driven to those inventions, I knew, because she could not stand boredom, as she could not stand most of the people in our world. I did not fear boredom, but I feared that if she was defeated by boredom, something colossal would happen, something deadly, something that would change her and me forever. I would do anything she asked me to, just so that she found life interesting.

And now, in her letters, I sensed an emergency. I would not be surprised if she wrote a letter next week announcing that Jacques was dead from a drowning accident or a sudden illness. I wondered if that would give me an excuse to return to Saint Rémy.

This game of sending me out to the world as a girl author was getting old. It was time for it to end, and this time, it was up to me alone to act.

~

THE NEXT DAY, Mrs. Townsend sent for me just as I was about to go out to the garden. I had planned to ask Meaker a few questions—whether girls in the past had left Woodsway because of family emergencies, and how one might arrange traveling from London to Paris.

"I think it's time for you to learn something new," Mrs. Townsend said, pointing to a typewriter on her desk. "I ordered a French typewriter for you. It's secondhand, but in good shape."

Typing was not included the curriculum. Calligraphy was. There was plenty of writing to do at Woodsway—essays on the arts, literature, and music, reflections after our visits to the theaters, museums, and galleries. Mrs. Townsend read them more for presentation than content. We wrote these essays in our best handwriting, and she would circulate a particularly good example to show us how neatly the work was done. Mine was never chosen. There was a typewriter in the classroom, but nobody used it. Mrs. Townsend had her own typewriter, which she used for the school correspondence.

I had always wanted to learn to type. At M. Chastain's office in Paris, I had seen several young women in smart outfits pounding away on the keyboards. It was one of those lives that I had sometimes imagined for myself. Working in an office was just like sitting in a classroom, following orders, getting things done, not attracting attention. The only difference was that I would bring home money instead of homework. After work would be my real life, which would be spent with Fabienne. What would she do during the day? I tried to place her in an office with a typewriter, or a department store with beautiful clothes, or a shop—a stationery or a chemist's, like the ones in Paris, where M. Bazin had photographed me, but none of them felt right for her. Perhaps she could be a gardener. She could easily do most of the jobs Meaker was doing; the only thing she needed to learn was how to drive an automobile.

Mrs. Townsend told me to try the typewriter. I touched a few keys without pressing them down.

"Do you know why I want you to learn typing?" Mrs. Townsend asked.

"Because it's a useful skill?"

"That, yes," she said. "But more importantly, you're an author. The typewriter, along with the fountain pen I gave you, should be the two loyal assistants in your pursuit. Now take a seat. Type a few lines. Don't worry about the right fingering yet. We'll work on that."

A piece of paper was already waiting, but I did not know what to type.

"Here," Mrs. Townsend said. She placed a notebook next

to me, the same kind as the ones she had given me for my book, though a size larger, and the leather cover was in a deeper blue. She opened the notebook. The first sentence was unfamiliar, so was the next. A couple of lines later I recognized a description I had used for Paris-Austerlitz, but Mrs. Townsend had changed most of the words, so it no longer read "the gray buildings outside the station looked stern, like the Parisians" but "the moment I exited the station, I was frightened by the stream of Parisians walking past me with cold indifference in their faces, and by the buildings behind them, gray and impassive."

Mrs. Townsend, who had pulled a chair over to sit next to me, was watching me closely. I tried to keep my face neutral.

"You see, the book is more or less the same one as you've written," Mrs. Townsend said. "I only smoothed out a few wrinkles. Let's plan for you to type an hour in the afternoon every day. And of course you will continue to write in your notebook."

I had not wanted to write the book in the first place. Now I had to type out what Mrs. Townsend had written. I wished I could tell her to do it herself.

"Why are you quiet?" she asked. "Do you not like the sound of my plan?"

"Do you think, Kazumi . . ." I said, trying to make my voice extra-sweet and meek, "do you think it's possible that I could take a trip to France?"

"Why?"

"I thought I would like to talk with M. Chastain about the book."

"Have you written him about it?" Mrs. Townsend asked.

"Not specifically about this book. We correspond occasionally."

"So you want to talk about writing this book with him? You can write him."

"But it's hard to explain things in a letter, don't you think?" I said.

"Tell me what's hard about it," Mrs. Townsend said. I could hear impatience in her voice. She never liked to be surprised. "Go on."

"A lot more can be achieved in a meeting than in letters back and forth," I said. "If I could meet with M. Chastain, he may have some good advice for the book."

"I don't think you need his advice to write. You've been doing exactly as you're told. With my assistance, we can get the book finished first, and then we can plan a meeting with him, preferably after the term is over. I cannot spare any time at the moment."

"I can travel by myself."

"That's impossible. I have full responsibility for you as your guardian," she said. "Besides, I don't see the point of going."

"What if I see a point?" I asked.

Mrs. Townsend's eyes narrowed, frosty with contempt and impatience. "You? What do you know about these things?"

I took a deep breath before saying: "Kazumi, may I have your permission to travel to Paris?"

"That I can't allow. Stop this nonsense and get to work," she said, raising her chin to indicate the typewriter.

"I'm not talking nonsense," I said. "I've followed all your instructions, Kazumi, but that doesn't mean I cannot tell what's good for me, or what I need for my work."

"What you feel you need doesn't matter," Mrs. Townsend said. "We know what's good and necessary for you."

I wondered who she meant by we.

"Don't forget that you've come here to improve yourself,"

Mrs. Townsend said. "You're not here to make decisions beyond your capacity."

"But you said I've been improving."

"Calm down, Agnès," Mrs. Townsend said. "There's no need to be hysterical."

"I'm not being hysterical."

"You are being emotional."

Being hysterical was among the gravest offenses at Woodsway. Being emotional was, too.

"I can't have every decision about my life made by others," I said.

"The girls at Woodsway, they all have decisions made for them by others. In what way do you think you're so special and different from them?"

I thought for a moment. "None of them writes books," I said.

"And precisely for that reason you should count yourself lucky that people like M. Chastain and myself take it as our responsibility to supervise and advise you. Now, now," Mrs. Townsend said, her voice softened but still cold, "I'm afraid you're too young to understand how things work. You're here at the school fully supported by the scholarship I've raised on your behalf. You and your parents have agreed to the terms of the scholarship. Are these things not clear enough for you? Now, please, no crying. That's one thing we don't have any use for."

~

THAT NIGHT I MADE UP MY MIND: I must escape Woodsway and never return. I would change into the clothes I had worn when I had traveled from Saint Rémy to Paris. I would pack all the letters I had received. I would bring the notebooks I had written in: my diary and my version of *Agnès in Paradise*. The book was not finished, but there were enough pages to show M. Chastain. I would leave the blank notebooks behind, along with the version of *Agnès in Paradise* Mrs. Townsend had rewritten, and her fountain pen.

I would have to bring one of the suitcases Mrs. Townsend had provided, but I would send her money for that—I would find a way. M. Chastain might be willing to give me a loan if I went to see him in Paris. He might even like what I had written and pay me for the book.

It was a shame, of course, that I had to leave behind my leather shoes with shining silver buckles, my dancing shoes, and my rambling boots, which might actually have been useful back at home; and all the dresses—the green satin, the blue velvet, and the rose-colored taffeta, with a belt that was made to look like a wreath of rosebuds; the misty-white blouse with pearly buttons, the tweed jacket that Margareta called smart, the straw hat with the lace ribbon that I so adored and had not yet had an opportunity to wear, and all the other nice things that no one in Saint Rémy had seen. I arranged my nightdress with the scalloped hem on the bed, spreading it out to mark the shape of my body and folding the two sleeves in front of the chest like an angel's. It was so soft and so pretty, but I knew that if I made an exception for it, soon I would make exceptions for the rest. No, I would not take anything from the school but only what truly belonged to me.

How should I run away without being noticed? The moment I arrived in France I would be free, but before that I would have to use my brain. I could slip away next time when we took a day trip to London, but I would not be able to bring my suitcase, and Mrs. Townsend might inform the police if she noticed something amiss. I could leave in the middle of the night, climbing out of my window—I would hide the suitcase in the garden before nightfall—and then I could walk all night along the train line, so I could take an early train to London from a station where no one would connect me to the school. Still, would someone find me suspicious and report me to the police? What would I say if I were caught?

Or I could ask for Meaker's help. Maybe on one of the days when Mrs. Townsend went to London by herself, I could ask him to drive me to the train station. I did not have any money, but he might be willing to lend me some.

To hell with *Agnès in Paradise*. What I should write instead was a thriller like one of those books the girls read behind Mrs. Townsend's back. *Agnès on the Run. Agnès Freed. Agnès Is Home.*

I stayed awake half of the night, thinking through different plans, perfecting every one of them. In the end I decided that the best way was to enlist Meaker's help. He would understand me, and he would do everything he could to help.

~

THE NEXT AFTERNOON I found Meaker in the orchard. It was a sunny day, and he was lime-washing the apple trees and crabapple trees. There was an extra brush in the can, which I knew was for me. I took the brush and started to work next to him.

"Were you ever married?" I asked when I finished with one tree.

"Me, no," Meaker said.

"Why not?"

He placed the brush in the can, so that the lime wash would not drip on the grass while he was thinking of my question. I rested my brush next to his, making sure that the handle stayed clean. I had not been a neat person, but I had begun to pick up some of the habits from Meaker.

"I suppose I'm not the marrying type."

"What type is the marrying type?" I asked. Jacques said

marriage was a stupid thing, so he would not be a marrying type, either. Why would Fabienne make it sound that he was in love with me, then? What use did Jacques and I have for love, if not marriage?

Meaker looked at me strangely.

"What?" I said.

"That's not a question you should be discussing with me."

"Then with whom? The girls? Mrs. Townsend? You know that would be like talking about . . ." I searched the words in my head. "It would be like talking about pig-minding with them."

"I don't get it," Meaker said.

"They won't understand anything I say. Pigs to them mean bacon and chops."

"I see."

I was not sure if Meaker did see what I meant. "The friend you talked about the other day—Wilfred—was he the marrying type?"

Meaker shook his head. I did not know if that meant he did not know, or that Wilfred, even if he had lived, would not have got married. Meaker indicated that he was going back to his work.

"The friend I told you about, Fabienne, she and I are not the marrying types, either," I said.

He nodded, though I could not tell if he actually heard me, or understood what I was telling him. He was measuring and marking where the lime wash would end, so that all the trees would have a uniform look when we were finished.

"Meaker, can I ask you for something?" I said. "It's very serious."

He looked at me again, and this time he returned the brush to the can and spread a tarp under a tree for me to sit on. He himself took a seat on an overturned bucket.

"I need your help, but I need you to keep it a secret between us."

He bowed his head, indicating that he was listening to me. I explained to him that I had decided to go back to France. Could he help me find out which trains and boats to take from here to Paris? Also, could he loan me some money? "All I need is to get to Paris," I said. "Once I'm there I can find my way home. And I can send your money back from Paris."

Meaker listened with an expressionless face. There was something comforting about his face, like a tree trunk that would not alter its look despite the changing weather or the progression of seasons.

"Have you discussed this with Mrs. Townsend?" he asked.

"Of course not," I said. "It's a secret between you and me."

"Do you mean you want to run away?"

"Only going back home," I said, trying to sound confident so that Meaker would not be unduly alarmed. I told him that the following week Mrs. Townsend would be going to London for some business meeting, and that would be a perfect day for me to depart. "I'll leave a note to her and tell her I'm going home. I'll ask my Parisian publisher to telegraph her once I arrive. That way she doesn't need to worry," I said. "You see, I have everything worked out."

"It's a long way to go back to France by yourself," Meaker said.

"But if you tell me how to get there, it won't be too difficult. I have enough English to read the timetable. I can ask people for directions in English," I said. "Oh, will you also drive me to the train station that day? I promise I won't tell anyone."

"Why do you want to go home?"

"I hate it here," I said.

Meaker nodded, as though he had known that all along.

"I'm very unhappy," I said.

He shook his head. "That's not a reason to run away. Sometimes we have to carry on even if we feel unhappy."

"But my friend back home, Fabienne, she won't carry on if she feels unhappy."

"What do you mean?"

"Ever since I came here, she's been very unhappy," I said. "You see, she has no other friends at home. And her mother and her sister died when we were little."

"It's a hard world for orphans," Meaker said. I wondered if he, too, was an orphan, but I did not want to distract the conversation from the important topic.

"I want to go back home to her," I said. "I worry that she'd do something if I stay here longer."

"Do something, like what?"

"Like killing herself," I said, an answer that startled Meaker and me both. Fabienne would be the last person to kill herself. And yet I had no option but to make it sound convincing. "She could easily do that."

Meaker looked at his two hands dangling between his knees. "Perhaps you should speak to Mrs. Townsend."

"She won't understand."

"You should at least try," he said, no longer meeting my eyes. "I don't think I can help you."

He was saying that only because it was the right thing for him to say. Adults often felt the need to say the right things. That way they would not feel bad about making life hard for others, especially for children. I uncrossed my legs and moved closer to Meaker, putting a palm on his giant knee. "Of course you can," I said. "Nobody else will."

He stared at my hand but did not remove it. "You have to

let Mrs. Townsend know if you want to go home. You're too young to make the decision by yourself."

"She won't let me," I said. "Besides, I'm old enough to write books."

"That's different."

"I'm old enough to get married," I said.

Meaker looked up. Finally, I thought, I got his attention.

"For instance, if you asked me to marry you now, I would say yes. Then Mrs. Townsend wouldn't be able to call herself my guardian anymore, as you could be my guardian. You know, that postman friend of mine, he proposed to me once, only I turned him down." It was not an outright lie, I thought. M. Devaux had asked Fabienne to be his lover, and easily he could have asked me instead of her. And the distance between a lover and a wife was not that far.

Meaker's tanned face, copper-colored, turned into a deep red.

"No, I don't mean that you should propose to me for real," I said, hurrying to relieve him from his concern. "You're not the type to marry. I'm not, either. But you're my only friend here, and I need your help."

He stood up abruptly. "You really should go back to the house. I have work to do."

"Will you help me?"

He shook his head.

"But I'm so unhappy here I would rather be dead," I said. "Think about it. If your friend asked you to do one thing to save his life, would you say no to him?"

Meaker could still change his mind, I thought when he left me for his cottage. I picked up the brush and painted another tree. When he returned I would plead with him again, but he did not, and a few trees later, I got tired of waiting. The girls were beginning to enter the garden. I sniffed my hands and decided that I needed not wash before joining them by the pond.

A little later, I saw Meaker going up the path to the house. Rose, who was showing me a new bracelet her mother had sent through a London jeweler for the year-end dance, was surprised when I ran after Meaker. I told her that there was something urgent I needed to speak to him about.

"Please think again," I said to Meaker when I caught up with him. "You're my only friend here."

He stopped. "It's not my place to make friends with anyone here," he said. "I'm not your friend."

"But I think of you as a friend."

He repeated that he was never my friend, nor had he ever considered me a friend. His words had such a finality that I winced. Meaker, like Jacques, was supposed to be gentle, understanding, and not to say anything or do anything to hurt me. I wanted to raise my voice in protest, but he only nodded apologetically and left me standing by the azalea bushes.

Tomorrow . . . I said to myself, tomorrow I will try again.

But the next afternoon he was not in the garden. Before dinner, Catalina came into my room with the excuse of giving me a crystal pin to go with my blouse. "By the way, Kazumi told me to let you know: Meaker no longer works at Woodsway."

I turned violently around from the mirror. "What?"

"She said before she finds the new person, you're not allowed to go into the garden by yourself."

"Why?"

"Why what?"

"Why did she fire Meaker?"

Catalina shrugged. "She must have her reasons."

"Has he already left?"

"I don't know. Why?"

"I must see him now."

"Oh, don't be silly. The gong will start any minute."

"I know why Kazumi doesn't like him," I said. "She can't stand that he's my friend."

Catalina laughed as though I had told a good joke. "Don't let others hear you."

"But it's true. Meaker and I are close. In fact, we've been talking about getting married."

"No! Are you serious? Is that why you've arranged to see him every afternoon?"

Fabienne and I had raised ourselves to be the best make-believers. The world was often inconvenient or indifferent to us, and it was our ingenuity that made what was inconvenient and indifferent interesting: the stinging nettles left bloody marks on our legs as we ran, but we pretended that those were the nail scratches of the girls greedy for our attention; the leeches attached themselves to our flesh when we waded in the water, needy little creatures, which to us were like most men, who only pretended to have spines. The berries that filled our hungry stomachs could turn poisonous sometimes. Once, when we were seven, after eating too many of those crimson fruits, we had become certain that we would die by the end of the day—the prospect, rather than frightening us, had thrilled us, and we had gone to the cemetery, looking for a patch of space between stones, and, after a long search, settled on the ground where we would be buried together. But instead we had lived. We had always lived, because others had died in our places: Fabienne's mother and sister, my brother, a little boy we had tripped one day in the alley, who passed away the next day from some illness, the pigs and cows and goats and chickens and rabbits, new hatchlings dropped out of the nests, grasshoppers and katydids after the frost, M. Devaux's wife, whose death left him in a craze of desire for Fabienne, M. Devaux himself, who no doubt would die, too, long before our time was over. A hard life, unlike what we were taught at school, did not make us virtuous; the hardest life was the most boring, the most unrewarding. How else could we overcome this boredom but to bring ourselves up in our own make-believe, which, as we grew older, had become more elaborate, more exhilarating, and, most of all, closer to the truth? What was wrong with the muddy muck underneath our feet if we could give it the power to track unseen beings wandering around in the dark? What was a cold tombstone but a door that opened to our own secret, warm chamber? We were not liars, but we made our own truths, extravagant as we needed them to be, fantastic as our moods required. Built from scratch like our books, our games had banished M. Devaux when he became a trouble for us, catapulted me into this English finishing school, and made Meaker my only true friend in this foreign land. Our make-beliefs were our allies. How else could we thrive, if not for them: unseen, nameless, patient, always on our side?

~

OF ALL THE PEOPLE in the world, how many of them, looking into their own conscience, can say with unwavering certainty that they have never betrayed someone in their lives—ten, five, none? If so, why do we often make a fuss about betrayal? So many movies and books, so many broken marriages and torn friendships. The knives we stick into one another's backs—perhaps those knives have their own wills. They take a grand tour, finding a hand here and a back there. We cannot blame the hands, just as we cannot sympathize with the backs. They are equally recruited for the knives' entertainment. The world is never short of knives.

There are different ways to tell what happened to Meaker. You can say he betrayed me by reporting my escape plot to Mrs. Townsend. You can also say I betrayed him by robbing him of what had mattered the most: his livelihood and his solitude.

The next day, at the end of the morning lessons, Mrs. Townsend announced that Meaker was gone, and that in a few days a replacement would be taking over. She did not give any reason. I stared at her and she smiled back. "Do you have any questions, Agnès?" she asked.

I had to sit on my hands so I would not pick up the inkstand and throw it at her. The girls turned toward me, waiting for me to speak. There were no secrets in Woodsway. We were transparent creatures, with see-through bodies like the tiny shrimps in the spring creek. Two pinching fingers could easily crush us—the girls might not know that, but I did. Margareta, the most transparent of all, gazed at me with sympathy, bafflement, and misery in her eyes. Catalina shook her head ever so slightly, indicating that I should not fuss. It would be an embarrassment for everyone if I made a scene. But wasn't it embarrassing enough to be in this strange place, conducting our days as though everything we did were staged for a secret photographer? I looked around at those dainty girls. Once again I felt the urge to reach for the inkstand. Instead of throwing it at Mrs. Townsend, I could walk around the room with the ink bottle, pouring ink into everyone's hair, letting it drip down onto their faces and necks.

"Agnès, you look like you have something to say," Mrs. Townsend said.

I focused on my vision of the ink-covered girls for a moment longer.

"We've been waiting," Mrs. Townsend said.

"I meant to ask, Kazumi, if you have an address for Meaker."

The room was so quiet that you knew the girls were trying not to gasp. They must have all learned of my disreputable liaison with Meaker, and that I had even talked about marrying him. I did not trust that Catalina would be able to keep such a paramount scandal to herself.

"Why would you need that?" Mrs. Townsend asked, and, not giving me a moment to reply, added, "You and I can discuss this later."

"I just wonder if you wouldn't mind giving me his address," I persisted with a wickedness that would make Fabienne proud. "I plan to write to him. He's going to be in my book, you know?"

Eloquently Mrs. Townsend's girls expressed themselves with the minute dilation of their pupils, an unhurried folding or unfolding of their hands, the stillness of their backs.

"We won't waste everyone's time discussing your personal matters," Mrs. Townsend said, and told the girls that they were to get ready for lunch.

I stood up with everyone, but the girls seemed to flow around me as though I were a fallen branch in the middle of a creek. No one seemed to be in a rush, yet they all managed to block my path and walk past me, leaving me the last to exit the room. Mrs. Townsend ordered me to stay.

"You've behaved unacceptably," she said. "I think you owe me an explanation."

I could, as I used to, arrange the words in my head before speaking, but I was tired of looking for the right words. "You're horrible to Meaker," I said.

"I don't understand. Meaker was employed by the school, and it was necessary to terminate his position."

"Why?"

"He's encouraged some unhealthy attachment from one of my students. That's unprofessional, irresponsible, and immoral."

I wondered how much Meaker had told Mrs. Townsend

about my plan to escape. Oh, Meaker, how could you have been so stupid to fall for the trap of being a responsible and moral man?

"He didn't do anything to encourage me," I said.

"He wasn't a good influence," Mrs. Townsend said. "The fact that he put himself in a situation where you even discussed with him a plan to run away from the school—that alone was enough evidence that he should never be allowed to work in any school in the future."

"He didn't help me," I said.

"Whatever he did or didn't do is beside the point. The decision has been made, with the welfare of my students in mind."

"No, you let him go because you're jealous. You got rid of him because he's my friend. You can't stand that I have a friend. You want to have me all to yourself," I said.

True blind rage is like true blind courage—if you have ever seen a squirrel trapped in a cage or a bird fly into a room by accident, you will understand this. It does not matter that the squirrel's claws cannot shake open the cage, or the windowpane will not give way to the bird's thumping. For some—animals, children—despair and doom galvanize.

"He didn't help me run away," I said. "And I don't blame him. He obeys the rules. But you, you cannot get rid of me, so you punish me by getting rid of him. You are—"

Before I realized it, Mrs. Townsend was already facing me, her hands on my shoulders, squeezing so hard that I could not finish my sentence. "I am what?" she said. "Say it."

I did not know Mrs. Townsend could hiss like a peasant woman. "You . . . are . . . an . . . evil . . . person," I said in my best English.

Mrs. Townsend, her eyes still close to mine, squeezed my

shoulders harder, her small, plump hands hard as steel clamps. I gasped, though more from shock than from pain. Fabienne and I had trained ourselves to tolerate all kinds of pain.

"Listen," Mrs. Townsend hissed again. "Don't you dare test my patience like this." She shook me violently. Through my blouse I could feel her fingernails, though I was more frightened by her face, which, seen at this close distance, looked nothing like a human face. Growing up in the countryside, I was always aware that even the mellowest cow could turn vile without a reason, and a timid dog could become rabid.

"If you don't know how to obey me, you'll end up having nothing and being nothing," she said. "Do you understand?"

I did not speak. She shook me once more. "Do you understand?"

"I want to go home," I said.

"That's impossible. Let me remind you, the agreement between me and your parents is that you will be educated under my supervision for a whole year."

"I want to go home," I said again.

"Shut up," Mrs. Townsend said.

"Then I will tell the journalists that I didn't write any of my books. That postmaster in my village wrote them. And I will tell the journalists that I hate my school life here, but you forced me to write a book called *Agnès in Paradise*. And I will tell them that you're writing it for me."

Mrs. Townsend stared into my eyes for a long moment before letting go of my shoulders. I watched her return to her seat and tidy the notebooks and papers from the morning class. When she looked up at me again, her face was as smooth as a china plate. "I don't think you would gain anything by lying so to the press."

"It's not lying. I'd be telling the truth."

"But we have plenty of evidence that you're a habitual liar, don't we? You told Meaker that you were unhappy here, while I and all the other girls have gone above and beyond to embrace you and make you a special member of the Woodsway family. You told Meaker that you wanted to go back to your friend, but it was really her brother you've been eager to return to, isn't it? You're only using her as an excuse. What you can't let go is some little boyfriend back home, whom you've deemed more important than your career."

"I don't care about my career," I said. "You can have it."

Mrs. Townsend took a loud breath. I wondered if she was fighting the urge to hurl something heavy at me, the typewriter on her desk or the bronze paperweight, made in the shape of a Buddha. When she spoke again there was a coaxing tone, cold and greasy, in her voice. "I don't think, Agnès, you understand the situation enough to say anything about your career. Why destroy what you've worked so hard to build? Soon we'll finish *Agnès in Paradise*, and you'll get all the attention you deserve. You'll learn so many things here, and you're guaranteed a bright future whether you stay in England or return to Paris. Think of all the things you may be able to achieve under the right tutelage. Think of all the things I can do for you."

Four months ago, I would have found that future alluring because I would have believed in every word Mrs. Townsend said—ignorance had given me the right to hope then.

"I want to go home," I said. If Mrs. Townsend did not allow me to leave, I would say that all the time, to everyone I encountered. I would be like one of those children in fairy tales, who, robbed of their human forms and transformed into something else—a bird or a fox or a tree—never give up trying to prove that they once had human hearts.

"I must remind you, my dear Agnès, that you're committing career suicide."

"I don't care."

"You may be running late for lunch. Why don't you go ahead? I'll join you all at lunch shortly."

"I want to go home," I said.

"Go on, to lunch now," she said with a smile. "We'll have a conversation later. I have a great deal to consider."

I WROTE TO M. CHASTAIN TODAY," Mrs. Townsend said to me the next day, when she summoned me to her. "I think you should read the letter before I send it."

She handed me the letter. She regretted to inform M. Chastain that though I had made progress at Woodsway, my performance had proved unsatisfactory. "As you understand, Agnès's upbringing has resulted in her appearance and manner, uncouth beyond description. These I have done my best to improve. However, she has demonstrated little of what is supposed to be her innate intelligence and talent, and all my efforts in conveying to her the knowledge and wisdom she needs for her future writing career are unsuccessful. She has learned to speak a certain amount of English, and her French has improved, but having spent nearly five months with her, having, especially, devoted more time to her than to any of my students, I have come to the unfortunate conclusion that her original story of being a child prodigy from a squalid background is not to be trusted entirely. Particularly, she has made claims that have shed new light on her relationship with the former village postmaster, whose name you very generously included in your introduction to her first novel and printed on the cover of that book. She might have used M. Devaux to a degree beyond our speculation. Please understand, my dear sir, that I have written this to you confidentially. I understand that her second book will be published in the fall, as her first book continues to gain attention. I am giving you all the assurance that I shall keep this professional assessment between us. However, it has transpired that hours of my unrewarded work with her will not advance her career as a writer. To make matters worse, it has proven that her character, more than her appearance or manner, has become an impediment for me, for my other students, and for herself. I feel obliged to propose that we end her school career earlier than we originally designed."

So on and so forth the letter went for a few more paragraphs, discussing the mechanism of returning me to Saint Rémy, outlining traveling schedules. She did not leave any room for M. Chastain to disagree with her proposal.

"So?" Mrs. Townsend said when I returned the letter to her.

I shrugged.

"It's still not too late to reconsider," Mrs. Townsend said. "Once this letter is posted, you cannot change your mind."

"Why would I want to change my mind?" I said.

"I thought after a night of sleep you may gain some perspective. You can't be this stupid, or am I wrong again to even hope for that?"

I shook my head. I had wanted to go back home, and now I would be returned home. There was no triumph in this escape, as I would have felt had Meaker helped me. Still, it was an escape.

"What do you have to say for yourself?" Mrs. Townsend asked.

"I think you're wrong about me."

"Which part?"

"I didn't use M. Devaux," I said.

"You told Meaker that M. Devaux proposed to you," Mrs. Townsend said. "That alone has shed more light on your career than anything else."

Why couldn't Meaker see that his honesty was useless to him and to me? "But I didn't marry M. Devaux, did I?"

"That changes nothing," Mrs. Townsend said. "In any case, you told Meaker that you're extremely unhappy here at Woodsway. I would be unhappy, too, if I were you. This is not the right place for you."

That I could not disagree with.

"I would recommend that you keep quiet about our plans for you. I'll explain to the girls after you leave."

~

MY DEPARTURE from Woodsway, my return to Paris and then to Saint Rémy, smoothly arranged between Mrs. Townsend and M. Chastain's office, were not met by any press. In Paris M. Chastain confirmed that the second book Fabienne and I had written would be published as scheduled, still with M. Devaux's role highlighted. I could see that he had little of the enthusiasm he had had for me a year earlier, and I did not tell him that M. Devaux had barely helped with our second book.

M. Chastain did not ask any questions about my time at Woodsway. He did not ask if I would write a new book set in the school. He and Madame Townsend had had several phone conversations, he explained to me. Though initially he had been disappointed by Madame Townsend's decision, they had come to a mutual understanding that returning me to Saint Rémy would be best for everyone. My interview with him lasted a quarter of an hour. He wished me good luck and handed me off to his assistant, a new one, a young woman much more aloof than Mlle Boverat. She accompanied me to the train station, though for the entire journey she did not say more than a few necessary words to me.

Was there defeat, even humiliation, in my homecoming? Some people—those who had followed my adventure from a pig minder in the countryside to a published author in Paris to a work-in-progress as a society girl in England—must have thought so. They might have been baffled by the fact that, rather than offering a new chapter, my story simply faded—I vanished. My second book was published quietly and soon forgotten.

But their disappointment would not last. That year a girl named Françoise Sagan, who was four years older than me, made her name in literary history. The fame of Agnès Moreau, the peasant girl who failed to be transformed into a debutante, was no more than a twinkle of a firefly compared to the meteoric splendor of Mlle Sagan.

The next year Minou Drouet, a poet of eight years old, caught the attention of the public, enough to make Agnès Moreau sound like a middle-aged author, already irrelevant.

~

MY PARENTS received me as though I had been away for a brief trip and they had expected all the time that I would return to this old life unaltered. My mother had marveled at the beautiful and unpractical clothes I had bought back with me—Mrs. Townsend had insisted that I accept her generosity and keep the clothing, which, she pointed out, would be of no use to anyone else. "I hope one day you will understand how much you're indebted to Woodsway and to myself for this experience," she had said before I left. "Sometimes an educator's job is to plant a seed, even though the seed may take a long time to germinate."

An hour after I got home, I was already in my old overalls, which were tolerably small. The chickens, half of them hatched after my departure, did not know me, yet it did not stop them from swarming to me and clucking from eagerness: feed from my hands tasted no different than from my mother's hands. Our dog spent some time sniffling around my suitcases. A few times he sneezed—from the unfamiliar scents of fragrant soap and camphor balls from England, I was certain.

Saint Rémy felt like such a strange place, but it was strange in a way that my old gum boots were strange. Surely my feet, after the leather shoes with shiny buckles, after the satin dancing flats, would no longer fit? And yet the moment I slipped them on I was back to that peasant girl, Agnès. The smells of the barnyard surrounded me; the fields and the alleys, the villagers, my parents—all of them were here. The world of Saint Rémy was like the warm, shapeless mud after a summer rain, waiting for me to settle in again.

The past few months felt like a trance. No one stays in a trance forever, true, but no one, shaken awake, lives on without feeling a void inside. A trance is a displacement. A trance is a wound.

My parents told me that they were glad to have me back. Soon I would turn fifteen, old enough to start my adult life, and they did not think that I needed more schooling after the summer. If I would like to go into a factory or work in a shop, my father said, they would see what they could do for me, but what they really hoped, he said, was that I could stay on to help with the farm—until the day I married a man who could take over the toiling on the farm, though that they did not say. They did not have to.

My parents respected me a little more than before, but their love, which had always felt meager to me, had not changed. I was never an unloved child, but that was far from a badge one could proudly wear on one's shirt. I was fortunate not to have the desire, like some other children, to reciprocate their insufficient love with an overabundance of wishful love, hoping that would make a difference. My love for my parents was equally meager.

Later I understood that it was unfair of me to say that about them. When I was first married to Earl, he often took pleasure in teaching me things that I had not known. Once, he explained to me about the Mohs scale, which was used to test the hardness of minerals and gems. Diamond is the hardest, he said, and diamond can scratch any gem on the scale, but every other gem can leave only a scrape on those softer than itself. None of them would do anything to a diamond.

Perhaps I was born a material different from my parents. I was born a hard person, harder than most people in my life, so I have only myself to blame when I cannot feel the love of others, my parents among them. Love from those who cannot damage us irreparably often feels insufficient; we may think, rightly or wrongly, that their love does not matter at all.

The only person who could leave a scratch on me—then, and now—is Fabienne.

You cannot cut an apple with an apple. You cannot cut an orange with an orange. All those years we had made ourselves believe that we were two apples hanging next to each other on the same branch, or that we were two oranges nestled in a crate, or, even, that we were born with joined selves, like one of those oddly shaped radishes or potatoes, two bodies in one. But that was only our make-believe. The truth was, Fabienne and I were two separate beings. I was a whetstone to Fabienne's blade. There was no point asking which one of us was made of harder material.

~

"ARE YOU COMING TO SEE JACQUES?" Fabienne asked when she came out of her house. It was the day of my homecoming, late in the evening. I had written her ahead of time, announcing to her my liberation from Woodsway. I had wondered if she might ask my parents if she could accompany them to the train station, but only my mother was on the platform. I wondered then how I could have been so stupid. My father would not have wasted half a day of work. And it would have been Jacques, if he were real, to stand with my mother, waiting for me.

I looked at the unlit windows of Fabienne's house. Her father and her brothers should be out drinking by now. "Jacques—uh, is he home?"

Fabienne signaled me to follow her. In the alley some villagers greeted me, though like my parents, they had accepted my return without much curiosity. A girl a few years older than us asked me if I had learned to speak English, and I said yes. Good enough to go to America? she asked, meaning it as a joke, as she did not wait for me to answer before chasing her littlest brother down a slope.

In the cemetery there was a fresh grave. My parents had not talked much about the village news with me. I wondered who was buried there. Fabienne pointed to the grave. "There's your Jacques," she said.

I wanted to protest, saying that was impossible. Jacques could not be dead, because we were not dead.

"He thought you would never love him as much as he loved you. He thought you would never come back," Fabienne said. "That's where he ended up, for being impatient."

There was no Jacques, I told myself, but that was like saying my life at Woodsway had been only a dream. You can comfort yourself with those words, but the fact that you have to keep telling yourself means you do not believe what you say. Was there no Jacques? I had his letters in my suitcase, his handwriting different than Fabienne's, his words more affectionate than hers, more melancholy, too. I had written him words of love. "When did he die?" I said.

"Last week," Fabienne said. "Friday night."

I had been feigning normality among the girls at Woodsway then, so they would get to learn about my departure only after I disappeared from their world. God alone knew what Mrs. Townsend had told them, but whatever she chose to say would benefit only her and her school. I had not had the opportunity to say farewell to Catalina. Perhaps she would miss me for a day or two. But she, like all the other girls at Woodsway, was cultivated to bloom. My life belonged to the dirt, the worms, the manure, the rot underneath.

Fabienne studied me. There was something unreadable in

her face. She was my Fabienne, and yet she was a stranger. We stood farther apart than we used to. Perhaps she, too, saw in me a stranger.

"How did he die?" I asked.

"Oh, you know, he was getting restless. I told him to leave Saint Rémy, to go to the army or find a factory job, but he took Papa's shotgun and finished himself off," Fabienne said, thumping her forehead once with her fist. "Bang. Just like that. One shot."

I wished Fabienne had been kinder to the one person we had allowed in between us. Death was not the only way to keep Jacques away now that he was no longer needed. She could have said that he was living a soldier's life; she could have even said that he had fallen in love with someone passing on the train and followed her to another town. We would have told each other that he had gone away at just the right moment, and that whatever he had decided would not affect us. She and I were back together. That was all that mattered.

"Why, you don't look too sad," Fabienne said.

"How sad should I feel?"

"I don't know, you tell me," she said. "You know he was in love with you. And you kept saying you were in love with him, too."

I thought for a moment, and said that of course I was sad, but he was not the first one who had died.

"How heartless you sound," Fabienne said. "Poor Jacques. He died for love. What a silly reason to die."

Fabienne would never die for love; I would never dare to. "It's better that way," I said. "My brother, Jean, died without knowing love."

"Well, what difference does it make now? They're both dead. Rotten."

A few rooks were circling in the evening sky. She cackled at the birds, mocking them.

"Will you miss him?" I asked.

"The question is, will you?"

It had come back to us, this thrill of our leading each other into a new game: to talk about a dear boy without embarrassment because he was designed to be dear to both of us; to talk about a dead person who could only die in theory. "Yes, I think I'll miss him," I said. "Very much."

"That won't do him any good now," Fabienne said. She hopped over the new grave and reached for a low branch of an oak tree. She was agile as always. In no time she was sitting astride on a higher branch. "Come up here," she said.

I eyed her but did not move.

"Why, did you forget how to climb a tree?"

I walked over and tried to reach a lower branch, but, as my mother had pointed out earlier to my father, all the good food in England had filled me out nicely. I gave up the effort and climbed onto a nearby parapet. When I stood I was almost at eye level with Fabienne. "Be very careful," she said. "Don't break your neck."

That was when I thought I had the old Fabienne back. I did not mind her mocking me, just as she did not mind my being slow and clumsy. "What's going to happen to us now?" I asked.

"I was going to ask you that. What's going to happen to *you*?" Fabienne said. "Are you still writing that *Agnès in Paradise*?"

"No."

"Why not?"

I had not told Fabienne in detail why I had been sent back home. In my letter I had written that I did not like the school and I was bored with my life there. "That school is not a paradise at all," I said.

"I imagine not."

"What's going to happen to us?" I asked again. "What do we do now?"

"What do you think?"

"We can find a new game to play," I said.

"You mean, I should make up a new game for us to play?"

Why else, I thought, had I rushed to her house the moment I could get free from my parents?

"I'm tired of games," she said. "None of them are real."

"But we don't like real things," I argued.

She stood up in the tree, stretched, and then took off. In that split second, I thought she would be soaring into the sky, but simultaneously I thought she would break her leg on a tombstone. But she neither flew away nor stumbled on the ground. She climbed up the parapet and sat next to me. "You still don't understand, do you?"

Her voice was too gentle and too patient for my liking. "What don't I understand?"

"We had fun with our games because they made us feel real."

"But are we not real now that we're back together?"

"We are, but that's the problem. We're life-real now, not game-real."

"I don't know what you mean."

"You always need me to explain things to you," Fabienne said, her voice still eerie with gentleness. "Let me ask you: Were you truly in love with Jacques?"

I paused. I did not know what answer she would want to hear.

"Remember, you wrote all those words to him. Was it because he was a boy, so you could easily say those words to him?"

"That was part of the game, wasn't it?" I said. I had written those words to Jacques because he was Fabienne, and yet he was not Fabienne.

"Why did you love him when you could've loved me?" she said. "What does he have that I don't, other than he's a boy and I'm a girl?"

But I had loved her all my life. I had loved her before we knew what the world was, what love was, and who we ourselves were. But all these things I could not say.

"So when you wrote all those words to Jacques, they felt real, right?"

"Yes, but—"

She cut me off. "And Jacques felt real, too?"

I nodded, even though I did not entirely understand her.

"And when things like that happen, life feels real, right?"

I felt a knot in my stomach, as though she were patiently leading me up a dangerous path but I could not see where the snare was.

"But you can't always expect me to make things happen for both of us, don't you see?"

"I can do it with you, if you just tell me how," I said.

She looked at me, pity in her eyes. "Remember that one time when you thought I would kill M. Devaux? What if we had?"

"But we didn't want to kill him."

"We didn't know that we might want it one day," Fabienne said.

"What do you mean?" I said. I did not like to think about M. Devaux, just as I did not like to dwell on Meaker. They were men who had momentarily wandered into our world, but they, like Jacques, had to be banished.

"If we had killed him we might feel more real now. We would have a harder time, going through a trial, being sentenced to the guillotine, all those troubles, but they would be part of a real life, too, don't you think? No, don't interrupt me. You're going to say that we don't have to murder someone to feel real. You're right. We wrote the books. We got your name and pictures into newspapers. We got you to an English school. Then what? We are still us, you and me—nothing has changed for us."

"But I don't want anything to change. I just want us to spend the days together, like we always used to."

"For how long?"

"For as long as we want," I said. "Forever."

"You're an idiot, Agnès. We don't have forever. We don't even have a long time. Soon we'll have to get married. And have children."

"We don't have to do all those things," I said. "We can wait for a year and then move to Paris together."

"Then what? That won't make us feel real, don't you see?"

"I don't know what you mean by real or not real," I said. The daylight was fading fast, and there was a cool mist among the graves. How could this not be real, when we were sitting together with no one coming between us? The world would never interrupt us again.

Fabienne turned to me, and her face looked softer, as it always did when daylight faded. She circled my neck with both hands. Her thumbs, pressing on my throat, were cold. "See, if I were to strangle you now, they would sentence me to death and take me to the guillotine," she said. "Oh, don't look at me that way. You know I'm not going to hurt you."

I did not know. And I did not care.

"And what would they say about us? They would say I was jealous of your success so I killed you. Or they would say I've always been this crazy and nasty girl, and it's only a surprise that I didn't murder ten other people. They would put both of us in the papers. Someone at school would remember you as a gentle soul, someone in the village would tell the journalists that you were smart and pretty, someone would make up a story about you and weep to the camera. And then they would talk about the books you've written, and they would say it's a pity your life was cut short and you can't write more books. But that would be nonsense, right?"

I nodded. Her hands were not tight around my neck, and I had no trouble breathing. But for all I cared, she could keep her hands there forever, and she could talk about killing me forever. For all I cared, we could spend a lifetime dying in that cemetery. But I felt an ache inside me. Fabienne was right: we did not have that forever.

"People can be wrong about so many things. How can you and I be real when the world is so wrong about us?"

I said something, and she removed her hands. "What did you say?" she asked.

"I said: What does it matter that the world is wrong? We have each other. That's all we need."

There was a strange glistening in her eyes. Perhaps it was her tears. Or perhaps it was what a wolf would look like before it pounced on a hare. "You dream big, Agnès," she said, and I could hear something unfamiliar in her voice—like a sob that could not find a way to become a sob. "But you know it's not possible."

"Why not?"

"Because you know the world better than I do. You know

it so well that you can lie to my face now, saying we could live together forever, like in a fairy tale. But you know you're lying, right? You've been to Paris. You've been to England. You've smiled the way the photographers want you to. You've said the right words to the journalists. That poor old man M. Devaux once said that he and I were too smart for the world, but we wouldn't have pulled off anything successfully without an idiot like you."

I winced. I had never felt pained when Fabienne called me an idiot. But to know she and M. Devaux had shared something, in which I had not a place . . . He, like her, wanted to do something for revenge. They had used each other, and they had both used me. But revenge for what? "I only did what you told me to," I said. I was trying to soothe a pain in Fabienne, though I could not see where her wound was.

"But you always know what the world wants from you, and you always know how to give the world what it wants," Fabienne said. "No, don't deny it. At this moment we can both say, 'To hell with the world,' but it will change. In a year or two, you will change, and you will want me to change with you. Or you will change without bothering with me."

I wanted to scream that she was wrong. But I stayed quiet, feeling the coldness seeping into my body from the stone below. I knew what the world wanted from me, but I did not know what Fabienne wanted. If I refrained from saying that aloud, perhaps she would never discover the truth.

She let go of my neck. "Can't you see that we've already lived past the best time of our lives?"

The moment she said it, I knew she was right. She had made a game to deceive the world; we had succeeded, and now the game was coming to an end. I could feel my eyes, heavy with tears that would not change anything for us.

Being real was like being mad, like thrashing in the most feverish dreams, like being dead while alive, or living on and on after the world considered us dead and buried. But we were too young to die; we were too sane to submit ourselves to madness.

"What do we do, then?" I asked. It was still my job to ask questions, still her job to answer me.

Fabienne pressed her hands hard on my ears. I stayed still, and then heard her shriek, not through the air, but through our bodies. Even with my ears muffled I knew the shriek was terrifying, more animal than human. If a child cried for help, someone would hear it, but no help would come for us now, because Fabienne was no more than an injured animal. Somewhere in a house a baby would be awakened from sleep and cry. A dog wandering in the alley would be running home, frightened, with its tail tucked in.

Fabienne shrieked once more, and then pulled her hands away from my ears. In a voice nearly inaudible, she said, "It's going to be pain and pain and pain and pain from now on, don't you see it, Agnès?"

"There must be something you can do, no, we can do together?" I said. It was futile, but I must still try to say all the things that could be said.

She took her knife from her pocket and unfolded it. "You could kill me," she said. "Then they would sentence you and take you to the guillotine. They would make a story about you. And who knows, people might even think of some nice things to say about me when I'm dead."

Was there no other way for us to get out of this terrible pain?

"But you don't want to kill me. You want us to live together, happily, to a hundred years old," Fabienne said.

"Some people do live to be a hundred years old," I said.

"Not us," she said. "Listen, you should go home now. Your parents are probably wondering where you are."

"They know I'm with you."

"But I want to be alone now," she said. She placed the blade between her teeth and jumped off from the parapet before I could stop her. In a minute she climbed back up into the oak tree.

If she missed a branch and fell, if the knife got stuck in her throat, I would tell the world that I had killed her. But she was a good climber. When she reached a branch higher than before—and now I could barely see her—she took the knife out of her mouth to speak to me. "Go home, Agnès. There's nothing we can do for each other now."

I obeyed her order. I took the long way home.

~

A FEW YEARS AGO, two girls living in the town next to ours skipped a day of high school, took a walk out to the field, and, eventually, lay down on a train track. They said they had been bored with school; they had had a long conversation, and then fallen asleep. A train ran over them, waking them up to the rest of their lives: four legs were lost between the two girls, and yet they survived.

They denied that they had been suicidal. They had only been talking, dozing off when they got tired. It was a warm spring day. On other days they had also played truant, for a similar reason of being bored. On other days they had also fallen asleep in the field. One girl was quoted to have said to the journalist: "Yeah, you could call us stupid, but we still have each other. And you know what? No one else in the world will ever understand us as we do each other."

I thought about Fabienne when I read the news, which I

clipped out of the paper. Last night I took the cutting out and reread the report. There were pictures of the girls, already faded, from when the accident first happened. I studied them and could see little of myself and Fabienne in them. They were American, with long blond hair, broad shoulders, bright white teeth, healthy complexion—sturdy even after their tragedy. There was a picture of their crutches, two pairs laid side by side, bearing matching cartoon stickers.

By now the girls are young women, and they may be wearing matching pants covering their prostheses. I envy them as the girls they were, and I envy the young women they are now. This may be the most illogical thing anyone has ever said about them; the kindest, too. Life was real—and will always be, I hope—for them, in a way that Fabienne once wanted for us: and yet neither she nor I could make a real life for ourselves. We could not have achieved what those two girls did, letting the world take something from them, letting the world mark them both. And yet from that colossal loss, the loss for which people will always take pity on them, they have earned the right to laugh back at the world, at its people, who cannot understand.

I now know that so much of our story began with Fabienne's exultation and despair, both out of my reach. For as long as I could be the outlet of her exultation and her despair, life was bearable, even interesting, to her. I was the whetstone that sharpened her mind's blade; I was the orange that she cut into effortlessly. All the same, I could not save us. It was not boredom that defeated us, it was not defeat that made us drift apart. Not every child is born with an untamable force within her. It is the world's job to avert its eyes, writing that force off as childish tantrum, as immaturity. It is a child's job to forbear that force until she, too, can write it off and sail into a safer adulthood. Fabienne had no words to describe her exultation and despair, and I had no way to grasp them, but she was not alone in her extremes. The lucky ones have waited out the storms. The really lucky ones who have learned a few tricks to tame the untamable—however momentarily—have made their names. I am not sophisticated enough to claim that I understand those geniuses, but I know what they have put in their symphonies and concertos, what they have put on their canvases or in their books, is what made Fabienne shriek in the cemetery. Through her hands I had heard her pain: there was something immense in her, bigger, sharper, more permanent, than the life we lived. She could neither find nor make a world to accommodate that immense being.

~

FABIENNE AND I did not drift apart overnight, but through the summer and fall, even as we continued to spend time together, we both knew that it was futile. Quietness set in—not the quietness we used to share, the ease of two turtle-doves perched on a fence, neither making a sound but each attentive, ready to answer the other's cooing. We never talked about Jacques, and rarely mentioned England or the books we had written.

You can climb up a tree, and if you are agile like Fabienne, you can jump down without hurting yourself. But it was not a treetop where we found ourselves then; rather, we were at the edge of a chasm. Had we chosen to jump together, hand in hand, we would not have survived, but we would not have parted, either. But as so many people before and after us, I chose to retreat, and for the first time I led the way: she had no option but to follow. In that retreat it became impossible for us to stay together.

To the world we were two girls getting older, duller, closer to marriage, childbearing, and the rest of life's toil.

The next year, when my sister Rosemary, who lived in Deux-Sèvres, told me about an apprenticeship in a dressmaking shop, I decided to move away from Saint Rémy. I asked Fabienne if she wanted to look for a job nearby, knowing she would say no. My parents thought I was finally outgrowing a friendship that they had never approved of. But my parents, like the rest of the world, preferred only the least perturbing version of the truth.

Shortly after I moved to Deux-Sèvres, a traveling circus passed Saint Rémy. After they decamped, I heard, Fabienne disappeared. The village talked about her joining the circus—not a bad choice at all for that girl, people said. Even I made myself believe that: she was good with animals, she was good at flying high, too.

When I was seventeen, I met a cobbler's apprentice, and for a while I could imagine a life with him. A year later we got engaged, and, for reasons unknown to me, our engagement was reported by an evening paper: Agnès Moreau, who once enjoyed a short-lived fame as a girl author and now works as a seamstress, is engaged to marry Jules Gagnon, a worker in a shoe factory. The journalist made a joke about a cobbler being a perfect prince for Cinderella.

Reading the news, I knew I could not marry Jules. Imagination of happiness, after all, is more fragile than most other imaginations. I broke off the engagement and moved to Paris. I worked at a dressmaker's shop first, and a few months later found a position on the floor of a department store, selling women's sleepwear. It was there I met Earl, an American engineer, who, in his broken French, asked my help to buy presents for all the women in his family: his mother, aunts, and two sisters-in-law. To marry Earl, to move to America, to be never known again as Agnès Moreau, who failed to live up to a fairy tale's standard—all those things I have achieved, with determination, without sentiment.

In my American life, I encountered my past only once—or, I should say, only once did my past seek me out, in the form of a literary historian. The man, whose name I no longer remember, contacted me two years ago, saying he was working on a book about child prodigies in the 1950s, and it had taken him many months to locate me. I would not have replied to his letter but for his mentioning of a Mrs. Antonia Townsend, whose memoir, the man wrote, had a chapter about a former student named Agnès Moreau.

I agreed to meet the historian, who arrived with a full folder of material: press cuttings in French and English, many of them I was seeing for the first time in my life; copies of my enlarged pictures from an archival photograph agency, Agnès Moreau, a peasant girl, a young author, and a debutante-in-training; the French editions of the two books that bore my name. Only the first one, *Les Enfants Heureux*, had been translated into English, and the man pointed out the translator's name: she had since become a well-known literary figure in London, one of those things that he thought would impress me, and would make me more willing to open up to him. And there was Mrs. Townsend's memoir, published by a vanity press. The book, he explained to me, had little historical or literary merit. It was mostly an account of Mrs. Townsend's professional life as the founder and headmistress of a boutique finishing school, though in the early chapters there were some interesting tales about growing up in a Swiss boarding school her father had run, her hasty marriage to an Englishman sent out to Japan to teach in an agricultural college, and their traveling in Asia in the early 1930s. The historian had nothing more to report about Mr. Townsend but that Mrs. Townsend, after living in Japan with him for twenty months, had left the marriage.

Mrs. Townsend, after all these years, was finally able to realize her author's dream. For a brief moment, I considered asking the man if I could keep the book. After I'd read it, I would know her a little better, more than I could say of M. Devaux, Meaker, and those professionals—editors, journalists, photographers. All of them, once upon a time, came into my life by accident, as though they had pushed the wrong door and found themselves on a neglected stage. All of them exited quickly.

But if I asked the literary historian for the book, he would ask something from me in return, so I only scanned the chapter he flagged for me, titled "A Faux-Prodigy." In the chapter, Mrs. Townsend had written about my stay at the school. I was described as a child with a primitive mind and a feral appearance, nearly illiterate, with a tendency for tantrums. Though she would refrain from making a conclusive statement about my achievement, the girl she had known, Mrs. Townsend wrote, had shed some interesting light on the rumors that, unlike Françoise Sagan and Minou Drouet, Agnès Moreau was merely a hoax. How else could we explain her complete disappearance from the literary world?

I told the man that he seemed to have gathered more material about my life than I myself possessed. I declined to answer any question, to argue for or against my history.

A YEAR AGO, my mother wrote to me that Fabienne had returned to Saint Rémy. She claimed to have married a famous clown, who had recently died and left her some money. Perhaps there was something true to her story, my mother wrote, as there were a few calculating men after her these days. No doubt she would marry again.

Perhaps it was one of those men who fathered the child whose birth killed her.

Why had she returned to Saint Rémy, which, like all the places in the world, has never known us, and will never know us? I did not think of writing Fabienne then, but I now wish I had.

A long time ago, when the game of writing was only an idea, like the idea of growing happiness, Fabienne said that we should write books together so people would know how it felt to be us. That, I now know, was the only mistake she made. What we wrote was about many things, but not about us. When the books were read by others, we were nowhere to be found.

The real story was beyond our ability to tell: our girlhood, our friendship, our love—all monumental, all inconsequential. The world had no place for two girls like us, though I was slow then, not knowing that Fabienne, slighted, thwarted, even fatally wounded, tried to make a fool of that world, on her and on my behalf. Revenge is a story that often begins with more promises than the ending can offer.

And there she is now, in a grave in Saint Rémy, all the pain over. Tonight I wish she were here, so I could tell her that once again, I have written a book, once again with her help. Somewhere, I believe, somewhere she is laughing. You are still that silly goose, she says. You dream big, Agnès.

But she is wrong about me, just as the world was wrong about us. If my geese ever dream, they alone know that the world will never be allowed even a glimpse of those dreams, and they alone know the world has no right to judge them. I live like my geese.

I have interrupted that living to write: the story of a faux-prodigy, which is the real story of Fabienne and Agnès, as real as on that day when we were in the graveyard, wanting, and unable, to kill each other; wanting, and unable, to save each other.

ACKNOWLEDGMENTS

My deepest gratitude to the Guggenheim Foundation, the Windham-Campbell Prizes, and the American Academy of Arts and Letters for their generous support during the writing of this novel.

Sarah Chalfant: Your clarity and steadfastness sustain me. Jacqueline Ko, Charles Buchan, and the others at the Wylie Agency: Thank you for taking extraordinary care of me and my work.

Mitzi Angel: Your editorial vision is a thrill, a delight, and a lifesaver. Molly Walls, Na Kim, Lauren Roberts, and the rest of the FSG team; Kishani Widyaratna and the rest of the Fourth Estate team: Thank you for all your work to get the novel into the world.

Edmund White, Rupert to my Eglantine: What would the last two years have been like without our five-o'clock book/giggle club?

Mona Simpson: LMWM—there is no deeper truth to a writer's life than that, and thank you for being part of it with me.

Elizabeth McCracken: Thank you for the geese and goslings, Scotch eggs and pork pies; thank you for the love effable and ineffable, sent for real and sent in imagination.

Brigid Hughes: Thank you for the marigolds and the turnips, for turtledoving, and for all the placeholders.

A Note About the Author

Yiyun Li is the author of six works of fiction—*Must I Go, Where Reasons End, Kinder Than Solitude, A Thousand Years of Good Prayers, The Vagrants,* and *Gold Boy, Emerald Girl*—and the memoir *Dear Friend, from My Life I Write to You in Your Life*. She is the recipient of many awards, including the PEN/Malamud Award, the PEN/Hemingway Award, the PEN/Jean Stein Book Award, a MacArthur Fellowship, and a Windham-Campbell Prize. Her work has also appeared in *The New Yorker, A Public Space, The Best American Short Stories,* and *The PEN/O. Henry Prize Stories,* among other publications. She teaches at Princeton University.